Her eyes blazed and narrowed.

She launched herself at him with a vengeance.

For Ian, it was like doing battle with a whirlwind. He ground out a curse, caught her wrists, and forced her arms behind her back.

Still, she fought him, refusing to be subdued, refusing to acknowledge his superior strength. She called him every vile name she could think of, then inhaled upon a sharp gasp when he suddenly enveloped her with his strong, sinewy arms.

Without warning, his mouth came crashing down on hers. She moaned in startled, furious protest and struggled anew within his embrace.

But it was no use. Ian would not be denied. She had been kissed before, but—*heaven help her*—never like this!

WILD
TEXAS
ROSE

Catherine Creel

FAWCETT GOLD MEDAL • NEW YORK

A Fawcett Gold Medal Book
Published by Ballantine Books
Copyright © 1993 by Catherine Creel

Library of Congress Catalog Card Number: 93-90534

ISBN 0-449-14785-1

Manufactured in the United States of America

First Edition: December 1993

To a real Texas gentleman, Roy Gene Crow. Thanks for being a wonderful father, and for loving your "passel of grandchildren" so much.

❧ Prologue ❧

Texas . . . 1876

"You're a hellion, girl. Always have been." The tough old rancher heaved a sigh and shook his head ruefully. "I guess I've got no one but myself to blame for that. But I'll be hanged if I'll let you end your days as a dried-up old maid. I want grandchildren, do you hear? A whole passel of them. And just so you know, I don't aim to have one foot in the grave before that happens. You might as well set your mind to it here and now. Damn it, Callie Rose, it's your duty!"

"My duty?" Callie Rose Buchanan blinked across at her father in stunned disbelief. Outrage immediately followed. "How utterly charming! You make it sound as though I'm one of the brood mares, waiting patiently out in the barn for an 'introduction' to the stallion with the best bloodlines! And since you have decided to lecture me on the subject of duty, why the blazes aren't those four goshalmighty, wonderful sons of yours present? Lord knows, they've had ample opportunity in which to do *their* duty. Why, I'm surprised the whole countryside isn't already peppered with little Buchanans!"

1

"That's different! And—"

"The devil it is!"

"—even if it wasn't, a *lady* doesn't go around talking about such things!"

"No one has ever accused me of being a lady!"

"Then it's high time they started!" The lean, gray-haired patriarch of the Buchanan family scowled darkly as he turned to pour himself another generous shot of whiskey. "By thunder, you must have learned something at that fancy school back East. I'd hate like hell to think I wasted my money."

"You did waste it—every single penny!" retorted Callie Rose. That wasn't entirely true, of course: She was now well versed in the social graces and could use her accursed womanliness to the best advantage. But what did that matter? She certainly had no intention of calling upon her newly acquired skills. A caustic little smile touched her lips when she reminded her father, "I told you it would do no good."

"It would have done plenty if only you'd tried," he said accusingly, with another paternal glower in her direction.

He downed the last of the fiery, amber-colored liquid and allowed his fingers to tighten about the glass. His gaze narrowed as it flickered over the striking young woman his only daughter had become.

She was a beauty all right, he thought, his heart swelling with pride in spite of his annoyance with her. Silken curls, black as midnight and reaching nearly to her hips, framed a deceptively angelic countenance. The simple white shirtwaist and blue cotton riding skirt she wore fit her supple yet well-rounded curves to perfection. She was tall for a woman; it was clear she took after his side of the family in that respect. And her eyes . . . hell, her eyes were so blue and full of fire they'd put genuine sapphires to shame.

"You look just like your mother standing there," J. D. murmured, half to himself. He cleared his throat in the next instant, set his glass down atop the polished surface of the sideboard, and rounded on a mutinous Callie Rose again.

The fading afternoon sunlight warmed the windowpanes and filled the parlor with a soft golden glow. The room had a comfortable, well-worn look about it. J. D. suddenly found himself recalling that night long ago when his daughter, barely six years old, had taken it in mind to house her latest "pet" inside the oak rolltop desk sitting against the far wall. Come morning, the skunk had announced its presence with a familiar, unpleasantly distinctive aroma. It had taken the better part of a month to air the place out.

J. D.'s eyes lit with wry humor at the memory. Just for a moment, his resolve wavered. But he told himself that what he was doing was for her own good. She needed a husband, and *he* needed to see her settled before the year was through.

"You'll be twenty soon," he pointed out, with a grimness that Callie Rose would have deemed laughable if not for the fact that it was *her* advanced age he was worried about. "It's time we found you a husband. And since you've chased away every able-bodied man who's come courting for the past four years, we're going to give those young bucks over in Europe a shot at it. Maybe one of them will catch your eye."

"It would serve you right, J. D. Buchanan, if I never came home again!"

"You'll be back. Just make sure you lasso a man with enough money to pay for all the visits you'll be making. And try to get one with a title while you're at it," he advised, his mouth twitching irrepressibly. "Truth be told, I sort of like the notion of having a son-in-law with the handle of 'duke' or 'earl.' Yes sirree, I'd really be able to lord it over Hiram Griffith and all those other sonsabitches who keep saying only a cross-threaded fool would take on a wildcat like you."

"I can't believe I'm hearing this," Callie Rose sighed, feeling mingled resentment and dismay. "Do you truly expect me to spend the whole summer—?"

"I do."

His aplomb made her temper flare. She lifted her chin in an eloquent gesture of defiance, her eyes blazing their magnificent, deep blue fire. She was well matched for pride and stubbornness by the man who had sired her. But he had a good forty years on her. And he knew just what to do whenever she dug in her heels.

"You'll go," he decreed in a low tone edged with steel. All traces of amusement had vanished now. "I've given my word."

There it was—the dreaded truism that had ended many an argument between J. D. and his five headstrong offspring. No Buchanan *ever* went back on his word. They all knew that just as surely as they knew what would happen if they were witless enough to bring dishonor on the family name.

Callie Rose gave an inward groan.

"For heaven's sake," she exclaimed, "I haven't even been home a month yet!"

Cursing the sudden tears that sprang to her eyes, she folded her arms across her chest and swept past her father to take up an angry stance before the lace-curtained window. The battle was already lost, and she knew it. Still, that didn't mean she was going to accept defeat gracefully. Not this time, not when her entire future depended on it.

Her bright, stormy gaze was drawn to the corral, where her two oldest brothers were helping the hands break in some of the new horses. Sam and Billy would lend their support, she told herself confidently. And she knew she could count on Jake and Clay to back her up as well. But would their intervention do any good?

"Martha will be around to fetch you first thing in the morning," J. D. announced behind her.

"What?" Incredulous, she whirled to face him again. "You might at least have given me a few days' warning! Why, I—I can't possibly be ready to leave by then!"

"You can pack a few things and buy whatever else you need when you drop anchor over there. I'm sure Martha will take care of everything. She always does." He smiled faintly, then sobered again before warning, "You do as your cousin says, understand? I'm counting on her to make sure you behave yourself. Seeing as how she's a widow, and on the shady side of thirty besides, she ought to be a big help when it comes to finding a man with enough gumption to take you in hand."

"This latest scheme of yours is doomed to certain failure, J. D.!" Callie Rose asserted hotly. "If you think you can force me into marriage, you are very much mistaken. As God is my witness, I'll run away before I allow that to happen! Great balls of fire, do you really think sending me to the other side of the world is going to make any difference?" she demanded, closing the distance between them now. She shook her head. "I told you before, I won't marry at all unless I can find a man who will treat me with true respect instead of like—like some mindless, weak willed little ninny who exists only to do his bidding! And since I doubt very seriously that such a man exists—I've certainly seen no evidence of it thus far—I'd say there's a good chance I'll remain a spinster for the rest of my life!"

"And *I'm* saying it's time you put those damned clap-trap notions out of your head and remembered you're a woman!" His face reddened in anger as his gaze bore down into the unflinching luminosity of hers.

"I can assure you that I'm in no danger of forgetting it! But you're the one who raised me to think for my-self. Why should the fact that I am a woman—?"

"Enough!" J. D. ground out. There was a dangerous gleam in his eyes, while his mouth had tightened into a thin line of barely suppressed fury. "I won't hear any more on the subject. My mind's made up. You're going . . . and that's that."

"Tell me then"—she challenged him recklessly, her voice laced with bitter sarcasm—"should I follow the example set by my brothers and allow some of the 'young bucks' to sample my charms before I decide which one's to have the honor of fathering your grand-children?"

J. D.'s hands clenched into fists at his sides. He muttered a curse that would have singed the ears of a more gently bred female.

"God willing, there's a man out there who'll be able to tame you!" he uttered between clenched teeth. That said, he stalked from the room, jamming his broad-brimmed felt hat down upon his head on the way out.

Callie Rose glared after him. Her heart ached at the dismal prospect of being away from the ranch again, and she was infuriated by her father's persistent efforts to see her wedded and bedded and heavy with child.

It was all so damnably unfair, she mused with a long, frustrated sigh. If she hadn't had the misfortune to "blossom" into a woman a few summers ago, she would still be enjoying the same free and easy life her brothers led. She longed for those days in the not so distant past when she had been treated like one of the boys. . . . Why the devil couldn't she have been born a man?

She would have to go, of course, she told herself as she wandered back to the window and raised a hand to the slightly yellowed lace curtains. J. D. would certainly never relent now. And her threat to run away had been an empty one; she couldn't bear the thought of leaving the Diamond L forever.

"So be it," she murmured, her eyes kindling with fiery determination. She would go to Europe with Cousin Martha. Yes indeed, she would play the part of the dutiful daughter—*but only up to a point*.

There would be no husband. Not now, not ever. The man who could tame Callie Rose Buchanan hadn't been born yet . . . and never would be!

🌟 ONE 🌟

Scotland ... three months later

Callie Rose stood alone at the foot of the hill, her gaze moving appreciatively across the wild, rugged beauty of the Highland countryside. At moments like this, it wasn't difficult to imagine that she had been transported to another world. The silence surrounding her was almost eerie, broken only by the wind, which, capriciously, either tore at her full skirts and upswept hair or caressed her cheek with a tantalizing lightness.

She inhaled deeply of the cool, salt-tinged air and raised her face toward the sun's gentle warmth. Tugging her hooded, velvet-lined cloak more closely about her body, she congratulated herself once more on having had the good sense to purchase a pair of red flannel drawers upon her arrival in Inverness two days ago. They were far from fashionable, but, as she had archly told a disapproving Martha, the chance that anyone else would see them was remote at best. She wore them now beneath a two-piece walking suit of emerald green wool. A white linen chemise, a petticoat of heavy white muslin, black woolen stockings, and a pair of French kid boots completed the ensemble. In spite of her precautions, however, there were times when it seemed the wind cut right through to her skin.

The afternoon certainly promised to be a chilly one. Of course, it was impossible to predict the weather with any real degree of accuracy. One moment it appeared the long, clear summer day would stretch into an equally serene night, while the next, dark and ominous clouds would suddenly gather overhead to send rain pelting downward with a vengeance. In that respect, at least, she thought with a soft smile of irony, Scotland was not so unlike Texas. There was a popular saying back home that said, "If you don't like the weather, wait around for a little while and it'll change."

She wandered farther down the hillside. All about her, light and shade played together over the empty glens where the proud, fiercely loyal clans had once battled one other—and England—for control of the land. Heather bloomed in all its purple glory amid the grass and bracken carpeting the hills, while the nearby mountains towered heavenward to disappear into the beckoning thickness of the clouds.

It was indeed a mystical place, she reflected with an inward sigh. A place of legends and solitude, and an almost seductive charm. Nowhere else had she witnessed such incredibly long and beautiful twilights; this far north, the sun hardly set at all. Still, it was a lonely region, full of rocks and caverns and lingering echoes, its narrow, thinly inhabited valleys cloaked by frequent mists, its deep, fjordlike lochs holding secrets no mere mortal could ever hope to fathom.

She was enchanted by everything she had seen thus far, although her delight was tempered by a certain nag-

ging sense of disappointment. While she couldn't say
exactly what she had expected to find in the Highlands,
there was something missing; it was as if she were waiting on the brink of some other—imminently earth-
shattering—discovery.

Chiding herself for being such an overimaginative
fool, she tugged the hood of her cloak up over her
tightly pinned curls and looked to where her horse
grazed peacefully beneath a tall oak tree.

She had disregarded Martha's warning about galli-
vanting off alone. The widow, who at that moment no
doubt believed her young charge had followed her advice and joined a "suitable group of lady tourists," had
elected to remain behind in the warm, homey comfort
of the Caledonian Hotel. Martha was nursing a bad
cold. The illness had come upon her quite suddenly during the long yet spectacular railway journey from Edinburgh, and it was beginning to look as though she
would be unable to fulfill her duties as chaperon for the
rest of the week.

Free at last, mused Callie Rose. At least they had
been able to do a bit of exploring about the self-
proclaimed capital of the Highlands before the poor
woman had taken to her bed. Inverness had proven to
be a pleasant surprise, boasting of elegant spires, arched
bridges, and a beautiful, red sandstone castle. Situated
on the southern side of the river Ness, it was the only
town of any real importance north of Aberdeen. It
lacked Edinburgh's ancient buildings (owing to the re-
grettable fact that, throughout the years, it had frequently been burned to the ground by marauding
clansmen), but it held a charm all its own, and she knew

she'd never forget how the sound of bagpipes had filled the air when she and Martha had finally stepped off the train.

What a vast difference from London, she reflected as she paused and drew in another deep breath, then frowned in remembrance. These past several weeks had been an endless whirl of fellowship with oh-so-polite society, of visiting grand and glorious estates and dancing with rich and titled (and boring) gentlemen who had spent the entire time either talking about themselves or else proclaiming their undying love and devotion after only a few days' acquaintance. She'd had all she could stand of unwanted admirers who bedeviled her at every turn.

That unpleasant business with the young Duke of Albemarle had proven to be the last straw. She had rejected several other proposals of marriage, of course, but her rejection of *his* had proven especially scandalous. The news had spread throughout the city like wildfire. Her reputation as a heartbreaker had only been reinforced as a result, but she hadn't cared. Nor had she cared when Martha had cautioned her that no man alive would ever be able to measure up to her impossibly high standards. That suited her just fine; she wanted nothing more than to forget all about men and marriage and everything else save her exploration of a mysterious land, where the Buchanans had first gotten their start.

It was difficult to say exactly why she had felt a sudden desire to see Scotland. Until now, she had never been particularly interested in visiting the country where her grandfather had been born. She had only a hazy memory of him—a tall, dark-haired fellow with a perpetual frown on his lined and craggy features. He had died shortly before her fourth birthday. J. D. hadn't told her a great deal about him. It seemed the two men had quarreled too much for comfort. But she did recall hearing how he had journeyed to America as a young man with nothing but a few coins in his pocket and a dream of finding a better life.

Angus Buchanan. She repeated his name silently. According to J. D., Angus had possessed the devil's own temper. That particular trait had, without a doubt, been passed on from father to son. And on to the next generation in turn.

She glanced back toward the crumbling ruin that had once been a magnificent, turreted great house. Sadly enough, the ruin atop the hill was all that remained of the Buchanans' ancestral estate. It had been abandoned many years ago—apparently a short time after Angus Buchanan had taken himself away to America—and according to local legend, it was still haunted by the ghost of a sixteenth-century Buchanan whose jealous wife had exacted a severe (and highly permanent) revenge for his philandering.

"You'll be wanting to stay away from that evil place!" an old woman in the nearby village had cautioned Callie Rose earlier in the day. Mary Crawford had been the only one to respond to her inquiries with anything more than a polite, yet firm, denial of any knowledge on the subject. The villagers' reluctance to speak of a man who had once been a neighbor was very strange. And very frustrating.

"A blood feud between the Buchanans and the MacGregors—that's what Angus left behind when he took the coward's way out!" the tiny, silver-haired Mary had revealed enigmatically.

"What do you mean, a 'blood feud'? Why did my grandfather . . . ?"

"Angus Buchanan." Mary had spoken his name one last time before shaking her head and perversely refusing to elaborate. "No, I'll not speak ill of the dead." With that, she had pivoted about and disappeared inside her thatch-roofed cottage.

Callie Rose frowned at the disturbing memory. Mary Crawford's words still burned in her mind. It was all so damnably mysterious . . . *a blood feud between the Buchanans and the MacGregors.* What had happened all those years ago? And who the devil were the MacGregors?

Thunder suddenly rumbled in the near distance.

Startled from her reverie, she whirled and saw that a boiling mass of clouds loomed threateningly on the horizon. The heavy, unmistakable smell of rain electrified the air.

"Damnation," she muttered. Her eyes traveled back to her horse, and she toyed briefly with the idea of trying to outrun the approaching storm. But she realized she'd never make it back to Inverness in time. And she had no intention of spending the remainder of *her* Scottish holiday in bed with a cold.

She cast a dubious look toward the old mansion. It wouldn't offer much in the way of shelter, yet she had little choice. If the storms she had witnessed these past two days were any indication, there would be a brief, violent downpour, followed by a gentle rain that could last well into the evening. But there was always the possibility that the skies would clear again within the hour. Either way, she concluded, it could certainly do no harm to try and wait out the worst of it. Martha wasn't expecting her back for another two hours yet.

Tugging the hood lower on her head, she hurried forward to untie the horse's reins. She took a firm grip on the bridle and led the frightened animal up the hill as the wind began to assault the earth with a ferocious howl. Her long skirts swirled wildly about her legs, and she raised a hand to shield her eyes from the dust and other debris stinging against her face.

Another loud clap of thunder split the air, only to be answered an instant later by a flash of lightning that lit up the entire cloud-choked sky. The sun had disappeared by now, and along with it any hope of deliverance from the damp, bone-chilling cold that settled over the land.

Callie Rose took refuge within the partially roofed rectangle that had once been the dining room. She breathed a sigh of relief at having reached its protection—however inadequate it was—in time. Releasing the bridle, she watched as the horse moved instinctively to the far corner of the darkened ruin.

A sudden shiver ran the length of her spine, and she pressed closer to the stone wall in an effort to shield herself from the wind. She tossed a quick look overhead. The storm had not yet broken, though the atmosphere was charged with an anticipation that teased at her nerves.

"*Rain*, confound it!" she murmured impatiently. She folded her arms across her chest and shivered again, wishing for all the world that she were back at the hotel with the sniffling, sneezing Martha.

Without warning, a dark figure loomed behind her.

There was no time to struggle. A sharp gasp of alarm broke from her lips as she was suddenly scooped up by a pair of strong, muscular arms. With terrifying swiftness, she was spun about and thrust facedown across a man's broad shoulder.

"Let me go!" she cried in a shrill, breathless voice. Struggling violently within her unknown assailant's grasp, she tried without success to catch a glimpse of his face. "What the hell do you think you're doing? Put me down, you—"

"*Silence!*" he ground out. His powerful arms tightened like a vise about her legs as he bore her purposefully out of the house.

Callie Rose battled a wave of light-headedness. Her heart pounding with a combination of dread and indignation, she realized that no one, absolutely no one, was around to help her.

"Who are you?" she demanded in growing panic. The folds of the cloak obscured her vision as she hung, ingloriously, like a sack of grain over the man's shoulder, but she caught a glimpse of the red, black, and white plaid kilt he was wearing. "Damn it, you can't do this! *Put me down!*"

She fought him like a wildcat, kicking and twisting and pummeling his back with her fists, but to no avail. He carried her to a waiting horse, tossed her roughly onto the animal's back, and mounted behind her before she could do anything more than snatch the hood away from her face. He clamped an arm about her waist and gathered up the reins.

"Let me go!" she screamed once more. She jerked her head around, only to suffer another sharp intake of breath when her furious sapphire gaze met the burning, emerald green intensity of his.

Her eyes widened in astonishment.

He was without a doubt the most handsome man she had ever seen. No more than thirty, with bronzed, chiseled features, a strong mouth and determinedly set chin, a full head of thick, reddish-brown hair . . . Great balls of fire, she thought dazedly, what could he want with her?

"At your service, Miss Buchanan," he declared softly, his deep, resonant voice laced with sarcasm. He spoke with the lilting brogue of a true Highlander, though an educated and highly insolent one.

"How do you know—?" she started, only to break off when he yanked her back against him. She tensed and gave a strangled cry of protest as her hips came into intimate contact with his hard-muscled thighs. Beset by shock, confusion, and a fear she would never own up to, she momentarily ceased her struggles.

With a faint, triumphant smile playing about his lips, the stranger set his booted heels to the flanks of the magnificent black stallion beneath him. The horse sprang forward on command.

"No!" Callie Rose screamed, coming to life once more. She clawed at her abductor's arm and made a desperate attempt to fling herself from the horse's back.

But it was too late. With relentless force, the man

held her captive before him while the stallion galloped wildly across the deserted, windswept countryside.

They had not traveled far before the storm released its vengeful fury at last. The heavens opened up with a great roar. Thunder and lightning added their volatile accompaniment to the deluge as the wind lashed and wailed and wreaked havoc with the north country's summer calm.

Callie Rose gasped when the first cold drops of rain struck her face. She bent her head, quickly pulling the hood of her cloak into place again. She squirmed with renewed vigor, but the Highlander bit out a curse and tightened his arm about her so that she could scarcely breathe.

Dear God, this can't be happening! she told herself, with an inward groan of dismay. Kidnapped by a stranger. A devilishly handsome Scotsman who knew her name. Where was he taking her? And why?

Whatever his identity, whatever his reasons, she had to get away! Her mind raced feverishly to come up with a plan. But it was difficult to think clearly when she was getting soaked to the skin and the wind kept trying to steal each breath she took. Clutching at the horse's thick mane, she closed her eyes tightly and offered up a silent, desperate prayer for strength, for wisdom—and for the courage to do whatever was necessary to gain her freedom.

She lost all track of time as they rode through the storm-tossed darkness. Soon, the rain gentled into a slow, steady downpour, and she was able to raise her head and look about. The landscape was unfamiliar to her, though she sensed she was being taken farther and farther away from Inverness. Acutely conscious of the Highlander's body pressing against hers, she would not allow herself to think about what he intended to do with her once they reached their destination. She would think of nothing other than escape. . . .

No words passed between them. And then, finally, the horse slowed its frenzied pace.

"Dhachaigh," the kilted stranger murmured in a low tone.

Callie Rose started at the sound of his voice. She did not understand what he said, yet she quickly turned her gaze in the same direction as his own. Her eyes widened in surprise.

In the distance just ahead sat a castle, rising straight and solid over the land. With its twin Scottish baronial tower houses, imposing battlements and turrets, and gently sloping, heather-mantled grounds, the massive stone palace looked like something out of a fairy tale. *Or a nightmare,* Callie Rose mused, with an involuntary shudder.

"Is that where you're taking me?" she demanded, twisting about so that she could fix her captor with a seething, murderous glare. The rain was nothing more than an annoying drizzle now, but the damage had been done. Every stitch of clothing she had on was wet, and it was all she could do to prevent her teeth from chattering when she lifted her head proudly and informed him in a furious rush, "I don't know who the devil you are or why you've done this, but I'll be damned—"

"All in good time, Miss Buchanan," he replied grimly.

"You cowardly, boneheaded bastard, let me go!"

While she struggled anew in his iron grasp, he guided the horse up the hill toward the castle's east entrance. There was no one in sight as they rode through the gate and into the main courtyard.

Reining the stallion to a halt at long last, the handsome, auburn-haired stranger swung agilely down and reached back up for Callie Rose. She struck out at him, then suddenly balled her hand into a fist and landed a hard, punishing blow to his chin. It was her turn to smile in triumph as he swore underneath his breath. Her victory, however, was to be short-lived.

"You have the spirit of a true Buchanan!" her captor pronounced, with angry, begrudging admiration. His green eyes filled with a dangerous light. "Aye, but you've yet to learn what it means to tangle with a MacGregor!"

She gave a small, breathless cry as he yanked her down from the horse. Tossing her unceremoniously over his shoulder once more, he carried his kicking, cursing burden inside the keep. A young man materialized in their wake to lead the horse away to the stables.

Callie Rose had no opportunity to see if the interior of the castle was as grand as the walled splendor on the outside had promised. She continued to struggle in vehement, and highly vocal, defiance as she was conveyed across the great hall, up a wide staircase, and then up a much narrower, winding set of steps to the openness of an arched doorway.

The next thing she knew, she was being set on her feet and thrust none too gently inside the firelit warmth of a room. She stumbled forward, her sodden skirts clinging to her legs and leaving a trail of water on the stone floor. She hastily regained her balance and whirled to confront the man who had dared to abduct her.

It was the first time she had been able to get a good look at him. What she saw provoked a wealth of emotion within her—not all of it unpleasant.

Though she was tall for a woman, he towered above her by more than six inches. She swallowed a sudden lump in her throat as her wide, luminous gaze traveled the length of his taut and powerfully muscled body.

He was wearing a rough tweed jacket, a plain white shirt beneath it, and the pleated tartan kilt that reached only to his knees. Hanging from his waist was the traditional leather *sporran*, a small pouch used in place of pockets. The lower half of his legs was covered by heavy knitted stockings, while on his feet were a pair of sturdy buckskin brogues. His head was bare; the firelight played across his face and lit gold in the gleaming, reddish-brown thickness of his hair as it curled damply just above the collar of his jacket. He had flung his black Inverness cape over his left shoulder, revealing a knife called a *sgian dubh* tucked into a sheath on the outer part of his right stocking. And at the moment, his dark brows were drawn together in an ominous frown.

To Callie Rose, he looked every inch the fierce Highland chieftain he was.

Her pulse raced alarmingly. In spite of the fact that he was clad in what her brothers would have derisively termed a "woman's getup," she had never seen such an all-out *masculine* man in all her life. For the first time since leaving Texas, she stood face-to-face with someone who, if physical characteristics counted for anything, could very definitely hold a candle to the five male members of the Buchanan family.

His eyes seemed to bore into her very soul. She took an instinctive step backward, pulling the folds of her cloak protectively about her body.

"Who are you—and why have you brought me here?" she asked, with a haughtiness that belied her wet and bedraggled appearance. Her long black hair had escaped its pins to fall in a tangled mass about her face and shoulders, tiny rivulets of water coursed down the flushed smoothness of her cheeks, and a puddle was forming on the floor beneath her.

"My name is Ian MacGregor. You are a guest at Castle MacGregor. Your presence, my dearest Miss Buchanan, was required to fulfill a promise."

She could have sworn she detected a note of mocking amusement in his deep voice. The possibility made her see red.

"Damn your eyes, I am not your guest—and I am sure as *hell* not your dearest!" she retorted in a blaze of temper. "And what kind of promise is it that makes you lay hands on an innocent woman and carry her off to some godforsaken place in the middle of nowhere?"

"Innocent?" He uttered the word ironically, like a challenge. The merest ghost of a smile played about his lips, and his gaze softened as it flickered briefly over her. She looked like a half-drowned kitten—or rather, a dripping wet, infuriated tigress. The thought prompted his smile to become real. But he sobered again in the next instant and told her, "Since I've no desire to add your death to my list of crimes, you had best get into some dry clothes. You'll find whatever you need in there." He gave a curt nod toward a huge, carved oak wardrobe in one corner of the room.

"You really are out of your mind if you think I'm going to stay here!"

"You have little choice in the matter."

"But you—you can't do this!" she sputtered in wrathful disbelief.

"I can and will," he vowed masterfully.

"But, *why*? Why have you taken me prisoner? And how long are you planning to—?"

"I'll explain everything once you've had a chance to warm yourself. However, rest assured I mean you no harm." He turned away now, his tall, virile frame filling the doorway as he prepared to leave.

Callie Rose's anxious gaze darted about the room in desperation. Her furrowed brow cleared when she suddenly hit upon an idea.

"Please, wait!" she entreated. Gathering up her heavy skirts, she hastened forward. She stopped dead in her tracks when Ian turned slowly to face her again. A knot of trepidation tightened in her stomach as a result of his proximity, but she had always been good at deception whenever it suited her purpose. She was therefore able to declare with a convincing air of proud and reluctant defeat, "You're right, of course. I can't stay in these clothes unless I want to risk pneumonia. So then, Mr. MacGregor, the least you can do before you go is to help me with this clasp." She raised her hands to the fastening of her cloak and tugged without success. "It seems to have gotten stuck."

Ian frowned, but did not hesitate before granting his

assistance. He stepped closer, his fingers moving to the engraved silver clasp.

It was now or never, thought Callie Rose.

Her eyes lighting with determination, she seized full advantage of the moment. She brought her knee crashing up against the front of her abductor's kilt, pushed past him, and made for the door.

Behind her, Ian ground out an oath—it was in Gaelic, but there was no mistaking it for a polite exclamation of surprise. His hand shot out to close on his beautiful captive's arm before she had cleared the doorway. She cried out in angry, helpless frustration as he yanked her back inside the room. He spun her about, his arms encircling her soft curves and forcing them against his hard-muscled warmth. He lowered his handsome face to within mere inches of the defiant, heart-shaped perfection of hers.

"Have you never heard it said, Callie Rose Buchanan," he queried in a low and splendidly vibrant tone, "that the aim of a lass is not to wound but to wed?"

She shivered at the sound of her name on his lips. His penetrating green eyes burned down into hers, and she was afraid for a moment that he actually meant to kiss her. But the fear quickly passed, and in its place came another burst of fiery outrage.

"I don't know what the blazes you're talking about," she hissed, "and what's more, I don't care! Now let go of me, you arrogant, dim-witted sonofabitch!"

She attempted to strike him again, but he easily caught her wrists and imprisoned both of her arms behind her back. Her full breasts were pressed intimately against the broad hardness of his chest, and he held her so close that she could literally feel his heart beating strong and steady against her own.

"You've a sharp tongue, haven't you?" he remarked, his gaze moving with a bold familiarity over her upturned countenance. "Aye, and a temper to match."

"I'm not the least bit interested in your opinion of me!" she cried hotly.

"Are you not? Perhaps you should be, Callie Rose. For I hold your fate in my hands."

"Go to hell!"

"It may well be that I am there already," he murmured, with a sardonic half smile.

He released her so abruptly that she gasped and staggered back against a small table. Subjecting her to one last intense, thoroughly disquieting look, he headed for the doorway again.

"I'll return within the hour," he promised.

"Don't bother!" she shot back, rubbing at her arms where they still tingled from his forceful, near bruising grasp.

His only response was to close the door on his way out. Callie Rose heard the sound of the key turning in the lock a moment later.

She muttered another curse and whirled about, flying across the room to the single window on the opposite wall. She unlatched the casement and threw it open. Her fingers curled upon the cold stone ledge as she looked out upon the rolling, misty landscape below. She was apparently in one of the tower rooms. It would be impossible to climb down from such a height, even if she could manage to fit through so narrow a space.

Surely there was someone else in the castle, she told herself, her eyes glistening with renewed hope at the thought. Ian MacGregor must have servants, women who cooked and cleaned, men who looked after the place for him. If she could just persuade one of them to help her . . .

" 'Guest' indeed!" she muttered, in truth more worried and angry—and strangely excited—than she had ever been before. With a heavy sigh, she turned away from the window. Her stormy gaze made a quick, encompassing sweep of the room.

It was small yet comfortably furnished. A roaring fire blazed beneath an oak mantelpiece, while an oil lamp burned brightly beside a pitcher and bowl on a washstand nearby. The ceiling was low and beamed with ancient timbers, the stone floor warmed here and there by hand-braided woolen rugs. In addition to the wardrobe, there was a rocking chair, a half-tester bed covered by a tartan blanket, and the table she had used to steady herself a few minutes ago.

Her eyes fell upon another door to the left of the washstand. She hastened forward, only to find that, while no lock guarded its usage, it led to a water closet rather than an avenue of escape.

"All the comforts of home," she observed, with bitter sarcasm.

She shivered again, but this time it was from a chill. Although reluctant to give Ian MacGregor the satisfaction of having his orders obeyed, she wasn't fool enough to catch her death of cold in order to spite him. Of course, she mused vengefully, it would serve him right if he had to explain a corpse to the authorities.

Crossing to the wardrobe at last, she opened it and noted with some surprise a single dress hanging neatly inside. A quick search through the drawers led to the discovery of all the necessary undergarments, stockings, a comb and hairbrush, and even slippers.

Could they belong to Ian MacGregor's wife? she wondered, then was startled to feel a sharp pang of disappointment at the thought. Frowning darkly, she snatched the dress down and carried it to the bed.

She cast a wary glance toward the doorway before finally drawing off her cloak. It fell in a heap about her ankles, and she kicked it aside for the moment as she hurried to unbutton the jacket of her walking suit. Soon, she stood in nothing but her chemise, drawers, and stockings. They were still damp, but she had no intention of exchanging them for dry ones. The last thing she wanted was for her "host" to barge in and find her standing naked as the day she was born. The very thought of it sent hot color flying to her cheeks.

She donned the borrowed gown, a simple white silk that buttoned up the front. Its form-hugging bodice and full, gathered skirt provided a remarkably good fit. But the neckline, low and rounded and trimmed with only a hint of lace, revealed a bit too much of her bosom; the dress had evidently been made for someone less endowed. A flat-chested mistress, perhaps, she thought with another scowl.

On the right shoulder, reaching across the curve of her breast to her waist, was pinned a plaid scarf. Her eyes widened at the sight of the yellow, red, black, white, and dark blue fabric, for she recognized it as the clan tartan of the Buchanans. She had purchased a length of it for her father in one of the many kilters' shops back in Edinburgh.

More baffled than ever, she tossed a quizzical look heavenward and set about putting her hair to rights. After dragging the hairbrush through its wet, luxuriant thickness, she spread her cloak and suit on the rocking chair before the fire. She sank wearily down upon the bed at last and drew the blanket up over her shoulders, allowing her thoughts to wander. Martha's face swam before her eyes.

Good heavens, she had forgotten all about Martha! Surely her cousin had begun to suspect that there was something wrong by now, surely she would insist upon immediate action . . . ?

A blood feud between the Buchanans and the MacGregors.

Her eyes filled with dawning realization at the sudden, unbidden memory of Mary Crawford's words.

"MacGregor!" she breathed, leaping to her feet. Was it truly possible that she had been abducted because of a quarrel that had erupted some seventy years ago?

To fulfill a promise, Ian MacGregor had said.

She gave a low groan and raised a trembling hand to her throat. Her wide, troubled gaze shot back to the doorway.

He had promised her an explanation. He had also promised that she would come to no harm. What other promises had he made? And how the devil could she trust a man who had treated her so roughly, a man who had subjected her to a wild, bone-chilling ride across the storm-swept countryside and then imprisoned her in his castle without so much as a by-your-leave? He had to be crazy. Stark, raving mad. Either that, or so damned overbearing and cocksure of himself that he didn't care what anyone else thought.

Her temper flared to its most dangerous level yet. She flung the blanket aside and determinedly searched about for something to use as a weapon. Her mouth curved into a smile of satisfaction when she spied an iron poker hanging below the fireplace mantle.

She grabbed the poker and returned to the bed, sitting down to wait. When Ian MacGregor returned, she would be ready for him.

❧ TWO ❧

The wait was mercifully brief.

Her eyes opened wide when she heard the door opening. Forcing herself to rise slowly, she stood beside the bed and tried to ignore the wildly erratic pounding of her heart. She clutched the poker in one hand, concealing it behind her full skirts. She held her breath and watched while Ian ducked his head beneath the low-arched doorway. The former chiefs of the Clan MacGregor had apparently been a good deal shorter.

Without a word, he stepped inside the room. His piercing, deep green gaze warmed with admiration—and a far more perilous emotion—as it sought and found the woman who had captured his interest.

She looked incredibly beautiful as she stood facing him—stiff and proud and angrily defiant across the room. Her long, unbound tresses cascaded about her like a shimmering black curtain, while her skin shone smooth and silken in the golden firelight. His eyes strayed to where her full, creamy breasts swelled enticingly above the deep décolletage of her gown.

Callie Rose felt her face flame. She was tempted to snatch up the blanket and wrap it about her again, but she'd be hanged if she'd give Ian MacGregor the pleasure of knowing how deeply affected she was by his "interest." To make matters worse, he was even more damnably appealing than before. In fact, he was downright magnificent.

He had changed into dry clothing as well, trading his tweed jacket for one made of black dress cloth with silver buttons, and his plain white shirt for one with ruffles at the neck and cuffs. A length of plaid was draped over one shoulder. His tartan kilt was identical to its predecessor, though adorned on the right side with a decorative pin, while a black sealskin *sporran* had taken the place of the other. His stockings and shoes were also of a higher quality now, and on his head he wore a blue Balmoral tam, in the center of which was fastened a brooch proudly displaying his clan crest—a lion's head with a crown.

The Lion of the MacGregors, Callie Rose mused silently, her own gaze kindling with ire as his bold scrutiny continued. Yes, by thunder, it was appropriate. The scoundrel was like some glorious, flame-haired male animal. And she was his prey.

"I trust you are more comfortable now?" he inquired politely, though his voice brimmed with sardonic humor.

"Comfortable?" Her eyes shot invisible daggers at his head while her fingers clenched about the tool's wooden handle. "Tell me, Mr. MacGregor, how could I possibly be *comfortable* when I am here against my will?"

A faint smile touched his lips before he turned to close the door. Callie Rose's heart leapt in renewed alarm. She would have struck then, but there wasn't enough time.

"Why did you do that?" she demanded, casting a significant frown toward the door. "Are you afraid someone will hear me scream for help?"

"There's no one to hear, save for a handful of loyal servants. But I would have privacy while we speak."

Her breath caught in her throat when he began slowly advancing on her. She stood her ground, her whole body tensing in readiness. She was surprised when he moved past her to take up a stance before the fire.

"My methods were admittedly extreme," he began, bracing a hand against the mantelpiece. His gaze momentarily fastened on the flames dancing below, and when he spoke again, it was half to himself. "Yet there wasn't time to do it any other way."

"Time to do what?" she asked, with furious impatience. Her eyes shifted with a will of their own to the doorway, but she hastily forced them back to Ian's handsome, somber features. "Why did you bring me here?"

"I told you. To fulfill a promise."

"What promise?" she demanded, her voice rising.

"The one I made to my father," he replied, with maddening equanimity. "The same one he made to his."

"Confound it, what *are* you talking about?" She inched ever so cautiously toward the foot of the bed now, taking care to keep the poker concealed within the gathers of her silk skirts.

"You've been in the Highlands for two days now, Miss Buchanan. Have you heard nothing of the feud between our clans?" he queried, his wonderfully lilting accent more pronounced than ever. It did not occur to her at the moment to ask him how he knew so much about her.

If she had known him better—if she had known him at all—she would have noticed the roguish light in the fathomless, gold-flecked depths of his eyes. As it was, she was too preoccupied with thoughts of escape to give more than passing attention to Ian MacGregor's splendid green eyes. His words, however, were another matter.

"I heard about it only this morning!" she replied honestly. "But if you're trying to tell me that you kidnapped me because of something that happened long before I was even born—"

"Och, lass, you've a great deal to learn about the Scots," he observed, his tone laced with what sounded suspiciously like a mixture of annoyance and affection. He folded his arms across his chest and gave her a brief, wry smile. "What else did Mary Crawford tell you this morning?"

"How on earth did you know . . ." she started to demand in surprise, her eyes growing very round.

"I've made it a point to know everything about you, Callie Rose."

"You mean you've been *spying* on me?" Strangely enough, it sounded like an endearment every time he said her name. She cursed the wild leaping of her pulse and forced her thoughts back to the harsh reality of her predicament.

"Aye, you could call it that," admitted Ian, his manner completely devoid of repentance. "I suppose you'll be wanting me to explain. But first, we've the matter of the feud to clear up."

He unfolded his arms and moved across to the window. Callie Rose turned so that he would not glimpse her weapon. She was only a few feet from the door now.

"A great many years ago, when they were both not yet twenty," Ian told her, "your grandfather, Angus Buchanan, was betrothed to my grandmother, Lorna MacGregor."

"Betrothed?" she echoed in astonishment. She inhaled sharply at a sudden, disturbing thought. "Good heavens, are you saying that you and I are . . . that we are cousins?"

"No." His smile this time was perfectly devastating. "No, lass, we've no blood ties between us. Angus and Lorna were never wed. He left her standing at the altar."

"And that's what started the feud?"

"It is. Angus Buchanan fled to America and never returned, while my grandmother, shamed and brokenhearted, was forced into marriage with a kinsman. My grandfather, to be exact. On the day Angus dishonored her—aye, and brought disgrace upon his own family's name—the MacGregors swore vengeance against the Buchanans."

"But I had nothing to do with any of that!" protested Callie Rose, her head spinning. "I'm not even Scottish—I'm an American!"

She felt as though she had become lost in the pages of some awful, medieval horror story. They were living in the nineteenth century, not the fourteenth. . . . God help her, how could something so positively *barbaric* happen in this enlightened day and age?

"I'm truly sorry that my grandfather jilted your grandmother," she declared, though unremorsefully.

"But you have no right to do this! Why in heaven's name should I be held responsible because he got cold feet and—?"

"Angus was the last of the Buchanans. There are a great many other members of the clan, of course, but none of the direct line to be found this far north. Until you came, that is."

"So *that* is why you brought me here," she said with astonishment, her gaze filled with incredulity. "For revenge!"

"When my father lay dying more than five years ago, he exacted the promise from me," Ian revealed grimly. "In truth, I never believed I would be called upon to honor it. You can imagine my surprise when I discovered that Angus's granddaughter had arrived in Inverness." His eyes glowed with a touch of ironic amusement once more. "Fate plays strange tricks at times, would you not agree, Callie Rose Buchanan?"

"This is the most ridiculous, backward bit of nonsense I've ever heard of!"

"Perhaps. But I gave my word that, should I someday come upon a descendant of Angus Buchanan's here in the Highlands, I would seize the ill-favored person and bring him—or her, as the case may be—to Castle MacGregor as my prisoner. And that is precisely what I have done."

"You really are out of your mind, aren't you?" she charged feelingly.

"There may yet be a method to my madness," he murmured in a low tone. He moved closer, his gaze darkening with intent. "I had planned to release you before nightfall this very day."

"What do you mean, *had*?" A warning bell sounded in her brain. She warily backed away toward the door.

"I think vengeance would be better met if you were to remain here for several days. After all, I'd be unworthy of the name MacGregor if I failed to honor the true spirit of the promise. I am the clan chief now," he disclosed with a frown, his eyes glinting coldly. "What would my kinsmen think of me if I displayed so little regard for a blood feud? The old ways are still followed here." It was as if he were trying to convince himself as well as her.

"Why, you—you'll never get away with this!" she stammered. "My cousin is waiting for me at the hotel in Inverness, and you can be sure she will inform the proper authorities! They'll find me and haul you away in irons—and then, as God is my witness, you bastard— I'll see you hanged by your—"

"Thumbs?" he mockingly finished for her. "Tell me, Miss Buchanan, do all of the women in Texas have such a charmingly bold way of expressing themselves?" Another faint smile of irony tugged at his lips while he continued toward her. "You need have no worries about your cousin, for her mind has been set at ease. She has by this time received a message, delivered by one of my own trusted servants, informing her that you have decided to accept an invitation to stay with friends at an estate some distance north of the city."

"Cousin Martha is well aware of the fact that I have no acquaintances in Scotland!" she pointed out, with a scornful toss of her head. The raven curls bounced riotously about her half-bare shoulders, and two bright spots of angry color rode high on her cheeks. "She'll know the message is a fake!"

"Ah, but it will seem perfectly valid when she hears that your hosts are old acquaintances of your grandfather's. And since she is abed with a cold, I doubt the poor woman will decide to launch an investigation into your whereabouts. No, Mrs. Terhune will be glad you have found a way to entertain yourself during her illness."

He was only inches away now, towering above her as he had done earlier, making her feel quite small and vulnerable. She wasn't at all accustomed to the sensation; she didn't like it one bit. She had always been the one in control when it came to men. But *this* man, this redheaded Scottish rogue with the devil in his eyes, was unlike any of the men she had encountered before.

"You'll come to no harm here," he reassured her once more. His steady gaze locked into silent combat with hers. "Contrary to what you may think, I am not a complete savage. I've never before found it necessary to lock beautiful young women in the tower, but—"

"But you've decided to make an exception in my case!" she supplied acidly. Her hand itched to slap his face, but she was still waiting for the right moment to strike. She retreated another step. "If you had one decent bone in your body, Ian MacGregor, you'd let me go now!"

"Would I, lass?" he murmured softly. He lifted a hand to smooth a stray tendril of hair from her forehead. It was a tender, almost possessive gesture—and one that caused her stomach to do a strange flip-flop. "We've an old saying here," he told her in a low, vibrant tone that was scarcely more than a whisper. " 'It's dear-cost honey that's licked off a thorn.' Perhaps, Callie Rose Buchanan, the risk would be worth it."

She drew in her breath upon an audible gasp. Dismayed to feel a sudden, inexplicable warmth stealing over her, she decided to wait no longer.

She raised her arm and brought her chosen weapon crashing down toward Ian's head. He managed to deflect the full brunt of what would surely have been a painful, if not exactly life-threatening blow. The blackened tip of the poker, however, scraped across the top of his shoulder. Muttering an oath, he seized the length of iron and wrenched it out of Callie Rose's hand.

She did not wait to see what he would do next. Whirling about, she pulled open the door and dashed headlong from the room. Her long skirts tangled about her legs as she flew down the tower's winding steps, but she hastily snatched them up and continued her frantic bid for freedom.

Ian was upon her before she had traveled more than a few yards beyond the foot of the stairs. He caught her about the waist and hauled her back against his powerful, hard-muscled warmth.

"No!" she cried. Hot, bitter tears of defeat sparkled in her gaze. "Damn you, let me go!" With a scream loud enough to wake the dead, she kicked and twisted violently within his grasp.

"Cum do theanga!" he ground out. Once again, though his words were uttered in the old Scots tongue, their meaning was all too clear. "Silence, woman!"

"I will not be silent!" She would have screamed again, but he clamped a hand across her mouth and gathered her so tightly against him that she felt her feet leaving the floor.

"Would you be having your supper now, my lord?" someone calmly inquired from a nearby doorway.

Callie Rose gasped, abruptly ceasing her struggles as her eyes flew to where a plump, middle-aged woman in a plain black gown stood surveying them without a trace of surprise, or disapproval, on her features. Indeed, she seemed to find nothing at all unusual about the tempestuous scene before her.

"Aye, Molly," Ian replied in the same even manner. "Miss Buchanan is no doubt hungry after the long ride."

Molly turned and disappeared back through the doorway. Callie Rose found herself released in the next instant. She rounded on Ian with her blue eyes furiously ablaze, her color high, and her breasts heaving above the low-cut bodice.

"If you think I'm going to sit down at your table and behave as though I were an invited guest—" she started to say.

"That is precisely what you will do," he insisted, his tone dangerously level. His hand closed about her arm in an iron grip, while his own smoldering gaze raked over her face. "Like it or not, you will remain here until I decide to let you go."

"And when will that be?" Trying to jerk her arm free, she met with no success and had to settle for shooting him another rancorous glare. She would have surrendered to the impulse to slap him, but she was afraid he might just hit her back. After all, she didn't know the infuriating rogue at all. She had no idea what he was capable of doing. Yet, she had somehow sensed from the very beginning that he would not hurt her. Though she cursed herself for a fool, she couldn't help feeling that Ian MacGregor was someone who, under different and more normal circumstances, she might actually like to know better. . . .

His large hand seemed to scorch her skin, even through the embroidered white silk of her sleeve. She colored hotly when his eyes dropped to her revealing décolletage. Raising a hand to impatiently sweep several wayward tresses from her face, she had no idea how much her anger served to heighten her beauty.

"Well, Mr. MacGregor?" she prodded when he did not immediately answer. "How long are you planning to continue with this despicable little farce of yours?"

"I've not yet decided," he replied. He had, of course. He had decided the first time he had set eyes on her. But he wasn't ready to admit the truth yet, not even to himself. "Come," he commanded, urging her along with him. "We could both do with a bit of nourishment. And you'll need to keep up your strength if you're to continue your misguided attempts at murder."

There was no genuine anger or reproach in his voice, only humor for the absurdity of the situation. He couldn't blame her for trying to escape; he would have done the same. By all that was holy, he reflected, she was the most courageous, spirited, hot-tempered woman he had ever known. *And the most desirable,* an inner voice saw fit to proclaim. He swore underneath his breath and forced his gaze elsewhere.

"Next time I'll aim much lower!" she vowed meaningfully. Ian gave a quiet chuckle at that, leading her across the corridor to the privacy of a small, warmly lit dining room on the second floor of the castle.

Supper proved to be an ordeal in itself. Callie Rose ate only a small amount of the food set before her, even though the faithful Molly (who would not meet her gaze, did not respond to her impassioned declaration that she was being held in the castle against her will, and could obviously not be relied upon to offer so much as an ounce of assistance) served a delicious meal of game soup, haddock in brown sauce, steamed vegetables fresh from the castle garden, and Dundee cake topped with almonds. The wine was strong and sweet, and she drank far too much of it. The appetite of her "host," she noted resentfully, appeared to be quite healthy and little affected by a conscience that should by all rights be wracked with guilt.

She was in no mood to admire the elegant furnishings of the room. The ceiling painted with rich and colorful designs, the elaborately carved table and chairs, the brocade draperies at the windows and the chandelier blazing above, the superb china and silver and crystal—all received negligent attention as her eyes drifted frequently to the doorway. She knew it would be useless to follow through on the impulse to toss a wine goblet at Ian's head and bolt from the room. There was little doubt in her mind that he would still manage to catch her. Either that, or his servants would be hot on her heels before she could make her way outside to the stables.

She had no choice but to sit opposite him and bide her time. Chagrined at the prospect of spending the night within the walls of Castle MacGregor, she stubbornly refused to be drawn into a conversation with its villainous owner.

"Your reputation has preceded you, Miss Buchanan," he suddenly remarked as he lifted his glass of wine to his lips.

When she merely sat ramrod straight in her chair and offered no reply, he continued:

"I have many associates in London."

He was satisfied to note the slight narrowing of her beautiful eyes, though her adorable mouth remained tightly shut.

" 'The Wild Rose,' " he murmured, his own mouth curving upward. "Aye, it fits you."

Her only response was to fling him a look that would have chilled lesser men into silence.

"It might interest you to know that the young Duke of Albemarle is a particular friend of mine."

An expression of surprise played across her face now.

"You've been branded a shameless and coldhearted vixen. In short, Callie Rose, you appear to have worn out your welcome in the fair jewel of England," he finished, with a faint, humorless smile. If even half of what he'd heard about her was true, she deserved little mercy from him.

"How could you know about that?" she challenged, her curiosity getting the better of her at last.

"I was in London for a brief visit only last week." He lowered his glass to the table once more and met her fiery, inquisitive gaze. "Another example of fate's 'kittle' ways, wouldn't you say? You see, I arrived the very day you and Mrs. Terhune departed for Edinburgh. I soon found myself apprised of the exploits of a certain young lady from Texas, a raven-haired enchantress who had not only spurned Albemarle, but a good many other poor, foolishly captivated souls as well. Little did I know that the scandalous former darling of London society would turn out to be Angus Buchanan's granddaughter."

"Am I supposed to believe that you just *happened* to return to the Highlands at the same time I was visiting here?"

"Believe what you will," he offered grimly. "The fact remains that when I journeyed to Inverness yesterday, I was informed of your presence at the Caledonian. The hotel's proprietor, Mr. Ferguson, was only too happy to tell me everything he knew about you—that you were indeed Angus's granddaughter, that your chaperon, Mrs. Terhune, had taken to her bed with a cold, and that you had requested directions to the old Buchanan estate with the intention of traveling here today. Our friend Ferguson was also quite eager to remind me of the feud," he added dryly. "The matter is common knowledge among my esteemed and ever curious neighbors."

"And so you followed me out here!" Callie Rose said accusingly. Her face was flushed from the wine as well as indignation, and her eyes shone even more brilliantly blue than usual. "You were lying in wait for me the whole time!"

"That I was." A dark frown suddenly creased his handsome, sun-kissed brow, and his gaze smoldered before dropping to the glass he still absently fingered. "My duty to my clan demanded I seize this one chance to redeem the family's honor."

He'd been given little choice in the matter. True

Highlander that he was, duty and honor meant more than life itself. Whatever his initial reluctance to involve a woman in the whole bloody affair, it was done now. She was here and he could not be sorry for it. . . .

"Did it ever occur to you, Mr. MacGregor, that you might have approached me in a polite, reasonable manner and asked for my help in resolving the problem, instead of—of manhandling me so rudely?" She downed the last of her own wine and set the crystal goblet down so hard that the entire table shook.

"Can you honestly say you'd have consented to the terms if I had done so?" he parried, with one mockingly raised eyebrow.

"You might at least have tried!"

He said nothing, but subjected her to a long, intense scrutiny. Then, rising to his feet, he tossed his fine linen napkin to the table.

"It's time you returned to your room." His features had become inscrutable, and his eyes gleamed dully now. "The hour grows late."

"Late?" She cast a quick glance toward the ornate, eighteenth-century wooden clock atop the marble chimneypiece to her left. "Why, it isn't even eight o'clock yet!" Her heart filled with sudden dread at the thought of going back upstairs. Now that darkness had fallen, she felt more than ever uncertain about her fate. Ian MacGregor had promised she would be safe . . . *safe from what*?

"The day has been a difficult one for you." He did not pause to ask himself if it was his concern for her well-being that prompted him to cut the evening short, or if he was anxious to remove himself from her presence for another reason entirely.

Callie Rose started to protest when he came around to take her arm, but she knew it would do no good. She held herself proudly erect as she went along with him. Preceding him up the tower steps, she was unaware of the way his burning, appreciative gaze followed the seductive sway of her hips. She swept through the doorway and turned to face him.

"Are you going to keep me under lock and key the whole time I'm here?" she asked, her voice slightly unsteady. The fire had been tended during their absence, and a large metal bathtub sat before its comforting warmth. Lying on the bed was a long-sleeved nightgown of fine white cotton, embroidered with flowers.

"Would you not agree that such measures are necessary?" Ian asked reasonably. He glanced toward the waiting tub. "Molly's daughter, Jenny, will bring the water for your bath. If you require anything else, you've only to ring for it."

"You've thought of everything, haven't you?" Folding her arms beneath her breasts, she warned him, "Don't think you've won, Mr. MacGregor! I wasn't brought up to give in without a fight, and I'm sure as blazes not going to do so now! I *will* find a way to escape, and I *will* make you pay for this!"

"Would you start another blood feud between our clans?" he taunted softly, not the least bit troubled by her threats. His gaze flickered with bold significance to her décolletage once more before returning to her face. "It might not be such a cruel fate to have you as my adversary, Callie Rose Buchanan."

It was the wrong thing to say. Or the wrong way to say it. Whatever the case, she was bone-weary, her nerves were strung tight as a bowstring, and her head was spinning dizzily from the effects of too much wine on a near empty stomach. And it was all this damned, wickedly appealing Scotsman's fault.

"Ooooh!" she hissed. Provoked by his arrogance—as well as her own inability to conquer an attraction toward him—she became reckless. Her eyes blazed and narrowed.

She launched herself at him with a vengeance. Her hands came up, her fingers curling toward his face in an attempt to score its rugged perfection with her well-manicured nails. At the same time she raised her booted foot to land a punishing kick to his unguarded shin. Her full skirts swirled about her shapely, black-stockinged limbs, while her long raven tresses streamed in a wild mass about her face and shoulders.

For Ian, it was like doing battle with a whirlwind. He ground out a curse, caught her wrists, and forced her arms behind her back. Still, she fought him, refusing to be subdued, refusing to acknowledge his superior strength. She called him every vile name she could think of, then inhaled upon a sharp gasp when he suddenly enveloped her with his strong, sinewy arms. Her head fell back, and she found herself staring up into a pair of magnificent green eyes that seared ruthlessly down into the blazing sapphire depths of hers.

She could not look away, could not move. Several long moments of highly charged silence rose between them. She held her breath while his eyes raked over her becomingly flushed countenance, dropped to the curve of her breasts again, then returned to meet her wide, expectant gaze. Though she did not know it, he was engaged in another battle now, this one with himself. . . .

Without warning, his mouth came crashing down on hers. She moaned in startled, furious protest and struggled anew within his embrace.

But it was no use. Ian would not be denied. Consigning wisdom to the devil, he kissed the enchanting spitfire in his arms as he had longed to do all evening. The feel of her soft, voluptuous curves squirming against his hard-muscled warmth was enough to drive him to madness.

His lips, warm and strong and masterfully persuasive, demanded a response as his arms tightened about her. Callie Rose felt her senses reeling, felt her traitorous body swaying against him. Her eyes swept closed. She had been kissed before, but—*heaven help her*—never like this!

His mouth virtually ravished the sweetness of hers, his hot, velvety tongue plunging between her parted lips. She moaned again at the bold invasion and tried to turn her head away, but he entangled a hand within her thick curls and held her captive for his pleasure—*and her own.*

A wondrous, unfamiliar warmth spread throughout her body. She grew light-headed and could no longer summon the will to fight. Before she knew what was happening, she was kissing him back. Passion flared and the world receded. All else was forgotten as, for the first time in her life, she gave herself up to the intoxicating pleasure of being kissed by a man whose very touch set her on fire.

And then, as suddenly as it had begun, the kiss ended.

Callie Rose's eyelids fluttered open. Wearing an expression that was half confusion, half disappointment, she blinked up at Ian.

"You would tempt a saint," he decreed huskily, his gaze smoldering with the force of his own barely controlled desire. He scowled down at her. "But you'll not count me among your other conquests, Miss Buchanan. I am no young stripling to be bent at will. No, and by all I hold dear, the next time you lift your hand to me, you'll feel the flat of mine on your backside."

"Are you—are you threatening me?" she stammered indignantly, her throat constricting in very real alarm at the look in his eyes.

"I am indeed. And keep in mind, lass, that no MacGregor gives his word lightly."

He released her at last. She glared umbrageously up at him as she took a hasty step backward and rubbed at her aching wrists.

"If you ever lay hands on me again, you bastard, I'll kill you!" At that particular moment, she was quite certain she could shoot him stone-cold dead and never feel remorse for it.

"Someday, Callie Rose Buchanan," he predicted in a voice of ominous calm, "you'll pay the price for that wicked tongue of yours."

Torn between the desire to sweep her into his arms again and the urge to skelp her well and proper, he did neither. He resolutely turned and left her alone, telling himself that she had every right to her anger. He had not meant to kiss her; by damn, he had behaved like a lovesick fool.

Still, he thought with a frown, he could not regret what had happened. She had set a fire to raging in his blood; he had never wanted a woman as much as he wanted her. But it was more than that. Much, much more . . .

The truth hit him full force. He came to an abrupt halt at the foot of the steps and cast a look back up toward the room where his beautiful, defiant captive stood trembling in his wake. His handsome face became a mask of iron determination, while his green eyes darkened with a potent mixture of emotion.

Blissfully unaware of the fact that her entire future was being decided a short distance below, Callie Rose sank down upon the bed. Her lips still tingled as a result of Ian's passionate kiss, and she could not escape the disturbing memory of his arms about her. Refusing to acknowledge that she had felt anything more than outrage, she lifted a hand to her throat and shot another narrow, murderous glare toward the door.

She was furious with him for having dared to treat her like some painted-up floozy. And she was almost, but not quite, as furious with herself for having let him. How the blazes could she have done such a thing?

"Damn you, Ian MacGregor!" she muttered in a low, simmering tone. Her predicament, which had started badly enough with her abduction that afternoon, had steadily worsened since arriving at the castle. What would happen next?

A sudden thought sent hot color to her cheeks and her eyes opening wide. Good heavens, suppose Ian came upstairs during the night and—? *No!*

She sprang up from the bed and crossed to the fire-place. Her stormy gaze settled on the blaze, mirroring the shower of sparks that rose heavenward.

In Scotland, there would be no one to bedevil her, she had told herself back in London. She couldn't have been more wrong. Ian MacGregor was bedeviling her worse than anyone on earth had ever done—

A knock sounded at the door.

She spun about, her heart leaping in trepidation. But it was not Ian who pushed open the door. It was a pretty, brown-haired young woman carrying two large, steaming buckets of hot water.

"Good evening, miss. The master said you'd be wanting a bath." Her black cotton skirts rustled softly as she moved toward the bathtub.

"The master?" Callie Rose echoed. Yes, she mused derisively, it suited him. "You must be Jenny."

"Aye, that I am." Jenny cast her a tentative smile in response, then carefully emptied the buckets' contents into the tub.

"I suppose you know that I'm a prisoner here!"

"A prisoner, miss?" repeated the other woman, look-ing baffled as she straightened from her task.

"Mr. MacGregor kidnapped me! My name is Callie Rose Buchanan, I am an American, and I am being held here against my will! Please, you've got to help me!" she entreated, reaching a hand out to grasp the other woman's arm.

"I—I'm afraid I cannot."

"Don't you understand?" she cried in exasperation. "I have to get away! Your *master* is nothing but a common criminal! He has no right to do this to me, no right at all, and if you refuse to help me escape, then you're every bit as guilty as he is!"

"Lord MacGregor is as fine a man that ever lived!" Jenny startled her by declaring fervently.

"*Lord* MacGregor?" Great balls of fire, she wondered with a deep frown of displeasure, did the man have a title to go along with his dictatorial ways?

"I am truly sorry for your unhappiness, Miss Buchanan, but the feud must be settled. If you could but know—"

"The only thing I care to know is how to get out of this castle!"

"The days will no doubt pass quickly," Jenny offered in a comforting manner. "My mother's cooking can be matched by no other, and I would be glad to bring you books from the master's library, or perhaps a bit of needlework to do." Her attempts to soothe were in earnest, but so was her devotion to her employer. "Lord MacGregor is a good man, Miss Buchanan. Aye, and a fair-minded one. He'll see that you're returned safely to Inverness when the time comes."

"A good and fair-minded man would not have brought me here!" Callie Rose disputed passionately. "And as for the question of my safety, are you really so naive that you can't see the danger I'm in? I am, after all, completely at his mercy. He could take it in mind to do a hell of a lot more than just—" She broke off, colored hotly, and whirled to stare down into the flames again. "Do you want *that* on your conscience?"

"Why, miss, he would never do such a thing!" Jenny proclaimed in a shocked, breathless tone, her eyes growing round as saucers.

"Wouldn't he?"

Jenny's only answer was to shake her head vigorously in heartfelt denial as she hurried back to the door. Callie Rose gave chase, seizing her by the hand.

"Please, you must help me!" she implored one last time. "I'll pay you whatever you ask if you'll only—"

"No!" The young brune jerked free and scurried through the arched doorway. She hastily closed the door after her, turning the key in the lock before Callie Rose could do anything more than pull at the knob in frustration.

"Jenny!" she called out, but knew it would do no good.

She was trapped. Trapped in a place where the only people who could help her were fiercely loyal to the man who had turned her entire world upside down.

His face rose in her mind again, and something he had said earlier returned to haunt her.

Perhaps, Callie Rose, the risk would be worth it.

A shiver ran the length of her spine. She drew in a deep, wayward breath as she recalled the moment when he had swept her into his arms and kissed her with such compelling mastery. Scoundrel though he was, she couldn't deny that he had a way about him. Yes, an inner voice put forth, he'd probably had his "way" with dozens of women.

The thought gave her little comfort.

She glanced toward the waiting tub. Unhappily realizing that the night would be a long one, she heaved a sigh and lifted her hands to the buttons on the front of her gown. Her aching muscles demanded relief, and the bath was simply too tempting to pass up.

If Ian MacGregor decided to return, she told herself
while her eyes kindled with a determination that was a
perfect match for his, he'd have another fight on his
hands. He would soon learn that the word of a
Buchanan was every bit as sacred as the word of a
MacGregor. She would never surrender ... *never.*

❧ THREE ❧

Callie Rose awoke with a start.

She came bolt upright in the bed, her eyes opening wide as her heart leapt in alarm at the unfamiliarity of her surroundings. Memories, troubling and unpleasant in the extreme, flooded her mind in the very next instant.

Castle MacGregor.

She gave an inward groan, dropped her fiery sapphire gaze to the nightgown she was wearing, and snatched the covers all the way up to her chin. It hadn't been a nightmare after all, she told herself with a disconsolate frown. No, by thunder, it had been all too real. Too painfully—mortifyingly—real.

Dismayed to realize that she had fallen asleep in the midst of such danger, she shot an anxious look toward the window. Soft morning sunlight was already filtering into the room to chase away the ghosts and anticipated horrors of the night, while from the kitchens below drifted up the wonderful, mingling aromas of sausage, fried potatoes, oatcakes, and coffee.

She closed her eyes again for a moment and inhaled deeply. The appetizing smell was a pointed reminder that she had eaten next to nothing in the past twenty-four hours.

"Traitor," she muttered in condemnation of her growling stomach. Frowning to herself once more, she flung back the covers and shivered when a blast of cold air greeted her. The fire had long since burned itself out, and even though the day had dawned bright and clear, there was a lingering chill within the castle's thick stone walls.

She resolutely left the warmth of the bed and pushed her bare feet into the pink satin slippers waiting on the floor. The first order of business was to get dressed. Her own clothing had mysteriously disappeared during supper the night before, and she had no desire to wear the form-fitting white dress again. The dilemma would ordinarily have been of little consequence to her—the dictates of fashion were near the very bottom of her daily list of priorities—but Ian MacGregor had changed all that. Her whole body grew warm when she recalled the way his steady, penetrating gaze had fastened on her breasts. Truth be told, she had felt as though he had stripped her naked in his mind. . . .

She swore and pulled herself rigidly upright. Hurrying across to the wardrobe, she was in the process of searching in the compartments for a wrapper when her ears suddenly detected the sound of the key turning the lock.

"Dear Lord!" she gasped, coloring furiously as she glanced down at her nightdress again. The thought of confronting her rakishly appealing captor while protected by nothing but the thin white garment filled her with a dread she would never own up to. She started for the bed, intent upon using the blanket as a shield again, but the door eased open before she could reach it.

"Miss Buchanan?"

It was Jenny. Smiling a bit uncertainly, the young housemaid stepped inside the room. In one hand she carried a bucket of hot water, while over her other arm was draped Callie Rose's traveling suit.

"I'm sorry if I've wakened you, but the master said I was to come up right away. I've tidied your dress as best I could, and I thought you'd be wanting to freshen up." She glided forth to set the bucket down beside the washstand, then glanced at the window. "It looks to be a braw day, do you not think so? Aye, and my mother's got a fine breakfast on the stove."

"And Mr. MacGregor?" demanded Callie Rose, escape returning as her main consideration now. She moved closer to the door. Fully prepared to flee in her nightgown if need be, she swept the sleep-tousled black curls away from her face and tensed in readiness. "Where is he?"

"Lord MacGregor's waiting for you downstairs," Jenny answered, with a gentle correction. Her eyes sparkled softly when she added, "He said I was to tell you that he's purely famished and that if you've not joined him in ten minutes' time, he'll be coming up himself to fetch you—dressed or not."

"Why, that insufferable bas—" Callie Rose started to fume, her own eyes bridling with irritation.

"You'd best hurry!" cautioned Jenny. She crossed to the bed, lowered the green wool ensemble neatly to the covers, and turned to offer one last token of advice. "He's not a man to be trifled with, Miss Buchanan. No indeed. Fair and generous he may be, but he's got the devil's own temper sometimes. Mind you, he's never angered without reason."

"What the blazes has *he* got to be angry about? I'm the one being held prisoner!"

"You do not understand . . ." The young brunette sighed, shaking her head. "Perhaps, when you've been here a wee bit longer, you'll—"

"No! I'll never understand what he's done!" Callie Rose insisted stubbornly. She shivered at the cold and folded her arms across her chest. "How can you possibly justify this—this black-hearted villainy? For heaven's sake, are all of you here completely mad?"

"It must seem so to you," Jenny said, with a faint smile. She said no more on the subject, but nodded toward the fireplace. "We've little time now, so I'll tend to the fire as soon as you've had your breakfast."

"I'm not hungry!" As if to expose the lie, her stomach growled again.

"Are you not? Well then, I'm sure you can manage some tea, or some coffee if you'd rather."

Jenny slipped from the room with that, leaving Callie Rose in a quandary.

She was sorely tempted to put Ian MacGregor to the test. Faced with the option of either digging in her heels and staying right where she was, or obeying his damnably ungallant summons, she showed remarkable presence of mind by choosing the latter. The prospect of facing him again filled her with trepidation, but she told herself it would only make things worse to postpone the inevitable. Besides, what could she hope to gain by remaining locked away in the tower? At least downstairs, there was always the chance that she could find a way to escape.

After performing her morning toilette and donning her newly pressed suit, she inspected her reflection in the mirror above the washstand. Her eyes were bright with determination, and her color unusually high. She had brushed the tangles from her hair, and, finding no pins, had secured the thick, midnight-black tresses into a single long braid that hung down her back. Satisfied with her appearance, and feeling more like her old self now that she was wearing her own clothes again, she turned away from the mirror and sliced a narrow, calculating look downward.

"It's time you learned something about good old Texas gumption, *Lord* MacGregor," she proclaimed in a low tone edged with defiance and sarcasm. Her father's image suddenly rose in her mind. Drawing courage from all that he had instilled in her, and from the agreeable thought of what he would do to the arrogant Scottish rogue once she had escaped to tell her tale, she squared her shoulders, raised her head high, and swept regally from the room.

Ian was waiting for her at the foot of the stairs. An expression that was half-masculine impatience, half-warm amusement, crossed his face when he caught sight of his prisoner. Attired much the same as he had been the previous day, he looked particularly handsome and virile—*and dangerous*—this morning. He favored her with a faint, mocking smile, his gaze darkening with an emotion she was afraid to put a name to.

"Another minute more, Miss Buchanan," he remarked dryly, "and you'd have found yourself across my shoulder yet again."

"Is that a threat, Mr. MacGregor?" she countered, her eyes flashing down at him as she descended the last few steps.

" 'Tis a promise." He stepped forward to take her arm, his strong fingers closing possessively about her soft flesh. He gave a curt nod toward the dining room. *"Tha ar bracaist deiseil."*

"Let go of me! And why the devil don't you speak English?" She tried to pull free, but was not at all surprised when his grip remained firm. It infuriated her no end to feel the way her skin burned at his touch. God help me, she mused, while her heart pounded crazily at his nearness, the sooner I get away from here, the sooner I can return to normal! Something strange was happening to her . . . and it had started the first moment she had looked into Ian MacGregor's green eyes.

"My apologies, lass," he said, with a smile that could easily have taken her breath away if she had let it. "You see, it's long been a habit of mine to use the Gaelic whenever I'm home. I get little enough practice in London, or in Edinburgh, for that matter."

"I find it difficult to believe that someone like you is actually welcomed into polite society! But then again, perhaps your money and your title are enough to turn the heads of those simpering fools and make them overlook your lack of breeding. *And* your utter contempt for the law. You may have fooled them, but you can't fool me. I have no doubt whatsoever that you come from a long line of baseborn scoundrels!"

She had gone too far with the insult, and she knew it,

but she'd be hanged if she'd ever take it back. In that moment, she would have said or done almost anything to hurt him. He was far too attractive and cocksure for his own good, and he had treated her more roughly than she had ever been treated before. The memory of his kiss haunted her once more. For that reason alone, she would have gladly thrown caution to the wind and slapped his face again. But his response took her off-guard.

"Think of me what you will, Callie Rose Buchanan," Ian told her quietly, all traces of amusement gone as he pulled her about to face him and finally released her arm. "But never again make the mistake of insulting my family."

His rugged features appeared quite grim as he issued the warning, while his eyes had taken on a hard, cold look that made her believe he was entirely capable of carrying out his previous threat of retribution. That he would love to get his hands on her was obvious.

Callie Rose stiffened beneath his disquieting scrutiny. Opening her mouth to fling him a suitably scathing retort, she thought better of it at the last moment and lapsed into angry silence as he took her arm again and led her into the dining room.

Molly was waiting for them beside the table. Her face brightened when they entered the sunlit room, and she greeted Callie Rose with a welcoming smile.

"Good morning to you, Miss Buchanan! Would you be wanting some eggs this morning? Or maybe you'd like a bowl of porridge with your sausage? It would take me no more than a minute to prepare whatever you've a mind for."

"Just some coffee, please," Callie Rose answered. She took her place opposite Ian, sitting ramrod straight in her chair and obstinately averting her gaze from the piercing steadiness of his.

"Bring our guest a taste of everything you've prepared, Molly," he instructed the cook, who immediately took herself off to the kitchen.

"I said—" Callie Rose started to reiterate in displeasure once Molly had gone.

"I heard what you said. But I will not allow you to starve yourself. You'll eat heartily of this meal—aye, and every meal hereafter."

"You have no right to tell me what to do!"

"Have I not?" His mouth curved into a soft, foreboding smile. "I think, my dearest Miss Buchanan, that it's time you had someone to look after you properly."

"Oh, really?" she ground out, her eyes fairly snapping with ire. "And I suppose you think you're the perfect man for the job?"

"It may well be that I am the man borne to tame the 'Wild Rose,' " he parried.

"*What?*" Callie Rose said, breathing hard in furious disbelief. She stood abruptly and flung her napkin to the table. "Why, you—you rattlepated sonofabitch! I don't need looking after, and I sure as hell don't intend to let you or any other man run roughshod over me!"

"Sit down," commanded Ian, rising now as well.

"Go to the devil!"

Her temper flaring beyond control, she finally surrendered to the impulse to launch a crystal water goblet at his head. He startled her by catching the glass in his hand. She hadn't expected him to possess such lightning-quick reflexes, but then he had already proven himself to be a man full of surprises. *Not all of them disagreeable,* a tiny voice inside her saw fit to pronounce.

With a strangled cry of rage, she gathered up her skirts and made for the doorway. Ian was upon her in an instant, his arm capturing her about the waist. She struggled wildly in his grasp as he dragged her back toward the table. Then, suddenly remembering the small dagger he wore on the outer part of his right stocking, she bent over and pulled the weapon from its sheath. She lifted her arm and brought the point of the knife slicing vengefully downward across his sinewy forearm.

He bit out an oath, but did not release her. His hand closed like a vise about her wrist, and she gasped in mingled frustration and dismay as he forced her to drop the dagger. He spun her about to face him, his hands relentlessly gripping her upper arms. His gaze smoldered down into hers.

"By heaven, you little vixen," he uttered in a low, ominous tone, "I warned you against—"

"I don't give a tinker's damn about your warnings!" she retorted hotly. "I hate you, Ian MacGregor, and I wish I'd been able to plunge the blasted thing into your heart!"

For a moment, it appeared he would strike her. If the savage gleam in his eyes was any indication, he would have liked nothing better than to give her the thrashing of her life. But the appearance of Molly on the scene prevented any retaliation on his part—at least for the moment.

"Why, sir, you're bleeding!" the cook exclaimed in

horror at the sight of the bright red stain on the sleeve of his snow-white linen shirt.

" 'Tis nothing," he murmured quietly. Without another word, he propelled Callie Rose back to her seat. She wisely chose not to resist. Her face was flushed as she sank down into the chair, while the bodice of her suit was wrinkled and sadly askew. Feeling an inexplicable twinge of remorse for what she had done, she sat silent and speechless with her eyes downcast.

"I'll fetch some bandages," Molly declared, with a frown. She lowered the platter of food to the table before hurrying away again.

In spite of what had just happened, Ian couldn't help gazing at his beautiful captive with a mixture of admiration and desire. She was all fire and spirit. And passion. His loins tightened anew, his gold-flecked emerald gaze darkening to jade when he recalled the way her sweet lips had moved beneath the conquering warmth of his the night before. The memory of her response, of her soft, thoroughly enticing curves pressing against his body, had invaded his dreams and made him yearn for daylight.

Across the table, Callie Rose was acutely conscious of his eyes upon her. She straightened her bodice and ventured a surreptitious glance at him from beneath her eyelashes. Why the devil did the man have to be so incredibly strong? she lamented to herself, an audible sigh escaping her lips. And what had she ever done to deserve being cast into this predicament? The fates had apparently conspired against her; her every attempt at escape thus far had met with disastrous results.

Once again, Ian MacGregor had made it all too clear

that he meant to keep her there until it suited him to let her go. He deserved to be horsewhipped for what he had done. Indeed, her palm itched to strike him until he begged for mercy—which, of course, she could never imagine him doing. He was without a doubt the most overbearing, maddening, full-of-himself man she had ever come across. J. D. and her brothers would probably be inclined to string him up once they found out how he had treated her.

And yet, she realized as she stole another look at his handsome, inscrutable countenance, she didn't really want him dead at all. . . .

"Twice now, Callie Rose Buchanan, you have drawn blood," he observed with a faint, mocking smile as he idly fingered the bloodstained tear in his sleeve. He was satisfied when her eyes flew upward to meet his.

"Yes, and I'll do so a third time if you don't let me go!" she threatened, with a great deal more bravado than she was actually feeling.

"Perhaps I should seek to even the score."

Her cheeks grew warm at the look in his eyes. She didn't even want to consider what he'd meant by the remark. Cursing herself for ever having felt guilty, she reached for the silver coffeepot Molly had left on the table.

"If I were a man, you'd never have succeeded in keeping me here!" she muttered, pouring some of the hot, aromatic brew into a porcelain cup. Her hands shook a little; their unsteadiness was a perfect match for her emotions.

"If you were a man, I'd not have wanted to."

Her color deepened, and she was dismayed to feel
her pulse race. She quickly looked away.

"Do you not think it time we declared a truce?" suggested Ian. For once, his tone was neither dictatorial nor
brimming with amusement.

Her eyes widened before returning to his face. His
expression, she noted, was perfectly serious, and she
could have sworn his gaze held a silent appeal for understanding. That was ridiculous, she told herself in the
next instant. If there was one thing she had learned
about Ian MacGregor, it was that he did as he pleased
and damn the consequences.

"You could enjoy your stay at Castle MacGregor if
you so chose," he told her. "We've a lot to offer in the
way of entertainment."

"Then offer it to someone else!"

"No, lass, I cannot do that." His brow creased into a
mild frown as he shook his head. "You are the only
one—"

"I know, confound it! I'm the only one who can end
the feud between the MacGregors and the Buchanans!"
She heaved a loud, highly eloquent sigh of exasperation. "Don't you think this medieval travesty has gone
far enough? You've kept your promise! You brought me
here as your prisoner, so surely all of the 'requirements'
have been met! What possible reason can you have
for—?"

"There is yet another requirement to be fulfilled."

"*Another* requirement?" His words struck fear in her
heart. She took a deep breath before demanding, "What
are you talking about?"

"I will explain it to you when the time is right," he

replied enigmatically. His gaze burned across into hers, and when he spoke again it was in a voice laced with steel. "For now, you'd do well to keep in mind that my patience is fast wearing thin. The fact that you are here against your wishes cannot be altered. But I will abide no more of these ill-conceived schemes to escape. You will remain with me until such time as *I* decide to return you to Inverness. Och, woman," he finished, with a scowl of annoyance, "did you truly believe you could get away so easily?"

"You can threaten all you like, but it won't make any difference! I'll fight you to my dying breath!" she vowed, with considerable fervor.

"Be that as it may," he said calmly, unscathed by the murderous glare she hurled at him, "you can hereafter be treated with gentleness and respect, or else suffer for your actions. Guest or prisoner, the choice is entirely in your hands."

"Isn't this a case of the pot calling the kettle black, Mr. MacGregor?" she challenged, with biting sarcasm. "I'm supposed to behave with all meekness and civility, while you yourself are the one who's played the kilted barbarian at every turn! First you carry me off—in a raging thunderstorm, no less—and then you keep me under lock and key as if I were a madwoman, and then you—you try and ravish me!"

"If I had tried, Callie Rose Buchanan, you'd have been well and truly ravished," he asserted in a low, splendidly vibrant tone.

She inhaled upon a soft gasp. A fiery blush crept up to her face, and her gaze fell beneath the glowing intensity of his once more.

Molly chose that opportune moment to return with the bandages.

"I've brought along the iodine as well," she announced to no one in particular. She bustled forward, her eyes silently accusing as they shifted to Callie Rose.

Ian's attempts to wave away the woman's concern were ignored. With the familiarity of a lifelong acquaintance, she rolled up his sleeve to expose the source of what was now little more than a slight trickle of blood. She performed a quick but thorough examination—and concluded with a sigh of relief that the cut would not require stitching. After expertly applying the iodine and bandaging the wound, she shot Callie Rose another reproachful look and left the two of them alone again.

They finally had their breakfast then. Callie Rose followed Ian's directive to eat and swallowed her pride—as well as a generous portion of the sausage, potatoes, and oatcakes. A young man appeared in the doorway during the course of the meal. He said nothing, but Ian excused himself from the table and disappeared from the room for several minutes. Offering no explanation upon his return, he finished off his own plate of food while Callie Rose cast furtive glances in his direction and simmered with curiosity.

Afterward, he escorted her into the outer hall. Her eyes widened with astonishment when she spied her own valise sitting at the foot of the tower's spiral staircase.

"How did—?"

"I had Peter ride for Inverness at first light this morning," Ian explained, cutting her off with a brief smile.

"Mrs. Terhune was most eager to oblige 'your' request. And she sent you this." He withdrew an envelope from the waistband of his kilt.

She took the envelope from him and quickly tore it open. Pulling out the single sheet of paper within, she felt a sudden lump rise in her throat when she recognized Martha's handwriting.

"My dearest Callie Rose," the letter began, "I am so very relieved that you have found companions with which to share our last few days in Scotland. You can imagine my surprise when I learned of your plans to accept an invitation from people you had only just met. However, I do know how very impulsive you can be, and I am quite sure you will enjoy your stay with the MacGregors. I have been assured by Mr. Ferguson that they are of high moral character and that Lord MacGregor, in particular, is a charming and well-favored person."

Callie Rose paused here and tossed Ian a narrow, peevish glance. His mouth twitched in response. She compressed her own lips into a thin line of anger and returned her gaze to the letter.

"I am forwarding to you a portion of your baggage," Martha had written. "I have packed three of your best gowns, in addition to your riding habit, and, of course, several other necessary articles of clothing. I certainly hope you were not caught out in yesterday's storm without sufficient protection, and that you have escaped any threat of a cold such as mine, which, I am sorry to report, has worsened. Mr. Ferguson's wife has been kindness itself, and has offered to summon a physician for me today. Do not worry, for I am convinced I shall be recovered in plenty of time for our trip home. I look forward to being reunited with you at the end of the week. Until then, I wish you a pleasant visit with your new friends." It was signed, "Your loving cousin, Martha."

Crumpling the letter in her hand, Callie Rose found herself perilously close to tears. She did not see the way Ian's gaze softened, nor could she have guessed that he was battling the impulse to draw her against him in comfort. A fierce, protective urge rose within him, and he felt his heart twist at the sight of her distress. He cursed himself as the cause of it. Yet there was no other way. . . .

"Come along," he said quietly, his hand taking her arm in a gentle grasp once more.

"Where are we going?"

"It's time you saw more of the castle. Unless, of course, you'd prefer to limit your knowledge to the tower?" His eyes brimmed with affectionate humor as they traveled over her beautiful, heart-shaped visage.

"Surely you've got better things to do than spend your days in *my* company!" she retorted, with a flash of her usual spirit. She dashed impatiently at her glistening eyes and lifted her head to a proud, defiant angle.

"I've other things to do," acknowledged Ian, then added, "but none better."

He gave her little choice in the matter. She was honestly glad for his insistence; the prospect of spending an entire day in the lonely solitude of the tower room was a dismal one. In this particular instance, at least, enduring Ian MacGregor's presence was the lesser of two evils.

And he did prove himself to be a captivating guide. She had never been terribly interested in viewing the interiors of other people's houses, whether simple country homes or grand estates with all the accompanying formalities and conventions and general rigmarole. Martha had dragged her through far too many of the latter these past few weeks.

But there was something different about Castle MacGregor. She was surprised to realize that she actually wanted to learn all she could about it. For some inexplicable reason, she looked about with rapt attention as Ian led her through the rooms that had witnessed nearly four hundred years of MacGregor domesticity—blissful and otherwise. Was it the place itself that drew her interest, she wondered, or was it because she was, quite literally, a "captive audience?"

Whatever the case, she soon discovered that the rest of the castle was as elegantly furnished as the dining room. The ceilings were of ornamental plaster, each painted in a riot of ornamentation, while the wallpaper, draperies, and carpets—all of impeccable design and quality—appeared to be new. The main entrance hall on the ground floor, once the very center of activity in the castle, featured Romanesque columns and a monstrous grandfather clock that, Ian told her, was of seventeenth-century German origin and had been purchased by his father some forty years earlier. It had terrorized the castle's occupants ever since, chiming incessantly at irregular moments, and often with less than melodious results.

Opening off to the left of the great hall was a library, filled to the brim with shelf upon towering shelf of books, a massive oak desk, and two crimson leather chairs. Callie Rose surmised correctly that the room was where Ian spent most of his time whenever inside. It had a warm, thoroughly masculine feel about it. Her eyes drifted to where a portrait hung above the carved Flemish mantelpiece. The subject of the painting, a dark-haired man clad in the distinctive garb of a Highlander, bore a striking resemblance to the present chief of the Clan MacGregor.

"My grandfather," Ian told her. His deep-timbred voice held an unmistakable note of pride.

"Maybe you should be grateful Angus Buchanan left your grandmother standing at the altar," she said caustically, her bright gaze offering a challenge he was only too willing to accept.

"I am more thankful than you will ever know." Though only the merest hint of a smile played about his lips, his eyes were alight with an intoxicating mixture of desire and amusement.

She felt a dull flush rise to her face. She had succeeded in pushing the memory of last night's madness to the back of her mind, but his bold, unnerving scrutiny brought it to the fore again. Muttering something unintelligible, she whirled and escaped back out into the hall.

The drawing room opposite quite took her breath away. Termed appropriately enough "The Sun Room" by the servants, it was lovely and airy with tall windows and a curious, chapellike air. Though very large, it managed somehow to feel cozy, even intimate, with its floral chintz-covered sofa and chairs, a rose-patterned carpet, and delicate stenciling work on the door cases and half-paneled walls.

In every room was a wealth of antique furniture, priceless paintings, and memorabilia from the long, turbulent history of the Highlands. There were enough clan crests, weapons, shields, and tartan rugs to fill an entire museum. More than ever before, and in spite of her adverse circumstances, Callie Rose was beginning to gain at least some small understanding of the true Scotland, the one few visitors are fortunate enough to find. It was *her* heritage as well, she realized as her fascinated gaze swept across the evidence of the past, both near and distant. Angus Buchanan may have chosen to leave it behind all those years ago, but it could never be completely forgotten. The blood of a noble, fiercely independent people ran strong in her veins. Was it any wonder that she had turned out the way she had? The thought made her lips curve into a soft smile of irony.

With her head spinning from all that she had seen thus far, she allowed Ian to lead her back up the staircase to the second floor. The majority of the bedchambers, he informed her, were situated on either side of the landing. They made a brief inspection of all four rooms to the south, then the first three northward, before finally pausing in front of the door at the farthest end of the narrow corridor. Ian swung open the door and waited for Callie Rose to precede him inside.

She knew immediately that it was his room.

The color scheme was predominantly red and gold, and the walls were paneled in rich-grained wood. It was a very large room, so that even with the tall mahogany wardrobe in one corner, two matching gilt-trimmed chests, and several elaborately fashioned tables throughout, there was no danger of feeling cramped for space. Overhead were thick beams and a white ceiling featuring a trellis pattern, while a thick wool carpet blanketed the stone floor. A massive stone fireplace stood ready to vanquish the cold, though at present the room was warmed by the dazzling sunlight that radiated through the arched, leaded-glass windows.

It was the bed, however, that commanded the most attention.

Her eyes grew very round as they fell upon the great four-poster looming against the opposite wall. It was an unusual and quite magnificent piece of furniture. Several variations of the family crest, the heads of boars and other strange beasts, holly leaves and thistle, and even the likeness of its first owners (a bearded man and a delicate-boned woman) had been carved directly into the wood. It bore the date *1598* on the centerpiece beneath the heavy brocade canopy. The plump feather mattress, crowned with a familiar plaid coverlet, was so far above the floor that a man of lesser height would no doubt have required a set of steps to reach it.

" 'Tis a peculiar thing, is it not?" Ian said behind her. She colored guiltily and would have fled the room if he had not blocked her path. His eyes twinkled down at her. "My father confessed to an extreme dislike for it. He said sleeping in it was much like being surrounded by all the ghosts and ghoulies of the night."

"Then it is the perfect resting place for a devil such as you," she opined, her gaze falling as she took an instinctive step backward. Her heart gave a sudden flutter at the sound of his low, mellow chuckle. She raised her eyes to his face again, only to feel as though an invisible current suddenly passed between them.

"Aye, Rosaleen, that it is," he concurred in a husky tone that was little more than a whisper.

"Wha—what did you call me?" Feeling unaccountably breathless, she tried to look away but could not.

"Have you never been called by a pet name, lass?" His eyes, so incredibly green and full of deep secrets, seemed determined to melt her icy reserve.

"I fail to see how that's any of your business, Mr. MacGregor!" she shot back, taking refuge in her anger. "Or should I address you as *my lord*?"

"Lord and master would be preferable," he teased softly.

"I'll never call any man that!"

"Will you not?"

He moved closer, so close that she could literally feel the heat emanating from his hard-muscled body. She swallowed hard and was dismayed to feel her knees weakening. Still, she stood her ground, refusing to turn coward and run ... refusing to admit that she wanted anything more out of the encounter than to show Ian MacGregor that he could neither charm nor bully her into submission the way he had no doubt charmed and bullied dozens of other women. Yes, indeed, she could well imagine that *they* had swooned at his feet and been glad for the dubious honor.

The thought gave her little comfort. Her eyes blazing their resplendent blue fire, she folded her arms across her chest and tilted her head back to confront him squarely.

"It's clear you're accustomed to having things your

own way," she declared in tight, measured tones. "But where I come from, a gentleman wouldn't dream of treating a lady the way you've treated me."

"Aye, but have we not already established the fact that I'm no gentleman? Bastard, rogue, scoundrel—were those not the epithets you deemed suitable?" He smiled faintly before adding, "And you are like no other lady of my acquaintance."

She recalled having told her father that she was no lady at all. The memory provoked a wealth of emotions within her, none of which made a great deal of sense at the moment. Unfolding her arms, she gathered up her skirts. She felt the sudden need to get away.

"Have we finished the tour?" she demanded, with a coolness that belied her inner turmoil. "If so, I'd like to go back to my room."

"I would not have thought you a coward, Callie Rose."

"I'm not a coward!" Her eyes kindled anew. "I'm not afraid of you! By damn, I'm not afraid of any man!"

"Perhaps you should be," he warned, with another ghost of a smile. His gaze warmed with passion as it traveled over her face.

"Get out of my way!" She angrily tried to push past him, but he caught her by the arm and pulled her about to face him again. She gasped sharply, her eyes wide open as she squirmed in his grasp. *"Let go of me!"*

But he was in no mood to comply. With a forcefulness that made her pulse leap wildly, he swept her against his powerful, undeniably masculine warmth. She had no time to protest before his mouth descended upon hers.

The kiss was fierce and deep, ardent and merciless, and Callie Rose felt her blood turn to liquid fire in her veins. She made one last valiant attempt to struggle free, but Ian's arms tightened about her until she could scarcely breathe. His lips moved strong and warm upon hers, his tongue masterfully claiming the moist sweetness of her mouth.

She moaned low in her throat and swayed against him in unspoken surrender, giving herself up to the delectable assault upon her senses. With even more flash and fire than last night's incident had foretold, all else was forgotten as Ian's mouth branded hers. She trembled at the savage ecstasy of his embrace, and her hands clung weakly to his broad shoulders. Her full breasts were pressed intimately, tantalizingly, against the burning hardness of his chest; she was certain he could feel her heart thundering beneath her soft flesh.

Ian gave an inward groan and gathered her even closer. White-hot desire raged within him. His body ached to possess her. He wanted nothing more than to carry her off to the ancient four-poster and make love to her the way he had longed to do from the very first. The thought of stripping her naked, of feasting his eyes upon her sweet, voluptuous curves, made him burn all the more. By all that was holy, she was his!

But alas, the time was not yet right. He knew it to be true. *Soon,* he promised himself, though it was scant consolation at the moment. He wanted her so much that it was sheer agony to even think of putting a halt to the natural course of things. Still, a kiss could be forgiven; the loss of her virginity could not. He wanted more than that from her. A great deal more. And she would be angry enough when she discovered what lay ahead. . . .

With great reluctance, and a silent curse for his own damnably inconvenient sense of honor, he raised his head at last.

Callie Rose gasped in surprise when his lips finally relinquished hers. Flushed and breathless, she felt her feet touch the floor again. Her eyes were still suffused with passion's glow as they opened to meet the fathomless green depths of Ian's. Plagued by an acute sense of disappointment, she was confused when he smiled softly down at her and raised a gentle hand to cup her chin.

"We'd best continue our tour now, Miss Buchanan," he decreed in a low, splendidly resonant tone.

"What?"

Her sapphire gaze widened with disbelief. Damnation, she seethed as fury quickly rushed in, was that all he had to say after what had just passed between them? Twice now he had forced a violent display of affection upon her, and both times he had behaved as though it had meant nothing. Absolutely nothing. She would not think about what either of the kisses had meant to *her*, nor would she acknowledge the sharp pain in her heart.

Indignation chased away the lingering dullness of her mind—and her tongue.

"Take your hands off me, you bastard!" she stormed hotly, pushing at his chest.

"You are a fickle woman," he said with a brief, sardonic smile. He held fast as she clenched her hands into fists. "One minute you are a purring kitten in my arms, and the next you turn into a fire-spitting tigress."

"It will be a cold day in hell before you ever hear me *purr*, Ian MacGregor!"

His eyes filled with a roguish light. The challenge was hard to resist. Indeed, he was sorely tempted to kiss her again before letting her go, but realized that it would only plunge him into torment if he did. His self-control had taken enough of a beating already; he'd be a fool to test it any further.

Forcing himself to release her, he watched while she furiously tugged her bodice into place once more.

"My father will kill you for this!" she vowed.

"Have you abandoned all thought of it yourself?" He answered her quickly, his voice warm with affection.

"Never!"

"Never is a long time, Callie Rose. It may well be that something will occur to change your mind before then."

He tossed a quick, deceptively casual glance over his shoulder at the bed before repeating that it was time they were on their way. Callie Rose avoided all contact with him as she swept from the room. He smiled to himself in her wake, his eyes gleaming with anticipation as he thought of what the night would bring. . . .

She had already reached the staircase when he caught up with her. Though he made no move to touch her, she tensed in defensive readiness and eyed him warily.

"You can spend the rest of the day at will," he said. "In the drawing room if you like, or perhaps the library. The entire castle is at your disposal."

"You mean you're actually going to allow me—?" she started to ask in disbelief.

"I've some business to attend to elsewhere. However,

Peter has agreed to serve as your 'guardian angel' during my absence.

"Absence?"

"Aye, I should return within a few hours' time."

"Where are you going?" she queried, feigning nonchalance. Her eyes sparked with a reborn determination while her mind raced to think of a new course of action. He would be gone . . . surely she could manage to get away with so much freedom at hand.

"Peter is a trustworthy substitute," Ian advised, disregarding her question. She glared up at him as they paused and faced each other at the foot of the steps.

"You can assign a dozen servants to watch me, and I'll still find a way to escape!"

"Ah, but will you always want to leave?" he challenged in a voice that held an undercurrent of meaning.

"Why, I . . . of course I will!" The way he was looking at her suddenly aroused her suspicions. What the devil was he planning now? she wondered, her eyes narrowing as they searched his face.

"Begging your pardon, sir, but your horse is ready," a servant announced from a short distance across the hall. Callie Rose turned to see that it was the same dark-haired young man whose appearance had drawn Ian away from the breakfast table. He, too, was wearing a kilt, and he was nearly as tall and muscular as Ian. Frowning at the sight of him, she told herself with an inward groan that he would be a worthy adversary.

"Thank you, Peter," replied Ian. "Miss Buchanan will join you in the library in a few minutes."

Peter gave a curt, wordless nod and took himself off

to wait in the library. Ian turned to Callie Rose and issued one last warning.

"You will behave yourself while I am gone, or else you'll spend the remainder of your time here locked in the tower."

"Even that would be preferable to spending another minute with you," she proclaimed haughtily. She had believed the opposite to be true less than an hour ago, but that was before he had decided to insult her again. He had not only wounded her pride, he had made it impossible for her to forget how vulnerable she was as his captive. And how humiliatingly susceptible she was to his physical charms. She swore to herself that she'd die before she'd ever let him touch her again. And she almost managed to convince herself that she meant it.

"*Soraidh leibh,*" murmured Ian, bidding her farewell as his steady, penetrating gaze seared down into hers once more.

Feeling uncharacteristically flustered, she dropped her eyes to where her high-top leather boots peeked out from under her skirts. Ian took her arm then and led her toward the library. She half expected him to say something else when they reached the doorway, but he did not. Her eyes followed him as he turned and walked away. He moved with such an easy, masculine grace. . . . The pleated folds of tartan fabric molded his lean hips and made her wonder what he wore underneath his kilt. She felt guilty color stain her cheeks at the wicked turn of her thoughts.

God willing, she told herself firmly, this would be the last time she ever set eyes upon Ian MacGregor.

"Miss Buchanan?" Peter called out to her from

within the library. It was obvious that he was going to be a vigilant caretaker.

Callie Rose drew in a deep, ragged breath, and, after wondering how far she could get before the capable-looking Peter caught up with her, reluctantly accepted the fact that her opportunity had not yet come. With her troubled gaze wandering to the heavy, iron-banded wooden door Ian had just closed behind him, she heaved a sigh of defeat and turned her own steps toward the library.

❧ FOUR ❧

The next several hours seemed to crawl by at a snail's pace for Callie Rose. And apparently God was *not* willing that Ian MacGregor vanish from her life forever.

She was curled up on the chintz-covered sofa in the sunlit drawing room with one of Sir Walter Scott's novels, her bootless feet tucked beneath her and the faithful Peter sprawled comfortably in one of the matching chairs opposite, when Ian finally returned. It was late in the afternoon by then, and he had ridden hard, but the enchanting sight of Callie Rose drove all else from his mind.

"I'm pleased to see the two of you have not yet thrappled each other," he commented dryly.

Callie Rose started at the sound of that deep, familiar voice. Her eyes, growing enormous within the heart-shaped oval of her face, flew to the doorway. She was taken aback by the way her heart stirred at Ian's affectionate, mocking smile. Coloring rosily, she untucked her feet, jerked her full skirts down into place, and got up from the sofa. It was all done with such haste that the book toppled to the floor.

"We've managed well enough, my lord," Peter declared, with a crooked grin, unfolding himself from the chair.

It was considerably less than the truth. The hours of enforced togetherness had taken their toll on him as well. He had found it necessary on two separate occasions to intercept the headstrong Miss Buchanan when she had attempted to slip from the room after momentarily diverting his attention elsewhere. Once, she had thrown open a window and scrambled halfway through before he had pulled her back inside, and she had even resorted to threats and cajolery and bribery—without success—when everything else had failed.

In addition to all that, she had locked Jenny in the tower room when the poor lass (his own loving sweetheart) had accompanied her upstairs for a brief period of rest following the noon meal. He had been waiting at the foot of the stairs, of course, and had easily managed to catch her. She had fought him like a wildcat, screaming and cursing like no other highborn female he had ever known, and making him wonder if all American ladies were so markedly temperamental. It was only half an hour ago that they had finally settled into an uneasy peace between them.

"You can go now, Peter," said Ian, a touch of humor lurking in his eyes. "I've little doubt you are in need of a respite from your duties." He sauntered forward while Peter, casting his reluctant charge one last glance, left the room with no small sigh of relief.

"I'm surprised you trusted anyone else with the 'duty' at all," Callie Rose muttered. Feeling decidedly on edge, she bent and retrieved the book, then sank back down to put on her boots. "What would you have done if I had escaped while you were gone?" She tugged her skirts upward a bit so that she could tie the laces.

"I'd have come after you." His gaze darkened with more than a passing interest as it strayed to the trim shapeliness of her ankles.

"And given Peter forty lashes, I suppose?"

"Aye."

She looked up at him in startled disbelief, only to see that a mischievous smile was playing about his lips. Her eyes flashed as she yanked the second bow tight and rose to her feet once more.

"Aren't you at all worried about what's going to happen to you once I'm free to tell everyone the truth?" she challenged, her whole body tensing when he drew closer. He looked none the worse for his journey; his chiseled features appeared more tanned and healthy than ever, and his eyes even more impossibly green.

"Should I be?" A shaft of sunlight fell across his head as he approached, illuminating the streaks of gold in the thickness of his reddish-brown hair. "As I told you before, Callie Rose Buchanan, you've a lot to learn about the Scots. My countrymen and I are quite loyal to one another, sometimes to a fault."

"Are you saying that no one will believe me?"

"What I'm saying, sweet vixen, is that so long as you are in the Highlands, you—"

"Stop calling me that!"

She folded her arms tightly beneath her breasts and whirled about to take up an angry stance at the window. It was one of those spectacular, tranquil summer days, the likes of which are known few other places on earth, but she was immune to its magic at the moment. Her thoughts had frequently drifted to Ian during his absence, and though she was still loath to admit it, she had caught herself glancing at the clock at least a dozen times while anticipating his return.

"I missed you today, for all your wild, bloodthirsty little ways," he proclaimed softly, advancing on her from behind. Before she could guess his intentions, he slipped his arms about her and pulled her back against the length of his tall, lithely muscled frame. It was tempting fate, and he knew it, yet he had thought of nothing but her these past several hours.

"Why, you— Take your hands off me!" she sputtered indignantly, trying in vain to pry herself from his grasp. She squirmed and pushed at his arms. Her unintentionally seductive actions brought the well-rounded firmness of her bottom fanning against his manhood. He stifled a groan as desire, thunderous and near painful in its intensity, coursed through him like wildfire.

"Be still, lass," he warned huskily, his lips close to her ear. A shiver danced down her spine.

"Let me go!"

"Are you not accustomed to snuggling, Callie Rose?" He scowled darkly as soon as the words were out of his mouth, and his eyes smoldered with jealousy. The mere thought of any other man holding her like this was enough to make his blood boil.

"Of course I am! It so happens, Ian MacGregor, that I have enjoyed the attentions of a great many, far better men than you!" she taunted on sudden impulse. She was unprepared for the violence of his reaction.

"The devil you say!" he ground out. He spun her

about to face him, his eyes fiery and accusing as they bored down into the shocked luminosity of hers. "What else have you done with these 'better men'?" he demanded in a low tone simmering with fury. "By damn, woman, I will have the truth! Are you guilty of nothing more than a few stolen kisses, or are you as cruel and heartless and *knowledgeable* as those fools in London would have me believe?"

"How dare you!" she said, seething, then inhaled upon a loud gasp when his fingers dug into her arms. She stared up at him in furious bewilderment, her throat constricting with a fear she was trying hard to ignore. "You have no right to say such things to me!"

"The truth, I said!" He yanked her up hard against him. A soft cry escaped her lips, and she felt hot, confused tears fill her eyes.

"No!" She shook her head in an adamant denial, all the while painfully aware of his harsh, mystifying anger. Why should her past conquests, or lack of them, matter so much to him? "I—I don't owe you any explanations!"

"You're right, of course," he answered, surprising her with the sudden concession. "Either way, it would not change what is to be."

"Not change . . ." she echoed, her own voice trailing away. She shook her head again, this time as if to clear it, and demanded tremulously, "What are you talking about?"

"You wish to leave here, do you not?"

"More than anything in the world!" She added emphasis to the declaration by renewing her struggles with a vengeance.

"Then I have a proposition to put before you." With an iron will, he brought his emotions under control and forced himself to release her. He moved past her to the other side of the room.

Callie Rose made her way back to the sofa, sinking weakly down upon the cushions as she rubbed at her arms. She shot her fierce, handsome tormentor a vengeful glare and watched while he turned to face her again. His expression was quite solemn, his eyes gleaming dully as they sought hers. He did not take a seat, but rather stood—looking grim and commanding a few feet away.

"I told you there was one last requirement to be satisfied before your release," he began quietly.

"What is it?" When he did not immediately answer, her stomach knotted in dread. She waited, silent and breathless, as he crossed his arms against his broad chest and allowed only the suggestion of a smile to touch his lips.

"We must be wed."

"*Wed?*" Her eyes widened with a mixture of incredulity and outrage. She leapt to her feet and stormed at him, "Damn your eyes, Ian MacGregor! What makes you think—?"

"It would not be a normal marriage," he admitted, satisfied that the words he had chosen were true.

"Normal or not, I wouldn't marry you if you were the last man on earth!"

"Have you heard yet of what we call handfasting?" he asked, disregarding her protests.

"Handfasting?" The term sounded vaguely familiar. . . . Her eyes lit with the sudden recollection of a conversation she and Martha had overheard between three local women in one of the shops back in Edinburgh. The bonneted and shawl-mantled trio had been discussing the daughter of a mutual acquaintance, referring to the girl as a handfast bride and agreeing that she had done well in her choice of a husband. Martha had commented afterward that she herself had once read about Scotland's centuries-old handfast law in a book, and that, in her opinion at least, it was the tool of the devil because it allowed for certain "liberties" without benefit of a church wedding. In other words, she had blushingly told Callie Rose, a couple could live together in sin and suffer no condemnation for it.

"I can see you have some knowledge of the custom," Ian observed, with another faint smile.

"Yes," she conceded reluctantly, "but what in tarnation does that have do with me?" *Marriage.* Great balls of fire, she mused in a daze, had the man gone completely out of his mind? She had thought him daft before now, but this was by far the craziest scheme he had concocted yet. Her blood roared in her ears, and she heard him as if from a great distance away when he calmly went on.

"It is all perfectly legal. A man and woman must simply stand before witnesses and declare themselves to be husband and wife." He unfolded his arms and strolled across to the window. Turning his fathomless gaze outward, he raised a negligent hand to the heavy wood frame. " 'Tis more of a betrothal, actually. The final vows are spoken before a parson within a few weeks' time. If not, then the two parties involved are free to go their separate ways. Some have used it as a trial marriage, but it will be what we make of it and nothing more."

"And do you really expect me to go along with this latest example of backhanded nonsense?" she demanded, her voice laced with scorn.

"You will do so if you wish to leave Castle Mac-Gregor." He lowered his arm to his side and turned to face her once more. The look in his eyes was deadly earnest. "You will agree to the handfasting, or you will remain here as my prisoner for as long as I say. The choice is yours to make, Miss Buchanan."

"Why didn't you tell me about this in the very beginning? Why did you wait until now to—?"

"I did not make the decision until last night." That, too, was the truth.

"But, *why*?" She got up from the sofa again and walked behind it, her fingers digging into the floral-strewn upholstery as she fired a barrage of questions at Ian. "What purpose would a betrothal between us serve? Why is it required to settle the feud? I seem to recall, Ian MacGregor, that you were supposed to do nothing more than kidnap a Buchanan and hold him or her captive here for a few days!"

"Aye. That was my original intention."

"Then what you're telling me doesn't make any sense at all," she said, sighing, her head still spinning. "By thunder, it can't be necessary for us to become betrothed, because your father couldn't have known if the Buchanan you captured would be a man or a woman!"

"Nevertheless, it will make amends for the past," he insisted. "My grandmother's disgrace will be avenged, and our clans will know peace between them once more."

"So it is *your* requirement," she accused, her eyes narrowing.

"It is." His confession held no trace of remorse.

"What happens if I do agree to the lie? And how do I know you won't try to hold me to the betrothal, or maybe even try to—to force me into a 'trial marriage'?" The possibility sent hot color flying to her cheeks. She cursed the way her whole body stirred at the memory of his kisses.

"Could I not have done that already?" he pointed out, his eyes glowing warmly.

"Not and lived to tell about it!" she retorted. She was annoyed when he favored her with a long, indecipherable perusal.

"Once the handfasting has taken place, you will be able to leave whenever you please," he continued in a wholly businesslike manner.

"How do I know I can trust you?"

"Because I give you my word that it will be so."

She continued to eye him mistrustfully as she wandered to the fireplace with an angry, preoccupied air. What he was proposing was ludicrous, it was insane— and yet what choice did she have? She *had* to get away from him.

What harm would it do to play along with the charade? she pondered with another sigh. It wouldn't mean a thing, not really. No one back home need ever know about that part of his villainy. And after all, she told herself by way of justification, it wasn't as if she'd be standing in a church and swearing before God to love, honor, and obey the man. No, indeed, she'd be free to go afterward, free to resume her own independent and orderly life. And she'd never have to face Ian MacGregor again.

"You're sure this 'handfasting' will have no real significance?" she demanded, rounding on him now as she sought confirmation of all that he had promised. "It will truly be nothing more than a formality?"

"Aye, unless we decide to consummate the marriage."

"*That's* something that will never happen!"

"Then you've no worries, have you?" He came forward with an impassive look on his handsome face, though she was certain she glimpsed a strange light in his steady, viridescent gaze. "Is it a bargain then, Callie Rose Buchanan?"

"I—I don't know," she stammered indecisively, still hesitant to consent to the outrageous scheme. "You've certainly done nothing to earn my trust so far."

"Have you not been well treated here?" he asked challengingly, coming to a stop in front of her. The sofa was between them, yet his proximity filled her with apprehension. Lifting her chin, she met his gaze with her usual proud defiance.

"Well treated? Yes, if you don't count all the times I was threatened and manhandled and forcibly embraced!"

"Peter will be lashed at once," he pronounced, with a mock scowl of reprisal.

"I'm not talking about Peter and you know it!"

"*Is it a bargain?*" he asked once more. His eyes seared down into hers.

"Yes, damn you!" she finally acquiesced.

"So be it. We'll attend to the matter this very evening. Peter and Molly can serve as our witnesses." He began leisurely rounding the end of the sofa.

"Then it will all come to an end?" Her pulse raced anew as he advanced on her, but she refused to give way to alarm. She had suffered enough humiliation these past twenty-four hours; surely she could gather enough courage to see her through the remainder of this latest (and next to last, thank heavens) encounter with the arrogant rogue. "I'll be able to leave tonight?"

"Aye, if you still want to."

"Can there be any doubt of that?" she shot back.

"We must seal the bargain," decreed Ian. He towered directly above her now, his mouth curving into a predatory half smile.

"Very well." The last thing she wanted was further physical contact between them, but she told herself that it would be cowardly to refuse. With admirable composure, she offered him her hand. He did not take it. "Back home, Mr. MacGregor," she informed him, "we shake hands to seal a bargain."

"Here in Scotland, Miss Buchanan, we have a far better method."

She gasped when he abruptly slipped an arm about her waist, hauled her close with no pretense at gentleness, and brought his lips swooping down upon the parted softness of hers.

Moaning in startled protest, she swung a hand at his head, but he caught her wrist. She struggled against him and tried to push free, only to find both of her arms imprisoned behind her back in the next instant. His mouth virtually devoured hers while she felt herself growing light-headed.

He did not settle for a kiss this time.

She could do no more than gasp again as he took a seat on the sofa and pulled her masterfully across his lap. She squirmed and kicked, her eyes opening wide but fluttering closed once more when the kiss deepened. He clamped one powerful arm about her hips while the other supported her shoulders.

He gathered her close, as though she were a child to be comforted following a bad dream. But there was nothing in the least bit paternal (and nothing remotely nightmarish) about the way he kissed her. His warm lips moved demandingly upon hers, his tongue stabbing provocatively at the velvety sweetness of her own as he proceeded to "seal the bargain" in a manner that would have been understood just as well in Texas.

Though aghast at finding herself held captive against him with such complete, possessive familiarity, Callie Rose was unable to offer more than a halfhearted objection now. Her hands spread upon the rock-hard expanse of his chest, pushing feebly. She could feel his skin burning through the linen fabric of his shirt.

His hand swept upward to close upon her buttocks as she surrendered to his embrace. All thought of resistance gone, she responded to his kiss with an innocent and delightfully natural passion. Ian gave a low groan and battled a wave of desire so intense that he felt his own self-control slipping to a dangerously low level. . . .

Everything happened with dizzying swiftness after that. Callie Rose was scarcely aware of the moment when he began tugging her skirts and petticoat impatiently upward. She might not have realized it for several seconds longer if not for the rush of cool air upon her skin. It was too late by the time she thought to protest. Ian's hand delved beneath the bunched-up folds of wool and cotton, gliding up the long, shapely length of her black-stockinged leg, and closed about her derriere once more. Her only protection was the pair of red flannel drawers; she dazedly wondered what he would think of them.

His mouth finally left hers to trail a fiery path downward to where her pulse beat so feverishly at the base of her throat. He cursed the high neckline of her bodice, though he vowed to himself that he would pay loving tribute to her breasts before he set her free.

"*Breagha* Callie Rose," he murmured hoarsely. He claimed her lips in another fierce, intoxicating kiss. His strong fingers explored the full and saucily rounded curve of her bottom, prompting her to squirm atop his muscular thighs. It felt wickedly pleasurable to have him caressing her with such boldness. She could summon neither the will nor the strength to stop him.

His hand suddenly moved from beneath her skirts to the row of pearl buttons running down the front of her traveling suit. With an amazing deftness, he unfastened the top four buttons. Callie Rose was only dimly aware of what was happening, but enlightenment hit her full force when his mouth once again followed an imaginary path downward to where the ripe fullness of her breasts rose and fell rapidly beneath the thin white cotton of her chemise.

A soft cry broke from her lips. She opened her eyes,

instinctively struggling anew, but Ian's arm tightened about her, urging her farther upward. With even more masculine impatience than before, he swept the liberated edges of her bodice aside and yanked the lace-trimmed neckline of her chemise downward so that her bosom was almost completely laid bare for his touch.

He set his lips to wandering across the upper curve of her breasts, branding the exposed flesh, provoking such a wealth of hot, rapturous sensations within her that she was certain she would faint with the wonder of it all. She closed her eyes again. The deep yearning that had flamed to life at the first pressure of his lips upon hers was fast on its way to becoming a raging, all-consuming inferno.

No man had ever touched her breasts. No man had ever touched her backside. Indeed, if anyone had dared to try, she'd have made him rue the day he was born. Why then wasn't she fighting *this* man? And why the devil did she like what he was doing so very much?

The questions remained unanswered. She couldn't even hope to think straight, not with Ian's warm, sensuously persuasive lips at her breasts. With a will of their own, her hands crept upward to curl about the corded muscles of his neck. He pulled her higher, his mouth closing about one of the rose-tipped peaks.

"Ian!" she gasped, then moaned low in her throat. His lips suckled hungrily at her breast through the delicate white fabric, his tongue swirling about the nipple with tantalizing fervor. She caught her lower lip between her teeth to stifle a cry of pure pleasure. Her head fell back, her long, thick braid of hair tumbling all the

way down to the sofa while she squirmed restlessly on Ian's lap once more.

Wisely or not, he was determined to have more of her. His hand moved swiftly downward again, disappearing beneath her skirts. His fingers slid purposefully up to where her stockings were held by a pair of beribboned satin garters, lingered there only briefly, then stroked farther upward along the insides of her slender, silken thighs. He slipped his hand within the opening of her red flannel drawers and continued on toward the soft triangle of raven curls at the apex of her thighs.

Finally he claimed the sweet treasure he sought.

Callie Rose tensed in alarm at the first touch of his hand upon her moist, intimate flesh. It was like being touched by lightning. Her eyes opened wide. Her mind screamed a belated warning, for she instinctively realized now that she was in very real danger of losing what she had sworn no man would ever take from her.

"No! No, you can't— *no!*" she whispered brokenly. Crashing back to reality, she struggled atop him, pushing with all her might at his arm while at the same time trying desperately to yank her skirts back down into place.

Ian swore underneath his breath. His arms tightened like bands of steel around her, and his handsome face was quite thunderous as he raised his head. His magnificent green eyes seared down into the deep sapphire blaze of hers, only to soften in the next moment. He felt his heart twist with guilt—but no true regret—at the sight of her gathering tears.

"Let me go!" she hissed, writhing and kicking like

the wildcat he had once called her. "You randy Scottish bastard, let me go!"

"Randy?" he repeated softly. The term was unfamiliar to him, yet he could well imagine its meaning. "Aye, I suppose I am that." Though his deep voice brimmed with irony, he was anything but amused by the way his body still burned. He cursed again, silently this time, and released her.

She furiously scrambled to her feet, whirling about to go storming back across the room to the window. Her hands shook as she pulled her skirts into place and hastened to button her bodice.

Behind her, Ian slowly drew his tall frame up from the sofa. He frowned thoughtfully as his smoldering gaze fastened on the rigid, graceful curve of Callie Rose's back. What had just happened between them made him more impatient than ever for the night to come. His brow cleared, and he smiled to himself at the thought of the handfasting.

She would be angry. She would be defiant and shrewish, and there would no doubt be a terrible collieshangie before he had convinced her of the truth. But by heaven above, *she would be his*.

"Our bargain is sealed now, Miss Buchanan," he decreed, his tone low and level. His eyes glowed warmly as they traveled over her.

"Like hell it is!" She fastened the top button and spun about to confront him with a reproachful glare. "Damn you, why did you . . . ? You had no right to treat me like that!" she sputtered.

A wave of hot, embarrassed color washed over her, and she derided herself for being swept away yet again.

Until she had come to the Highlands, until she had been abducted by Ian MacGregor, she had rarely been tempted to allow a man to do anything more than hold her hand and perhaps even give her a chaste kiss or two.

This flame-haired scoundrel with a title (what exactly *was* his title, anyway? she mused with a flash of resentment) had certainly done more than hold her hand. A good deal more. And there had been nothing chaste about his kisses, particularly not the most recent ones he had forced upon her. Remembering how pleasurable it had felt to have his lips upon her breasts, she shivered and folded her arms across her chest—as though by doing so she could somehow purge the disconcerting memory.

"Perhaps you would prefer to remain at Castle MacGregor a few days longer," he suggested, one dark eyebrow raised mockingly.

"Perhaps you would prefer to go to the devil!" she flung back.

"It's said the devil is good to beginners."

"I find it difficult to believe you lack experience in *anything*, except maybe humility!" She placed her hands on her hips and vowed through tightly clenched teeth, "Our bargain may be sealed, and after tonight I'll be gone, but I'll still find a way to make you pay. And if you think this latest disgusting little episode changes anything—"

"Only a taste of what might have been." He pronounced it with a faint smile.

"Then I thank God from the very bottom of my heart that I will never have to endure the entire meal," she answered feelingly. Squaring her shoulders, she gathered up her creased woolen skirts and sailed toward the doorway. Ian made no attempt to stop her, but followed at a short distance behind.

"Falbh suas a staidhre." He was rewarded for using the Gaelic—a command for her to go upstairs—when she came to an abrupt halt and rounded on him once more.

"You can save your blasted 'Scots tongue' for the next woman you decide to torment!"

"You'd do well to learn a bit of the *Gaidhlig*, lass," he advised smoothly.

"No, Mr. MacGregor, I would not," she hissed, shaking her head in a vigorous denial, "since I have no intention of ever returning to Scotland."

"Ah, but intentions have a way of losing themselves."

"Not mine!"

"Why do you believe yourself to lack the caprice and other delightful traits that are so much a part of the fair sex?" His resonant, deep-timbred voice was full of amusement. "Are you not flesh and blood, Callie Rose Buchanan?"

"I ... of course I am! But I'm not like the other women you've known."

"That is certainly true enough."

Cursing the way her heart fluttered beneath his glowing gaze, she announced, "It so happens that I remember hearing a fascinating little proverb when I was in Inverness the other day. 'There's a cure for everything but stark dead.' "

"Oh, aye? And how do you think that applies to

me?" he asked. He resisted the impulse to tell her he'd much prefer to see her stark naked.

"Because that's what you'll be once my father finds out what you've done to me!" She had uttered the threat before, of course, but she had never believed herself to mean it any more than she did at that moment.

"I've a favorite proverb of my own," said Ian. He moved closer, his eyes twinkling roguishly down into hers. " 'Fools look to tomorrow while wise men use tonight.' "

She opened her mouth to respond, but no words would come. She settled for directing a highly expressive glower up at him, then muttered an oath and flounced away to the staircase. Ian gave unhurried chase.

Tonight, his mind repeated. He was no fool. . . .

🐲 FIVE 🐲

It was nearly time.

Afternoon had given way to twilight (or the "gloaming," as Jenny had called it). The sun's last, lingering rays cast a splendid rose-hued glow upon the hills. Above, the sky remained endlessly blue, marked by nothing more than the merest wisp of a cloud, while the air was heavy with the sweet perfume of the heather. Within the cool darkness of the Highland forests, rabbits, field mice, foxes, and deer settled in for a well-earned respite from their simple yet perilous endeavors. The coming night promised to be beautiful and moonlit and filled with dreams.

But there was a storm brewing within the great stone walls of Castle MacGregor.

Callie Rose faced herself in the mirror, only to frown in disapproval at what her eyes beheld. Ian had insisted that she wear the white silk gown for the handfasting ceremony. It was, he had explained, necessary for her to at least look like a bride, even if she never meant to become one in fact. The tartan sash decorating it was to identify her as a Buchanan, and would be replaced by the MacGregor plaid once they had offered up their declaration. The gesture would symbolize an alliance between themselves and their two clans.

The end of one blood feud and the beginning of another, she reflected vengefully. Dropping her fiery gaze to the bodice's low-cut neckline, she frowned again. She had yielded to the demands of her "future husband" with something far less than enthusiasm. Tradition apparently played a great role in everything the Scots did, she mused with an irritated sigh.

But what did it matter? She would be on her way back to America soon, back to Texas and the Diamond L and the loving bosom of her family, back to where men didn't carry young ladies off—and if they did, where they'd find themselves either shot full of holes or dancing at the end of a rope for their troubles. Strangely enough, she felt a sharp twinge of pain at the thought of Ian MacGregor suffering either one of those irreversible fates.

The faint scent of lavender wafted about her as she turned away from the mirror. She had taken a bath and washed her hair before supper, using a soap made locally in an old priory outside Inverness. Her long, luxuriant raven tresses cascaded softly about her face and shoulders—yet another requirement for the ceremony, according to Jenny, who had apparently witnessed her fair share of handfastings. It seemed that a woman's unbound hair was to signify both her innocence and the promise that she was coming to her husband with a free and willing heart.

"Free and willing . . . like hell," muttered Callie Rose, then inhaled sharply when a knock sounded at the door.

"Are you not ready yet, Miss Buchanan?" It was Peter's voice she heard.

"Yes," she called back, then added underneath her breath, "as ready as I'll ever be."

She left the room and preceded Peter down the narrow, winding steps. Fully expecting that Ian would be waiting for her at the bottom, she was surprised to find no sign of him. Her brows knitted together in a frown while her gaze made a quick sweep of the hall.

"Lord MacGregor and the others are in the drawing room," said Peter, noting her bemusement.

"Others?"

"Aye. 'Tis only fitting that some of his kinsmen attend the ceremony. If there were any Buchanans—"

"It isn't as though it will be a real wedding," she interrupted, her eyes bridling with annoyance. "And this is the first I've heard of the presence of guests."

He gave her a faintly quizzical look before leading her onward. They descended the stairs to the first floor, then moved across to the drawing room. The sound of voices, predominantly male, drifted out to them as they drew closer, and Callie Rose began to feel more than a touch of apprehension by the time she and Peter stood together in the doorway.

Her blue eyes grew very round, her whole body tensing at the scene before her. There were more than half a dozen kilted Scotsmen in the brightly lit room, only three women, and Ian MacGregor. She swallowed hard when her wide, luminous gaze lit upon him.

He stood tall and proud and solemn across the room. Attired in his dress kilt, black velvet jacket, and clan-crested Balmoral tam, he was breathtakingly handsome.

And, once again, he looked to be every inch a powerful, hot-blooded Highland chieftain.

His green eyes darkened with a mixture of desire and determination when they met hers. At a curt nod from him, a man standing ready in the corner with a set of bagpipes struck up a melody that held particular significance for all but one of those assembled in the castle that night. "MacGregor's Gathering," written by Sir Walter Scott and Alexander Lee, concerned the dark period in history, nearly three centuries ago, when anyone bearing the name MacGregor had been ordered to change it or else face the penalty of death.

Callie Rose listened to the piercing, haunting tone of the pipes and felt her courage slipping away. She wanted to turn and run, to call off the accursed bargain, but her pride would not let her. *No Buchanan ever goes back on his word.* Her father had taught her well. Too well, she thought with an inward groan.

All eyes were upon her as she lifted her head proudly and allowed Peter to lead her forward. She caught a glimpse of Jenny and Molly out of the corner of her eye, but her attention was so inexorably commanded by Ian that she couldn't be more than dimly aware of anyone save him.

Her legs felt weak and uncertain as they carried her closer to where he waited in front of the window, his magnificent frame outlined by the waning sunlight. With anyone else, the effect might have been angelic. It merely served to make him look all the more formidable.

She took a deep, steadying breath. Her heart pounded fiercely within her breast. She kept telling herself that the terrible ordeal would be over soon, that she would be free at long last. The prospect of spending the night in the safety of her own room at the hotel in Inverness helped keep her course steady.

Cousin Martha would be thunderstruck when she heard the truth. Unless the poor woman was on her deathbed, the two of them would leave Scotland tomorrow. She longed to be at home again, longed to forget all about castles and feuds and clans—and a wildly appealing, green-eyed rogue with hair the color of sweet red wine and the ability to tumble her emotions into absolute chaos.

Finally completing what had seemed like the longest walk of her life, she found her hand grasped by the strong warmth of Ian's. She felt a sudden tremor shake her, and raised eyes full of confusion to his face. He gave her a brief, bolstering smile, tucked her arm firmly through the possessive crook of his, then urged her to turn about and face the assembled guests with him.

The piper ceased his playing. An expectant silence gripped the room.

"Welcome kinsmen, to Castle MacGregor this night," Ian began on a formal note. He paused to cast his intended bride a warm, compelling look.

"On with the handfasting, lad!" one of the MacGregors exhorted, with mock impatience.

"Aye, we've waited long enough for this day," said another, his remark eliciting quiet chuckles from the others.

Ian smiled at their raillery. Taking Callie Rose's other hand now as well, he grew quite serious.

"I, Ian Robert Stewart MacGregor," he proclaimed

in a clear, undeniably authoritative tone of voice, "tenth Earl of Strathburn, do hereby swear that this woman is Callie Rose Buchanan, spinster, the only known granddaughter of Angus Alasdair Buchanan, late of Dalcross."

Earl of Strathburn, her mind repeated numbly. He wasn't at all like the other noblemen she had met. But then he wasn't like anyone else at all. And what the devil was that poppycock about her being a spinster? She was being termed an old maid at the age of twenty. J. D. probably would have found it funny—but only up to a point.

"And furthermore," continued Ian, "I do swear before God and these witnesses that I take Callie Rose Buchanan for my wife."

Her heart leapt in alarm at the sound of those words upon his lips. *My wife.* Her eyes flew up to his once more, only to discover that he was regarding her with what she could have sworn to be triumphant satisfaction. His hand tightened upon hers.

"You must give a similar vow, Callie Rose," he instructed quietly.

Plagued by sharp misgivings, she looked away. Her swift, anxious glance encompassed the room as she wavered again between compliance and cowardice. The seven tall strangers, all of whom wore the same identifying tartan as Ian, stared at her as though they shared some secret knowledge of the proceedings. Peter, Jenny, and Molly, she noted in mingled relief and suspicion, were smiling warmly at her. The other woman present, a buxom, opal-eyed blonde not much older than herself, shot her a glare full of such obvious enmity that her brow creased in puzzlement.

"Speak, lass," Ian prompted.

She looked up at him again. Something in his gaze provoked an answering fire within her own. Almost before she realized it, she was speaking the words he had vowed to hear from her since he had first held her in his arms.

"I, Callie Rose Buchanan . . . take Ian MacGregor as my husband."

Her face flushed guiltily at the lie. Heaven help her, wasn't *this* going back on her word? She certainly had no intention of honoring the betrothal. None whatsoever. And yet she had just declared herself to be wed to Ian MacGregor.

Was it right to sacrifice honor in return for freedom? she wondered unhappily, though she already knew the truth. Her father wouldn't think it a fair price. He would be ashamed of her . . . she was ashamed of herself. No matter how it had all come about, in spite of the fact that she and Ian both knew it to be a harmless deception, she should never have consented to it. In truth, she had taken the coward's way out after all.

"Then it is done," Ian decreed somberly. "The blood feud will be spoken of no more. Henceforth, there will be peace between our clans." Releasing her hands, he unpinned the tartan sash from her shoulder and slipped it off, then took the length of MacGregor plaid Peter handed to him and fastened it diagonally across her breasts. His eyes burned down into hers when he told her, "You are one of us now, Callie Rose MacGregor, and so you shall remain unto death."

Callie Rose MacGregor. The name sounded strange and ominous to her ears. And his last words sent another involuntary shiver down her spine. She had not expected him to declare their "union" everlasting. Why had he not warned her that the ritual would include a declaration of eternal bondage? Nothing was going quite the way she had envisioned.

Her head spinning, she heaved a ragged sigh and started to turn away. Ian, however, soon made it clear that he did not yet consider the handfasting ceremony at an end. A soft gasp of startlement escaped her lips when he suddenly enfolded her within the strong, passionate circle of his arms and captured her lips with his own.

It was no traditional kiss. He kissed her thoroughly, hungrily, without consideration for the fact that their embrace held a rapt audience. She gave a low moan of protest and raised her hands to push at his shoulders, only to feel her resistance melting away as his mouth tasted deeply of hers. And when he finally raised his head again, she saw that his eyes gleamed with a light that could best be described as tenderly wolfish.

Her face crimsoned while her temper flared. With a whispered curse, she impulsively lifted her arm to strike him, but his hand shot out to seize her wrist and force it back down to rest upon his shoulder. He treated her to a slow, mocking smile while she squirmed against him in helpless fury.

"Is that any way for a loving bride to behave, my lady?" he said, his low tone brimming with amusement. Before she could reply, he kissed her again.

"If marriages are made in heaven, Ian MacGregor,

you've few friends there!" one of his kinsmen opined loudly.

The room erupted into a roar of laughter and enthusiastic cheers of approval. Filling his lungs with air, the piper began to play a tune called, appropriately, "My Love She's But a Lassie Yet." Peter, Molly, and Jenny hastened to provide each man with a glass of whiskey (Scotch, of course), while the lone female guest, appearing anything but pleased with the outcome, retreated to the doorway for a few moments before disappearing altogether.

Callie Rose's eyes were shooting sparks up at Ian when he reluctantly drew his arms from about her. He maintained a firm grip upon her elbow as they awaited the congratulations he knew would follow. She stood simmering beside him, her whole manner stiff and defiant, her mind racing with thoughts of revenge.

The Highlanders raised their glasses high. The stirring, distinctive strains of the bagpipe drifted away into silence again. A toast was offered up for the future happiness of the newlyweds by the oldest member of the clan present, a gray-haired giant of a man who looked upon Ian with obvious pride and affection.

"To our beloved *toiseach*. And to his bonny bride. May their life together be long and full of bliss, and may their sons be fine, strapping lads who will honor the name of MacGregor and never let it be forgotten."

Amid hearty murmurs of agreement, the whiskey was downed by one and all.

Long and full of bliss . . . sons. His words burned in Callie Rose's mind. Stunned, she caught her breath and peered up at Ian. He had apparently neglected to tell the others of their bargain. But, why?

More confused than ever, she did not object when he led her forth to introduce her to each of his kinsmen in turn. She listened to their felicitations, but could manage only a wordless nod in response. Her troubled gaze frequently shifted to the clock on the mantelpiece; she consoled herself with the thought that she would soon be on her way back to Inverness. The prospect of traveling at night did not dampen her resolve in the least. She'd ride through hell itself to get away from Ian MacGregor. . . .

The whiskey flowed freely as the celebration wore on. Callie Rose's nerves had been stretched achingly taut by the time the monstrous grandfather clock in the hall chimed—sadly off-key and ten minutes early—the hour of eight. She would have fled long before, but her "husband" would not allow her to leave his side. And strangely enough, she had been loath to cause a scene in front of his kinsmen, whether to spare her own pride or his, she couldn't say. As it was, she remained to hear the booming voices of the guests raised in song, forced herself not to launch another attack (either verbal or physical) upon Ian when he inquired if she was enjoying the evening, and resisted the urge to tell every blasted MacGregor in the room that she was still a Buchanan and would remain one until her dying day.

The soft kiss of the summer's darkness had settled upon the land when Ian finally led her to the doorway. Slipping an arm about her waist, he ignored the resentful glare she directed up at him as he pulled her close.

"I thank you for coming," he told the eager, bright-eyed witnesses. His own eyes glowed with wry amusement, the hint of a smile playing about his lips when he added, "True MacGregors that you are, you'll no doubt understand my impatience to be rid of you. My bride and I will welcome you again, along with your own wives and children, when the handfasting is permanently recorded in the parish records. Until then, we bid you a safe journey home."

"Och, man, would you deny us the honor of the bedding?" one of the younger men complained, feigning reproof.

"The *bedding*?" gasped Callie Rose. Though she knew little enough about Scottish customs, she was aware of this one. In centuries past, the bride and groom had been put to bed by a group of close friends and family (either mirthful or solemn, depending upon the amount of celebratory spirits imbibed) and bade to make the most of the night. Some of the revelers had even taken up guard within earshot of the bedchamber to make certain the marriage was indeed consummated.

She paled at the thought. Her wide, anxious gaze sought the steadiness of Ian's once more. He shook his head slightly and looked back to his mischievous cousin.

"Might I remind you, Andrew MacGregor," he said, "that the custom has not been practiced since long before the two of us first drew breath. And by all that is holy, I've no desire to revive it this night."

His remark was met with another deep rumble of laughter from the assembled representation of the proud Clan MacGregor. It was the final straw for Callie Rose.

She had kept her part of the bargain. And she was tired of waiting for Ian to keep his!

No longer caring what anyone thought, she wrenched herself from his grasp and spun about to take flight across the great hall. She forgot all about her valise sitting packed and ready upstairs; her mind was set upon a single, desperate purpose. If she could just make it outside, she was certain she could conceal herself within the shadows and find her way to the stables. She would ride to Inverness like the very devil. And she would never look back.

Her eyes sparkled with certain victory when she approached the massive, iron-banded door that had once withstood the assault of marauding enemy clansmen intent upon killing every last MacGregor who had taken refuge within the castle. She reached for the latch, her fingers curling about it as she prepared to make good on her escape at last.

Once again, however, she had underestimated the iron will of Ian MacGregor.

She cried out when she felt his hand closing about her wrist. He allowed her no time to round on him, but scooped her up in his powerful arms as though she weighed no more than a babe.

"No!" she protested, writhing and kicking futilely. "I'm leaving now, and you have no right to stop me!"

"I've not finished with you, Callie Rose MacGregor." With his handsome face a grim mask of determination, he began carrying her toward the staircase.

"That is *not* my name! I did what you wanted—I went through with the handfasting—and you can't—"

"I can and will," he insisted in a low, resonant tone.

A warning bell sounded in her brain again, louder than ever before.

"What are you doing?" she demanded. "Where are you taking me?" Her fiery, bemused gaze traveled swiftly back to the drawing room. "What about your guests?"

"My guests are well aware that my presence is required elsewhere." That was true enough, he thought, a devilish twinkle of humor lurking in his eyes. He continued onward, his steps unhurried yet purposeful as he bore her up the stairs.

"But, you—you promised that I would be free to go after the ceremony!" she stammered in growing alarm.

"Aye, that I did. But I also said you could leave only if you still wished to do so."

"I *do* wish to do so, damn you! Right this very minute! Now put me down!"

"All in good time, lass," he murmured softly, his rugged features inscrutable now as he carried her down the carpeted, dimly lit landing to his room.

❧ SIX ❧

He set her on her feet as soon as they were inside. She pulled away from him and stumbled backward, watching in furious disbelief while he calmly closed the door.

"What in heaven's name do you think you're doing?" She was seething, so enraged she could barely speak. "I demand that you let me out of here at once!"

" 'Tis customary for newlyweds to spend the wedding night in each other's company." He turned to face her with another faint, sardonic smile. "Or perhaps you follow a different custom in Texas."

"We are *not* newlyweds!"

"Are we not? You stood before witnesses with me and declared yourself to be my wife," he reminded her. He began advancing on her, his splendid green eyes darkening with the promise of passion.

"Yes, but we both knew I didn't mean it! It was only part of the— Hell's bells," she exclaimed in a breathless, uneven voice, "you told me that this handfasting nonsense wasn't binding!" Panic rose within her as she retreated in a desperate attempt to avoid the inevitable. She was painfully aware of the bed behind her. It loomed every bit as large in the turbulence of her mind as it did in the candlelit warmth of the room. Swallowing a sudden lump in her throat, she looked at Ian with something akin to murder in her eyes and said accusingly, "You said it was only a formality, that it wouldn't be a real marriage at all!"

"No, lass," he said, with maddening equanimity, drawing even closer. "I said it would not be a *normal* marriage. And even you cannot deny that to be the truth."

"You lied to me, you bastard!" Still unable to believe what she was hearing, she flew to the other side of the huge, canopied four-poster and folded her arms tightly beneath her breasts. "I don't know what the devil you think you're doing, but—"

"We are man and wife now." Facing her across the tartan-covered width of the bed, he negligently tugged the hat from his head and tossed it to land atop one of the pillows. His gaze dropped with burning significance to where his bride's full, creamy breasts swelled enticingly above the deep décolletage of her gown. "And what I am doing, my own Wild Rose, is nothing more—or less—than any other husband would do."

"No!" She denied it vehemently, her cheeks flaming. "We are not man and wife and never will be! You tricked me, Ian MacGregor! Damn your soul, you were planning to keep me here all along!" She read the truth in his eyes even before he confirmed it.

"My mind was set upon you from the very first," he readily admitted. "Aye, and my heart as well."

"But, how can that be?" she demanded, stunned by the confession. Her own heart took to pounding erratically, and she was dismayed to feel a deep, inexplicable heat spreading outward from the vicinity of her abdomen. "There's no such thing as love at first sight!" She had voiced the same dampening opinion to the Duke of Albemarle. But the notion that *this* man had formed an attachment for her on such short acquaintance (granted, an acquaintance that was unlike any other) was highly unsettling. "Confound it," she said, breathing rapidly, "you don't even know me!"

"I know you." Amusement flickered briefly over his face as his gaze caught and held the blazing sapphire of her eyes. "I know that you are proud and obstinate, and more courageous than any woman I have ever before encountered. I know that you are intelligent and sharp-tongued, full of incredible spirit and passion, and that you will no doubt lead me a merry chase for the next fifty or sixty years. In truth, Callie Rose MacGregor, I know all I need to know."

His words sent her emotions into utter chaos once more. Speechless for the moment, she watched as he removed the length of plaid from his shoulder, shrugged out of his jacket, and dropped them both on the table beside the bed. He started slowly around the foot of the bed toward her. She finally found her voice again when his hands lifted to the buttons of his shirt.

"You can't do this!" she protested, her eyes growing very wide as it finally dawned on her that he meant to do more than simply hold her captive. *A great deal more,* an inner voice warned. And what was that he had said about fifty or sixty years? Great balls of fire, she thought dazedly, he really has taken complete leave of his senses.

Trembling, she inhaled upon an audible gasp and backed away.

"No matter what you—you think you feel for me, you have no right to keep me here!"

"I have every right."

"No, you don't!" She shook her head in a vigorous denial, her eyes flashing hotly while her long black curls swirled about her shoulders in glorious disarray. "You low-down, double-crossing snake, how dare you think you can get away with this! I only agreed to the handfasting in order to gain my freedom and you damned well know it! It was to be nothing more than a betrothal, a betrothal neither one of us ever intended to honor, and yet you—"

"I told you it would be what we made of it," he pointed out, impatient to get her into bed. As always, her anger only served to heighten her beauty. He unfastened the last button of his shirt, peeled it off, and gave her a thoroughly disarming smile.

But she didn't want to be disarmed. She didn't want to feel what she was feeling as her stormy—albeit fascinated—gaze traveled across the bronzed and powerfully muscled expanse of his upper torso. His chest was very broad, covered with a light matting of dark, reddish-brown curls, while his arms, rock-hard and sinewy, lent evidence to the fact that he was anything but a man of leisure. Indeed, he looked well able to crush the very life from an opponent if need be. And well able, literally *and* figuratively, to sweep her off her feet again . . .

With a strangled cry of denial, she bolted headlong for the door.

Ian was there before her. He caught her up in his arms and carried her back across to the bed. She screamed and cursed at the top of her lungs, fighting him as she had never fought before, but he tumbled her roughly down upon the feather mattress and lowered his body atop hers.

"No!" she shrieked, kicking and squirming wildly. "No, damn you! I won't—" She broke off with a sharp intake of breath when he seized her wrists in a steely grip and yanked them above her head. He brought one long leg across the flailing, black-stockinged shapeliness of both of hers, holding her captive beneath him while she continued to struggle in vain.

"You're mine, Callie Rose," he decreed huskily, his face mere inches from her own as his penetrating, gold-flecked emerald gaze smoldered down into the fiery blue depths of hers. "You've been mine from the first moment I set eyes on you. I had not planned to care for you. I sought nothing more than an end to the feud. Yet when I held you in my arms yesterday, I realized that I had met my match. By the heavens above, I want you more than I've ever wanted any woman!" he told her, passion raging hotly within him. "Body and soul, heart and mind. And were you not so damnably stubborn, you'd admit that you feel the same for me."

"I'm *not* yours!" she insisted in a defiant, quavering tone. "And I don't feel anything for you but—but complete and utter loathing!"

It wasn't true, and she knew it, but she was too infuriated at the moment to acknowledge the deep yearning that had blazed to life at the first touch of his lips upon hers. She had spent most of her life wishing she had been born a man; she wasn't ready to embrace her womanhood. At least not without a battle royal.

Narrowing her eyes vengefully up at the rogue who made her want to launch herself at him in unbridled fury one minute and burst into violent tears the next (blast it all, she had never been able to abide weepy females), she tried her best to pull her wrists free.

"I hate you, Ian MacGregor!" she bit out. "I despise you, and I swear I'll kill you if you try and force me to go through with this!" She was surprised to observe a soft smile tugging at the corners of his mouth.

"I was once told that fanned fires and forced love never did well. But the fire has burned hot and strong between us from the very beginning. And as for love—" He paused, his gaze searching hers while the candlelight played across the rugged perfection of his countenance. "No, lass," he declared, his voice wonderfully vibrant, "it will require no forcing."

"You can't possibly care for me!" she cried. Breathless and light-headed from her efforts to escape, as well as from the disturbing pressure of his body on hers, she drew in a deep, shuddering breath and accused hotly, "You only want me in your bed! I'm not as naive as you seem to think, you four-flushing sonofabitch! You're no different from any other man! You'd say anything to get what you want!"

" 'Tis true I want you in my bed. But all the more because of what is in my heart."

"Your heart is as black as your word!"

"And your tongue is ever in need of schooling," he parried, his resonant, deep-timbred voice laced with a provocative blend of desire and amusement. "You will yet learn to call me lord and master, Callie Rose MacGregor. Before this night is through, you will admit the truth."

"I'll see you in hell first!" she swore dramatically. "Now get off me, you bastard!" She writhed beneath him, arching her back and twisting her head from side to side on the pillow. The accursed tears started to her eyes now, and she choked back the sob that rose in her throat. "Let me go!"

"Never."

With that foreboding vow upon his lips, he finally put an end to the quarrel. His mouth descended upon hers in a kiss that was at once fierce and loving, his body pressing her farther down into the welcoming cradle of the mattress. She moaned in protest and tried to jerk her head away, but he transferred her wrists to the relentless grip of one large hand and brought the other down to entangle within her long, lustrous raven tresses.

His lips were almost punishing, demanding a response, while his tongue plundered the softness of her mouth. He kissed her with more sweetly savage hunger than ever before, passion setting him afire, his very soul stirring for the woman who had captured his well-guarded heart.

Time held no meaning. Fate had decreed their union; nothing could change it now. She was his. And by all that was holy, *he would make her know it.*

Callie Rose trembled beneath him. She found all thoughts of resistance melting away, felt her own newly awakened passions taking flight, and numbly realized that she wanted the kiss to go on forever. . . .

She was left gasping for breath when Ian suddenly

removed the conquering warmth of his lips from the
willing and responsive softness of hers, trailed a scorch-
ing path downward along the graceful column of her
neck, and did what he had been aching to do since he
had first seen her in the tight, low-cut silk gown.

He released her wrists and impatiently tugged the tartan sash aside to kiss the swelling, delectable curve of
her breasts. She uttered a soft cry of pleasure as his
mouth roamed appreciatively across the creamy flesh,
branding her already feverish skin with his lips and
tongue. Her hands came down to grasp at his shoulders.
She tried telling herself that what was happening
shouldn't be happening at all, that she would surely suffer a hundred and one—no, damn it, a *thousand* and
one—regrets if she surrendered, and yet she was powerless to prevent it.

While she lost the battle with her own conscience,
Ian's fingers swept up to the buttons on the front of her
gown. Exhibiting the same swift, remarkable ability his
bride had witnessed earlier that day in the drawing
room, he proceeded to liberate the row of tiny pearl buttons from their corresponding silken loops.

She inhaled sharply, but could offer nothing more
than a halfhearted objection as he unbuttoned her gown
all the way down to her waist. Somewhere in that small
part of her brain still capable of rational thought, it occurred to her that he seemed to know an awful lot about
getting women out of their clothes. She felt a sudden
twinge of angry resentment at the thought, and briefly
struggled again in spite of the fact that she longed, trai-
torously and quite shamelessly, for his touch upon her
bare skin.

But Ian would not be denied. His hand delved within the gaping edges of her bodice to close upon one of her breasts, its soft, rose-tipped fullness covered only by the thin white fabric of her chemise. He startled her a moment later when he yanked so forcefully on the neckline of her undergarment that it tore. She gasped, her eyelids fluttering open as she felt the searing warmth of his hand triumphantly claiming her naked breast. His fingers caressed her boldly, intimately, before he lowered his head farther to draw one of the delicate peaks within the moist heat of his mouth.

"Ian!" Callie Rose breathed tremulously. Straining against him, she threaded her fingers within the flame-colored thickness of his hair and closed her eyes once more. His lips gently suckled at her breast, his hot, velvety tongue swirling about the nipple with light and tantalizing movements that prompted her to give another low moan and squirm restlessly beneath him.

The flames of passion blazed ever higher, ever more intense and rapturous and irresistibly compelling. With his mouth still performing its sensuous magic at her breasts, Ian's hand moved to her skirts. He raked them up about her thighs and allowed his fingers to glide along the curve of her hip, and then underneath to her thinly clad buttocks. He rolled to his side a bit, pulling her close against him while his hand curled possessively about the alluring, well-rounded softness of her bottom.

And then his hand traveled back around to the inner seam of her open-leg drawers. Her eyes flew wide in renewed alarm when he touched her between her thighs.

"No!" she gasped out, fear and confusion threatening to vanquish desire. "No, Ian, you—"

"You're mine, sweet vixen," he reiterated in a hoarse whisper. *"Mine!"*

His lips returned to capture hers once more while his fingers, warm and sure and strong, found their way through the opening of her drawers to the triangle of delicate, soft black curls.

She tensed, inhaling sharply at the touch of his hand upon that secret, intimate place between her thighs. Passion streaked through her like lightning across a darkened sky, and a low moan rose in her throat as his fingers parted the silken petals of flesh to claim the sweet bud of her womanhood. He stroked her with a gentle yet urgent mastery that turned her blood to liquid fire within her veins.

This time, there would be no stopping him.

Her hands smoothed feverishly across the broad, hard-muscled planes of his naked back. Once again, she strained upward against him, her legs parting wider of their own accord. His mouth ravished hers completely and without mercy; she was a willing participant.

What they were doing was madness, of course, an inner voice admonished in a futile attempt to bring her back to her senses. It was sinful and wicked—*and absolute heaven on earth.*

His eyes gleaming with triumphant satisfaction at her sweet, unspoken surrender, Ian gave a low groan and pressed her back down into the mattress again. His own passions were surging nearly out of control—like thunder to her lightning. And though he had fully intended to render her naked and kiss every square inch of her enchanting curves, he could prolong the exquisite agony no longer.

Consoling himself with the thought that the night was still young, he tugged at the fastenings of her ruffled, lace-trimmed drawers. The trio of buttons held fast.

And he was all out of patience.

Callie Rose gasped against his mouth when she felt him tearing the inner seam of her drawers wider. She opened her eyes in startled apprehension and pushed weakly at his arms. But it was entirely too late to turn back now.

Slipping a hand beneath her hips, he positioned himself between her legs. She frowned in bewilderment. Having spent the majority of her life on a ranch, she was more familiar than most properly bred young ladies with the physical aspects of nature and thus now wondered how Ian intended to take her while the lower half of his magnificent body was still fully clothed.

The question in her mind was answered in a precise—and highly breathtaking—manner in the next instant. True Highlander that he was, Ian MacGregor wore nothing beneath his kilt.

He tugged up the pleated folds of tartan, lifted his bride's hips slightly, and began easing his throbbing manhood into the honeyed warmth of her feminine passage.

Callie Rose tore her lips from his and gave a soft, strangled cry of pain while trying to squirm away. But her actions could not prevent the final blending of their bodies.

"Easy, lass," Ian whispered against her ear. Secretly thrilled by the undeniable evidence of her virginity, he resolved to do his best to lessen the pain. "It will hurt only a little, and then no more."

She was in no mood to believe him. In spite of the fact that her whole body yearned for his possession, she continued to resist. A faint smile of irony touched his lips, for he knew full well that she wanted him as much as he wanted her.

Returning his hand to the tangled mass of hair at the back of her head, he forced her to his kiss once more. His fingers resumed their bold, inflaming efforts between her thighs, until she was once again near mindless with desire. He plunged deeper at last, his hardness sheathing all the way within her.

The pain was more of a dull ache, and almost immediately gave way to pleasure as his hips began tutoring hers in the captivating, age-old rhythm of love. She moaned and clutched at his shoulders for support, instinctively meeting his thrusts, her breath nothing but a series of soft gasps while she forgot about all else save for what was taking place in that ancient, canopied wooden bed. It seemed that she had been transported to another world, a special world inhabited by no one but herself and the man who was making her realize that there just might have been a purpose for having been born a woman after all.

She clung to him as though she were drowning, while his thrusts grew faster and deeper and his mouth trailed hotly downward to her breasts once more. And then they were both soaring heavenward. . . .

A breathless little scream broke from Callie Rose's lips. Consumed by a pleasure so intense that she was certain she would faint, she felt herself drifting slowly back to earth. Ian tensed above her a moment later, gave a low groan, and made her gasp anew as his masculine seed flooded her with its potent warmth. She struggled to regain control of her breathing, her arms falling away from his shoulders while she closed her eyes again.

It had all happened with such tempestuous haste; scarcely fifteen minutes had passed since he had carried her upstairs. And yet their whole lives had been changed in that time.

Ian rolled to his back in the bed and tugged his bride's pliant, well-loved body against him. She was feeling much too weary and contented at the moment to struggle.

For several minutes, there was only silence between them. Callie Rose lay in her husband's arms, her head spinning with a mixture of shock and confusion, and her whole body still tingling warmly. She would never have believed it possible to feel what Ian had made her feel. She would never have believed it possible to behave with such shameless abandon. But heaven help her, she *had* felt that way and behaved that way . . . and she had enjoyed every blasted, wonderful moment of it.

What the devil was she going to do now?

She heaved a ragged sigh and felt herself blush rosily at the memory of Ian's lovemaking. The damage had been done. His fierce, sweet mastery of her body could never be forgotten. And neither could her own damnably wanton response. She groaned inwardly, her color deepening.

Confound it, she thought with a flash of self-directed fury, she might as well join all those other "scarlet angels" down by the river when she got back home to Fort Worth. She was surely going straight to hell in a hand basket. She had allowed a man who was little more than a stranger to make love to her. *Love?* Her sapphire gaze clouded with guilt. No, it hadn't been love. What had happened between them had been provoked by nothing more than physical (highly physical) attraction.

She opened her eyes and stole a quick glance up at Ian's face. He had vowed that she would know the truth before the night was through. What truth? she wondered, her brow creasing into a pensive frown. It was certainly true that she found him hard to resist—damn it, *impossible* to resist. It was also true that he had tricked her into marriage, seduced her without any regard whatsoever for her feelings in the matter, and apparently intended for her to play the role of loving and obedient wife for the rest of her natural born days.

Righteous indignation brought her to life once more. Stirring in his arms at last, she pushed herself away from him and jerked the edges of her bodice together across the exposed curve of her breasts. She sat up in the bed and turned a narrow, hotly reproachful look upon him.

"This doesn't change anything!" she declared, her voice low and quavering with emotion. "If you think just because you were able to force me—"

"Force?"

His mouth twitched as he turned and raised himself up a bit, leisurely bending one elbow beneath him. He had settled his kilt back down into place. The soft glow of the candles burning on a table beside the bed cast intriguing shadows across the bronzed hardness of his naked chest and arms. His eyes gleamed as they took in the sight of his wife's charming, seductive dishabille.

Her hair was streaming about her in a tangled mass of black curls, her beautiful face was flushed, and her skirts were still bunched up about her thighs. In spite of the fact that he had taken her only a few minutes ago, he felt desire raging hotly within him once more.

"You—you *raped* me!" she said accusingly. She was startled when she heard his quiet rumble of laughter.

"It was anything but rape," he said, disagreeing, his gaze full of wry and loving humor. "I knew from the first taste of your lips, Callie Rose MacGregor, that your passion was as fierce as my own. If you would set aside your pride, you would know that we are perfectly suited to each other. Our marriage will no doubt have its share of battles," he predicted, with another brief, rakishly appealing smile. "But the peace that follows will be all the sweeter."

"We don't have a marriage!" she cried in extreme annoyance. She was trying desperately to ignore the wild leaping of her heart. It was no easy task, not with him lying there half naked, not with the memory of his kisses still burning in her mind. And on her flesh. She stifled a moan and clutched the silken fabric tighter across her breasts. "You can't keep me here! You may have succeeded in having your way with me once, but—"

"Aye, and I'll have it again before the night is through," he vowed softly.

She suffered a sharp intake of breath, her blue eyes widening and filling with a mixture of alarm and excitement. No, by thunder, she told herself rigorously, she couldn't let it happen again. *She couldn't!*

With a blistering oath, she swung her legs over the

edge of the bed and scrambled down from its great height. Ian shook his head with slightly exasperated amusement at the prospect of yet another chase. Drawing his tall frame up from the bed, he blocked her path to the doorway once more. She avoided his grasp and took refuge behind a velvet-upholstered chair, then gasped in dismay when he merely knocked the chair aside. Whirling about, she tried to set a course back toward the door, but he twisted his hand within the full gathers of her skirts. She cried out as she felt herself toppling downward.

Ian caught her in his arms, cushioning her fall with his own body. She lay atop him for a moment, breathing heavily from her efforts and seeking in vain to keep her bosom fully covered, before stirring with another furious burst of defiance.

"Let me go!" she stormed, only to gasp again when he suddenly rolled her beneath him. Imprisoning her there on the carpeted floor near the bright, chill-conquering warmth of the fire, he raised up on his knees and took one of her feet in his hands.

"Wha—what are you doing?" she stammered, hastily sweeping the hair from her face.

" 'Tis time, you little savage, for your husband to see what manner of woman he has married," he decreed.

"No!"

While she tried to squirm away, he untied the laces and pulled her boot off. She brought her other foot up to kick at him, but he caught it as well and tossed her other boot aside to join the first. His fingers moved purposefully to the bodice of her gown.

"No!" she protested again, lifting one hand to strike

at the broad target of his chest. "No, damn your rascally hide, you can't do this!"

"You've nothing to be ashamed of, my bonny bride," he said, undeterred by her blows. "That much I know already."

"I'm *not* ashamed."

She struggled in vain to prevent him from stripping the gown from her body. He sent it flying to land across the upended chair, then did the same with her petticoat before beginning to tug at her satin garters.

"Stop it!" she cried shrilly. Clutching at the torn edges of her chemise's lace-edged neckline, she flung a number of unladylike curses at his handsome head while both of her stockings were rolled down and pulled off.

Her pulse racing wildly, she finally managed to turn over. She scrambled up onto her hands and knees, preparing to flee once more, only to inhale sharply when she felt Ian's hands on her drawers. He yanked them all the way down to her knees. She crimsoned at having her bottom bared to him, and groaned inwardly to realize the humiliating, highly vulnerable position she was in.

The next thing she knew, he was rolling her over on her back again and leaving her to cover herself as best she could with her one remaining garment while he climbed to his feet. He stripped off his own shoes and woolen hose, removed the *sporran* hanging about his waist, and unfastened his kilt. All the while, his penetrating green eyes seared down into the blue fire of hers.

"I'll make you pay for this!" she vowed, sitting up

and crossing her arms protectively against her breasts. Her fiery gaze shot to the door.

"I've little doubt of it," he shot back, with the merest suggestion of a smile. He took off his kilt now, standing before her in all his naked, masculine glory.

She swallowed a sudden lump in her throat, and her eyes grew round as saucers as they traveled up and down the whole magnificent length of him. There was not an ounce of fat on his body. His stomach was perfectly flat, his thighs lean and hard-muscled, his long legs athletic. A tremor shook her, and she felt herself growing warm all over when her enthralled gaze fastened on the cluster of dark curls between his powerful thighs—and the remarkable, awe-inspiring evidence of virility that sprang forth from those curls.

"Look at me that way any longer, Lady MacGregor, and you'll find yourself well and truly ravished on the floor," he warned, more than half in earnest.

Callie Rose started guiltily at that, her cheeks flaming anew. Muttering something unintelligible, she jumped from the carpet like a shot and raced to the door yet again. Ian was upon her in an instant, his arm slipping about her slender waist.

"Och, woman," he growled in mock irritation as he pulled her back against him, "would you have my kinsmen see you like this?"

"Better them than *you!*" she retorted acidly, still refusing to admit defeat.

"No other man shall gaze upon what is mine alone," he told her in a voice edged with steel. All traces of amusement were gone as he swept her up in his arms and bore her determinedly back to the bed.

"Haven't you done enough for one night?" she charged, wriggling in his grasp. Disconcerted by the familiar heat spreading through her, she waged another losing battle with her own proud, defiant nature.

"Chan eil." He shook his head, his eyes splendidly aglow as he favored her with a look that was both hungry and hotly possessive. "We've only just begun, sweet vixen."

He lowered her to the soft, shadowy warmth beneath the brocade canopy and imprisoned her body with his own. In a matter of seconds, he had tugged off her chemise. There were no barriers between them now, save for those she had erected about her heart.

She gasped sharply when bare flesh met bare flesh. Another shiver coursed down her spine as her enticingly feminine curves fitted with rapturous perfection against her husband's powerful, muscular hardness. She could not help but be aware of his arousal. He encircled her with his strong arms and drew her close, his lips descending upon hers with a gentle yet compelling urgency that stilled her weak struggles and sent a veritable flood tide of longing washing over her.

Ian MacGregor was, indeed, a man of his word. He soon set about fulfilling the promise he had made himself. Raising his body upward, he masterfully turned his wife facedown in the bed. She could manage only a lame protest as he swept the thick, shimmering curtain of her hair aside. He bent to his task with relish, his warm lips branding her skin down along the graceful curve of her back.

Her arms tensed about the pillow when his mouth settled upon her bare bottom. She gasped and tried to raise up in the bed, which only served to bring her backside even closer to his appreciative gaze. His hands smoothed about her hips. He explored every saucy, delectable curve of her bottom, his lips provocatively nibbling, his tongue teasing at the rounded flesh with a bold playfulness that both shocked and delighted her.

She moaned and squirmed restlessly in his grasp. And though she blushed at the wicked caress, she could summon neither the will nor the strength to put a stop to it. Wicked it might be, but she could not deny that it gave her pleasure. Heaven help her, a great deal of pleasure . . .

Ian proceeded to bestow a series of light, seductive kisses across the backs of her slender thighs, then down each of her long and shapely legs. When he finally rolled her to her back again, her eyelids fluttered open and she gazed up at him in expectation. But he gave her no time to consider what he might do next.

With a soft smile of triumph playing about his lips, he captured the willing softness of her mouth in another long, forcefully beguiling kiss. Her hands crept up to his neck as the kiss deepened, as the simmering fires of passion blazed higher once more. She kissed him back, her tongue doing sweet battle with his while his hands made thorough appraisal of her naked curves.

His mouth relinquished hers to roam across the flushed smoothness of her face, down to the pulse throbbing at the base of her throat, and then lower to the beckoning fullness of her breasts. His hands came up to caress the creamy, rose-tipped flesh, joining with his lips and tongue to pay loving tribute to her womanliness. She entwined her fingers within his sun-streaked auburn hair, straining farther upward and feeling herself grow light-headed with desire.

And then his mouth was traveling lower.

He trailed a searing path downward across her stomach, his tongue dipping teasingly within her navel before he slid his body farther toward the foot of the bed and allowed his lips to wander across her pale, quivering thighs. But when his mouth crept toward the triangle of soft raven curls between, she felt compelled to resist.

"No!" she gasped out, tugging on his hair. Great balls of fire, she thought as she turned beet red from head to toe, surely what he was intending to do was forbidden. Forbidden by whom? an inner voice piped up to challenge in the next instant. "No, Ian, you—"

"You will call me lord and master yet," he repeated, his voice full of that intoxicating mixture of desire and amusement she had already come to know so well. He gave her a soft, devilish smile. She trembled and sought futilely to squirm away.

"No!"

But he would have her burn for him the way he did for her. Disregarding her shocked protests, his hands clasped her about the hips in a firm, merciless grip. He held her captive for his pleasure—and for her own. His gold-flecked gaze darkened before he lowered his head once more.

A breathless cry escaped her lips. She shuddered with passion at the first touch of his mouth upon her moist, silken flesh. Her eyes swept closed, and she caught her lower lip between her teeth as his tongue skillfully darted and dipped and circled.

"Ian, please!" she entreated, her fingers clenching within the flame-colored thickness of his hair.

"Am I your lord and master?" His own voice was low and vibrant with emotion.

"Ian!"

"Say it," he commanded. He was every bit as anxious as she to bring the exquisite torment to its ultimate and satisfying conclusion. Her gasps and moans, the taste of her upon his lips, turned his own blood to liquid fire.

"Ian, I—"

"Say it."

"All right, damn you! Lord and master!" She complied in a broken yet defiant whisper, certain she could bear no more.

His eyes gleamed with exultant satisfaction as he quickly brought his body upon hers once more and rolled so that she was atop him. Perplexed, she pushed herself upward a bit, her thighs straddling him. She stifled another scream of pure pleasure as he lifted her hips and brought her down upon his awaiting hardness.

"Ian!" She breathed his name, feeling as though he had touched her very womb. Her hands tightened almost convulsively upon his shoulders, while her long hair cascaded down about her to tease at his naked chest. She met his gaze for only a moment—before closing her eyes and obeying the pressure of his hands upon her hips. She rode atop him, reveling in each of his thrusts.

Beseiged by sensations more intensely pleasurable than she had ever known, she no longer cared whether or not her surrender was a mistake. She no longer cared about anything other than this wondrous, near painful ecstasy she felt whenever she was in Ian MacGregor's arms. He had conquered her resistance and stormed the defenses of her reluctant womanhood; never again would she wish she had been born a man. And though she did not yet realize it, this proud, masterful, sinfully appealing Highland chieftain had stormed her heart as well. . . .

The fulfillment was mutually explosive. Callie Rose gave a soft, shuddering cry and collapsed upon her husband's chest. He took his own splendid release, then cradled her tenderly, their bodies remaining joined for several long moments.

In the sweet and languid aftermath of their passion, they lay together in the bed while the candles burned low and the fire crackled and hissed softly beyond the hearth. Ian gathered his bride's supple nakedness close to the hard warmth of his.

"I love you, Callie Rose MacGregor," he declared, his deep emerald gaze reflecting what was in his heart. "I've never loved before, nor will I love any woman but you from this day forward."

She caught her breath. Her own heart stirred at the sound of his voice, and even more so at the words he had spoken. But her mind told her it was impossible for someone to fall in love so quickly. It simply did not happen. While she was certainly no expert on the subject, she had always heard it said that people had to be acquainted for a considerable amount of time before they could know the true extent of their feelings for each other. And yet . . .

Releasing her breath upon a sigh, she instinctively

settled her body even closer against Ian's. Her actions were in direct contrast to the denial she offered him.

"I'm *not* a MacGregor."

"Are you not?" His low, mellow chuckle made her pulse quicken. "I beg to differ, sweet vixen. We are man and wife now, in every sense of the word. Lord and Lady MacGregor." He smoothed a warm hand possessively over the curve of her hip. "Indeed, I would say we had both served the honor of the clan quite well."

"Honor?" She pushed herself up a bit to cast him a challenging look. "It's high time, you arrogant sonofabitch, that you learned—"

She broke off with a loud gasp when he bestowed a hard, familiar slap on her bare bottom.

"But a taste of what you'll get if you don't learn to curb your tongue," he warned, his eyes holding only a touch of humor.

She compressed her lips into a tight, thin line. There were sparks in her own gaze, and her cheeks flamed with angry indignation, but she had already learned not to push him too far. Besides, she was much too tired to engage him in another battle just now. Later, she promised herself, she would seek revenge for the blow to her dignity.

He pulled her back down to him. Her eyes swept closed again, she finally drifted off to sleep with the strong, steady pulsing of his heart beneath her cheek.

❧ SEVEN ❧

Callie Rose awoke to the touch of her husband's lips upon hers. Her eyelids fluttered open, and she found herself gazing up at the rugged perfection of his countenance as he bent over her.

"Would you sleep the day away, my lady?" he teased, his eyes winningly aglow.

She looked to the window and frowned. Surprised to discover that it was morning already, she drew herself up into a sitting position in the bed. She swept the wildly disheveled mass of curls away from her face, recalled the fact that she was naked, and hastened to snatch the covers up over her breasts while coloring hotly.

Ian's mouth curved into an indulgent smile at her actions. He stood to his full height beside the bed, fully dressed and impatient to start wooing his reluctant bride.

"Do you not think it a bit late for such maidenly modesty?" He was unscathed by her narrow, vengeful glare. With another brief smile, he told her, "The water's been heated for your bath. And though Molly offered to serve us breakfast in bed, I told her we would be down shortly."

"Why is it you have only three servants to look after the castle?" she asked at a sudden thought, feeling awkward and embarrassed in spite of all that they had shared in the night. *The night.* She groaned inwardly as the vivid, highly disturbing memories flooded her mind. It didn't help any to see Ian MacGregor looking so handsome and commanding . . . and happy. Damn him, he appeared neither weary *nor* remorseful.

"We've no need for others," he stated, resisting the temptation to join her in the bed. The same memories were in his mind as well. "I seldom entertain guests while I am here. My business requires me to be away more often than I would wish."

"Your business?"

"Aye. When my father died, it fell to me to oversee the shipping business and other holdings. Though I would much prefer to remain here at Castle MacGregor, I spend more than half the year in either Edinburgh or London."

"And have you—have you ever been to America?" She cursed the way her whole treasonous body warmed beneath his gaze. It seemed absurd to be sitting there in his bed, naked as the day she was born, discussing everyday matters with him.

"Once, when I was a good deal younger. I've not been anxious to return there."

"Well, *I* have!" she retorted, her blue eyes flashing up at him. "Last night never should have happened, but nothing has changed!"

"Nothing?" he asked softly. His eyes dropped with bold significance to where she was clutching the sheet about her breasts, then lower still.

"Confound it," she swore, while a fiery blush stained her cheeks, "you know what I mean!" She raised her head in a proud, defiant gesture that belied the vulnerability of her present condition. "We're not really married to each other. The handfasting was—"

"Perfectly legal, just as I told you. We are bound to each other every bit as much as if we had repeated our vows before a parson." He folded his arms across his chest and allowed himself the luxury of contemplating what he would do to her—and teach her to do to him— when night fell once more. It was difficult to keep his distance and carry on a conversation with her, when all he really wanted to do was kiss her until she begged for mercy. Still, he was determined to show her that they were equally matched *out* of bed. "Indeed, my dearest wife," he proclaimed, "last night changed everything."

"That may be true under Scottish law, but it won't matter once I get back home to Texas!"

"This is your home now."

"Like hell it is, you bas—" She caught herself just in time. Eyeing him rebelliously, she remembered the hearty swat her backside had received in payment for the impetuosity of her tongue. And she was still in too precarious a situation to make this redheaded scoundrel pay for it.

"You'll find all you need in there," he said, changing the subject as he nodded to indicate a door to the right of the fireplace. "One of the first things I did when I became laird of the castle was to install a permanent bathroom—with running water heated by virtue of a special furnace—next to the master bedchamber." A faint smile of irony touched his lips when he added,

"Perhaps I realized that one day my new bride would appreciate the convenience."

"Perhaps you should realize *now* that your new bride doesn't want to be a bride at all and would be only too happy to bathe in ice-cold water for the rest of her life if it meant she'd never have to set eyes on you again!" She was surprised when he blithely turned and headed toward the bedroom door.

"Breakfast will be served in half an hour," he cautioned. "And make certain you dress in your riding habit."

"My riding habit?" Her brows knitted together in a puzzled frown.

"Aye. It has occurred to me that you could do with a bit of fresh air." He opened the door and paused to remind her, "Half an hour. Any longer, and I will give myself the pleasure of finishing the job." Musing that he would be well satisfied if she decided to put him to the test, he finally left her alone.

Callie Rose stared after him, her eyes flinging invisible daggers in his wake. She heaved a sigh and tossed back the covers; she was every bit as desperate for a bath as he had thought she would be. Padding hurriedly across the carpeted floor, she flung open the door to the bathroom and found a huge, claw-footed tub within. She set the water to running, then spied her valise sitting on a chair in the corner. At least she would have her own clothing to wear.

Recalling Ian's warning, she chose not to linger too long in the comforting warmth of the water. Her body was plagued by an embarrassing soreness (she ached in places she hadn't even known to exist before now), and she was anxious to escape the confining walls of the castle, even if the escape would be temporary and she'd have to endure the company of the only man who had ever made her doubt herself.

Her thoughts returned to the previous night as she emerged from the tub and quickly dried her glistening curves with a large, thirsty towel embroidered with the lion crest of the MacGregors. Closing her eyes against the memory of Ian's lovemaking, she shivered. It was still difficult to believe that she had actually let him touch her the way he had—and on three separate occasions at that. He had awakened her in the night with a seductive kiss upon her unsuspecting lips, and had then proceeded to do a good deal more while she had felt her body fill with longing and wondered if it was all some wickedly romantic dream.

It had been no dream.

"Damnation," she muttered, closing her eyes against the recollection of her own shameful responses. Nothing had been the same since Ian MacGregor had forced his way into her life. Nothing would ever be the same again, she mused with an inward sigh. The thought sent her eyes flying wide. Flinging the towel aside, she opened the valise and pulled out her clothing.

When she joined Ian at the foot of the staircase, she was attired in a two-piece riding habit of black grenadine. The jacket was fitted, closing down the front with half a dozen large brass buttons, while the divided skirt clung to the curve of her hips before flaring outward. She wore a white lawn shirt underneath, her high-top boots, and a pair of soft leather gloves. And since her cousin had neglected to send along her hat, she had once again secured her hair in a single long braid.

"You're a bonny sight this morning, Lady MacGregor," her husband pronounced, with a warm smile.

"Save your compliments for someone fool enough to believe them," she told him, though her retort lacked conviction. She blushed at the possessive admiration in his gaze. No matter how determined she was to turn her thoughts away from the previous night, they would not be controlled. She found it difficult to behave with anything even approaching normalcy. How in heaven's name *could* she after all that had happened between them?

Several conflicting emotions played across her face as she stood there, acutely conscious of his eyes upon her. Drawing in a deep breath, she offered no resistance when he took her arm and led her into the dining room.

They shared a breakfast of smoked herring, potatoes, griddle cakes, and tea, with Callie Rose avoiding Molly's sympathetic gaze the whole time. She knew that the older woman was well aware of what had taken place after the handfasting ceremony. Although she had never been a "shy and retiring young maiden," she found herself shifting uncomfortably about in her chair at the prospect of facing Peter and Jenny. They, too, would know. She wondered—with a faint smile of bitter irony—if she looked different than before.

She glanced up and caught Ian surveying her as though he would like nothing more than to carry her back upstairs; she swore inwardly and dropped her stormy gaze to the table.

Afterward, they headed outside. It was another cool, gloriously fresh summer morning. The sky was ablaze with the sun's golden radiance, the air was filled with the mingling aromas of wood smoke and wildflowers, while the sweet trill of bird song drifted along on the gentle breeze.

Callie Rose felt her spirits lighten the moment she emerged into the sunshine. She willingly accompanied Ian across the green-mantled grounds to the stables.

"You really do intend for us to go for a ride?" she asked, her eyes sparkling with eager anticipation when they met his.

"I do," he confirmed. His mouth curved into a soft, mocking smile. "From what I recall, you are an excellent horsewoman."

"I learned to ride before I could even walk." She pulled her arm free and lifted her head proudly. "I wasn't brought up to be the kind of woman who sits inside all day with her gossip and her embroidery."

"And your mother approved of your unconventional education?" he queried, with deceptive nonchalance. He was anxious to learn everything about the woman who had captured his heart. *Everything.*

"My mother died when I was still very young," she replied, her sapphire gaze clouding.

"As did mine."

She was startled at the way her heart twisted in compassion when she observed the sudden shadow of pain crossing his face. It was odd, but she had never really envisioned him with a family. He'd had one the same as everyone else, of course, and yet he was so very much his own man. Independent and overbearing to a fault—a great deal like J. D. Buchanan now that she thought about it.

"I—I suppose you were sent away to school as soon as you were old enough," she murmured.

"Aye. To Edinburgh in the beginning, then England, and then to the Continent. But my heart was ever in the Highlands," he remarked, with another brief smile.

"It is quite beautiful here," she acknowledged, only to mentally chide herself for the concession in the next instant.

She couldn't believe they were carrying on a polite conversation as if all was right with the world and they hadn't spent the night the way they had. For heaven's sake, she thought in a whirl of confusion, this was the same man who had forced her into marriage—and into his bed! By all rights, she should be seeking revenge, not details about his past. Or his present, or his future.

She folded her arms tightly across her chest. Until now, there had been nothing but fire and fury and passion (granted, an overwhelming degree of passion) between them. And yet, strangely enough, it seemed natural to be talking with him like this.

"What about you, lass?" he asked. "Have you never left your home before?" He regarded her steadily while she nodded and frowned.

"My father sent me back East to a boarding school for a while." A rueful little smile touched her lips when she found herself adding, "J. D. Buchanan is a force to be reckoned with. Once, when I was twelve, he arranged for an unmarried aunt to come and stay at the ranch. She was supposed to turn me into a lady, but the poor woman didn't last a month. He gave up after that. At least until I turned eighteen and he—"

The sentence remained unfinished. She had been on the verge of revealing her father's determination to see her married. The thought of it prompted her eyes to kindle anew, and she felt a dull flush rise to her face before she looked away.

Dear Lord, she wondered disconsolately, how was she ever going to face J. D.? And her brothers? And everyone else back home? They'd never understand how she could have surrendered to Ian MacGregor after all he had done. She'd never understand it herself. . . .

They had reached the stables by now. Ian took her arm again and led her inside. The building was made of stone, its cool semidarkness filled with the pleasant and familiar scent of hay. Callie Rose saw that there were a dozen stalls flanking the center, cobbled run, and she looked farther to observe a black carriage, polished and resplendent with an identifying coat of arms, sitting ready behind double wooden doors at the farthest end of the building.

Peter was still in the process of saddling their mounts. His attractive features split into a broad grin when he caught sight of them.

"Good morning, my lady," he said, nodding respectfully at Callie Rose. He told Ian, "There must be another storm brewing out to sea, for the horses are fair to jumping this morning."

"I'll keep that in mind," Ian replied, with only the hint of a smile. He stepped forward to help complete the task. Callie Rose wandered back toward the doorway, her blue eyes alight with a secret purpose.

The ride would provide her with the perfect opportunity to escape! She was certain she could manage to get away once she and Ian had left the outer walls of Castle MacGregor behind. Her pulse leapt with excitement at the prospect. But at the same time, a sudden, inexplicable heaviness gripped her heart. . . .

"Ready, my love?"

Ian's voice startled her from her reverie. She whirled guiltily to face him, the telltale color flying to her cheeks. She quickly regained her composure, however, and even managed to affect an air of only casual interest in the coming ride.

"Of course." She moved along with him as he and Peter led the horses outside. The mount he had chosen for her was a beautiful sorrel mare.

"Her name's *Ban-sith*, my lady," Peter told her, smoothing a hand along the animal's shimmering, dark red neck. "It means 'fairy woman.' We call her that because she's just a wee bit flighty. But you'll have no trouble with her so long as you keep a firm grip on the reins."

"Thank you, Peter," she said, casting him a preoccupied smile. She gathered up the reins and lifted a hand to the saddle horn, preparing to mount up. A soft gasp escaped her lips when Ian's hands suddenly closed about her waist. "I don't need any—" she started to protest, but he tossed her up into the saddle and then had the audacity to stand smiling up at her in wry, loving amusement while she jammed her booted feet into the stirrups and cast him a speaking glare.

"I would take no chances with your safety, sweet vixen," he declared in a voice meant for her ears alone.

"I'm damned well able to take care of myself!" she shot back. Though she was tempted to urge her horse into a gallop then and there, she knew the time was not yet right.

"Aye," murmured Ian, swinging agilely up onto his own mount. It was the same magnificent black stallion he had been riding when he had abducted her. "So much so that you were carried off by me."

"No other man would have done such a thing!"

"No other man would have been fool enough to try," he quipped dryly.

He reined about and set a course toward the castle gate. Still bridling at his arrogance, Callie Rose hesitated only a moment before following. Peter watched the two of them ride away. He shook his head, his eyes twinkling at the thought of the battles still to come. At least his Jenny would be a sweet and biddable wife once they were wed . . . *or would she*?

Ian led the way across the rolling, unspoiled countryside. He was ever aware of Callie Rose's presence a few lengths behind him. The little wildcat seemed intent upon outdistancing him; he smiled to himself and touched his heels to the stallion's flanks. The powerfully built animal surged forward, but the smaller mare soon closed the gap at her rider's expert command.

Their horses galloped neck and neck for nearly a mile, until Callie Rose seized her chance. She tugged on the reins, directing her mount off to the south while Ian continued eastward.

It was now or never, she thought, then was dismayed to experience a sudden, overwhelming reluctance to carry out her plan. She frowned and sliced a quick glance over her right shoulder. Her eyes filled with a contradictory mixture of triumph and disappointment when she saw that Ian was not yet giving chase. He was still riding toward the morning sun, apparently unconscious of the fact that she was no longer in the race.

Bending low over the horse's mane, she made straightaway for the nearby trees. She was convinced she could lose him within the heavily wooded forest even if he did manage to catch up with her. And once she emerged into the heather-strewed meadow on the other side, she knew she could find her way to Inverness . . . back to the life Ian MacGregor had so rudely disrupted.

Ignoring the sharp pain in her heart, she rode like the devil himself was after her, giving the animal beneath her the freedom to choose its own path across the hills. The fragrant darkness of the forest soon enveloped them. She held tight to the reins and battled the instinct to slow the mare's dangerously frantic pace.

I love you, Callie Rose MacGregor. Ian's words echoed over and over again in her mind as she felt sudden tears stinging against her eyelids. She drew in a deep, shuddering breath and bent even lower to avoid being swept from the saddle by the threatening outreach of the limbs. Though she dared not risk a backward glance, she sensed that Ian was not behind her. Her horse thundered along, its hooves flying sure and steady above the forest floor.

She could see the light of the clearing just ahead now. Freedom seemed increasingly certain. But still she took no joy in it.

The memory of these past two days would have to be

vanquished, put from her mind and never called up again. She'd have to try and forget about the green-eyed Highlander who had briefly (yet so very thoroughly) made her his wife. It would be best if she made no mention of the handfasting to her father and brothers. As a matter of fact, she decided with a frown that reflected her inner anguish, it would be best if she made no mention of her "husband" at all. . . .

The sorrel mare broke from the trees at last. Raising her head, Callie Rose dashed angrily at her eyes and finally allowed her troubled gaze to make a broad, encompassing sweep of the landscape.

A sharp, breathless cry escaped her lips when Ian suddenly materialized beside her. He had skirted the outer edges of the forest to head her off. His horse fell into pace beside hers, and his hand shot out to grasp her bridle.

"No!" screamed Callie Rose. She struck out at him, but he would not let go. He forced her mount to an abrupt halt—and in spite of her efforts to prevent it, slipped an arm about her waist, plucked her out of the saddle, and transferred her to the stallion's back. She cursed, struggling in helpless outrage while he imprisoned her before him, only to gasp when he dismounted and dragged her roughly down to the ground.

"A MacGregor holds what is his!" he decreed, his eyes burning down into hers while his fingers clenched about her arms. She was forced to stand on tiptoe to confront him.

"I'm not yours!" she denied hotly. She raised her hands to push at his chest, but he swept her up against him. The look on his handsome face was one of barely controlled fury, and his gaze darkened with an almost savage gleam as he brought his face close to her own.

"Damn it, woman, do you not realize that you might have been killed careening through the trees like that?" he ground out.

"I wasn't 'careening'!" she was quick to refute. "And it so happens, Ian MacGregor, that I could ride circles around you and never be the worse for wear!" She squirmed within his grasp again, her eyes brilliantly ablaze. Two bright spots of angry color rode high on her cheeks, and her breasts heaved beneath the fitted bodice of her jacket. "Now take your hands off me!"

"You will never leave me," he decreed in a voice that was raw with emotion. "No, nor will you ever again try to—"

"I *will* try! And I'll keep on trying until—"

It was her turn to be cut off. He silenced her with the hard, fiercely demanding pressure of his lips upon hers. She moaned and felt her whole body quiver. His arms locked about her, gathering her close. In no time at all, her hands were gliding up to his shoulders. Her knees weakened and her senses reeled as they always did beneath the rapturous onslaught of his embrace.

His anger joined with her own to provoke the ever-smoldering passion between them to a consuming, white-hot flame. Before she quite knew what was happening, they were lying entwined atop the sweetly scented cushion of grass. Ian unbuttoned her jacket and pulled it off. Her white lawn blouse soon followed, and then the divided skirt as well. He virtually tore off his own shirt, before lowering his body atop hers once more and capturing the parted softness of her lips in a kiss that took her to heaven and back again.

He yanked the hemline of her chemise upward, baring her ripe, satiny breasts to his touch. His fingers caressed her boldly, hungrily, his mouth roaming downward to tease the rose-tipped peaks with such merciless, sensuous persuasion that her head tossed restlessly to-and-fro on the heather. His hand insinuated itself between the opening of her drawers, and he began stroking her delicate pink flesh. Her breath became nothing but a series of soft gasps, her thighs parting wider and her back arching as her hands smoothed feverishly across the bronzed hardness of his back.

And then he was turning her facedown in the grass, his strong fingers already tugging on her drawers. The undergarment was soon down about her knees, and then eased all the way off, but when she thought he would roll her over again, he surprised her by pulling her back against him and returning the exquisite, skillful warmth of his hand to the secret place between her thighs.

When they were both near mindless with desire, he urged her forward onto her hands and knees, tossed up his kilt, and took her from behind. She trembled and gave a strangled cry of pure pleasure as his throbbing manhood sheathed to the hilt within her well-honeyed feminine passage. He tugged her back against him once more, his thrusts gentle at first but quickly growing swifter and bolder. Her hips moved in perfect unison with his, and her hands crept behind her to clutch at his lean, powerfully muscled thighs.

The position was a new and sinfully enchanting one; she wondered through a haze of passion how it was that

Ian knew so many ways to make love. It was wicked enough to share this sweet madness with him in the cloaking darkness of the night, but it seemed downright wanton of her to be doing so in the light of day, out in the open. Still, she was not the least bit inclined to complain.

Their union was, like the first, all flash and fire and heat of the moment. Their passions soared ever upward, until Callie Rose felt as though she had somehow been taken out of herself, as though her very soul had joined with Ian's. The sensation shook her deeply; though her body was left fully sated, her heart and mind yearned to know why she found it so difficult to bear the thought of leaving him. . . .

In the soft afterglow of their loving, Ian stretched out on his side and drew her body back against the welcoming length of his. He slipped an arm about her waist, his chin tenderly nuzzling the top of her head.

"You cannot deny what is between us, lass," he murmured in that wonderful, vibrant tone of his. She had pulled her chemise down into place, but it shielded very little from his penetrating gaze. "Aye, you must feel it, too."

"I don't know what the blazes I feel anymore," she said, sighing. It was the first time she had ever admitted any doubts, either to herself or to him. Lying there in the thick, fragrant shelter of the meadow with his body pressed against hers and the warm sunshine setting them aglow, she was more confused than ever. She shivered as the cool breeze swept across her thinly clad curves, then sighed contentedly as Ian gathered her even closer to his virile warmth.

"I love you, Callie Rose. And you love me. Why else do you think we were wed?"

"I ... you only married me because of *this*," she said, casting a significant glance down to where his arm rested possessively across her. Though he could not see her face, he knew she was referring to what had just happened between them. "And maybe the feud had something to do with it as well," she added. She was surprised to hear his quiet laughter close to her ear.

"You little fool," he said huskily, the term more of an endearment than an insult. "Neither lust nor revenge could have prompted me to marry. 'Tis true that I wanted you, and that I was bound by the promise to my father. Yet as I told you before, I knew from the first that you were the only woman destined to be my bride." He smiled again and pressed an affectionate kiss to the silken smoothness of her temple. "I could have taken you in the very beginning and left us both the wiser for it."

"I suppose that's what you did to all the other women you brought to Castle MacGregor!" she uttered mockingly, her eyes kindling with fire at the thought.

"There have been no others." He was delighted by the jealousy he detected in her voice.

"Like hell." She frowned and stirred in his arms at last, turning her head so that she could direct a narrow, accusing look up at him. "I have very little doubt, Ian MacGregor, that you have broken hearts all over Europe."

"Perhaps a few," he allowed, an unrepentant smile tugging at his lips. His features sobered in the next instant. "But I'll not break yours. No, nor will I allow my own to be broken." His gaze darkened as it seared down into hers. "Do you not yet understand? You are mine. I will never let you go!"

"But you—you can't keep me here forever," she stammered weakly.

"Can I not?" he said challengingly, with supreme confidence. Lifting a hand to cup her chin, he told her, "Our courtship was admittedly brief, but we've a lifetime to become better acquainted. We are man and wife now. And so we shall remain."

"But none of this makes any sense!" she argued once more. "People don't—"

"People do," he asserted. His gaze softened as it traveled over her beautiful, heart-shaped countenance. "Why is it so difficult for you to believe the evidence before you? Have you never considered the possibility that you would one day fall in love?"

"No, and I don't want to consider it now!" She tried to rise, but he pulled her back down beside him. "Confound it, I don't want to love you!" She breathed unevenly, cursing the tears that sprang to her eyes again. "I don't want to love anyone! I just want to go back to the Diamond L and forget any of this ever happened!"

"You could never forget."

"Well, I could damned sure *try*!"

"Stop fighting it, lass," he commanded softly. He smoothed a hand downward, over the enchanting curve of her hip. "We were meant to be together. Aye, and nothing will change that."

"I'll find a way to escape," she vowed in stubborn defiance. She was battling against her own emotions as well as his. "Next time, I'll succeed!"

"There won't be a next time." His sun-kissed brow creased into a scowl, while his green eyes filled with a dangerous light. "By heaven, woman, I'll skelp you good and proper if you ever again put yourself in such danger."

"I'm not afraid of you!" she bit out, struggling in earnest now. She wasn't entirely certain what the term *skelp* meant, but she'd be hanged if she'd let him keep running roughshod over her. "You can take your threats and—"

"Do not make the mistake of pushing me further," he warned grimly.

Seizing her arms, he rolled her to her back in the grass and came up on his knees to straddle her body. She glared up at him, continuing to fight in spite of the powerful temptation to surrender.

"Heed me well," Ian directed in a voice that was whipcord sharp. "Though I love you more than life itself, I will not allow you to persist in these childish, ill-conceived attempts to leave me."

"Childish?" she echoed furiously.

"Aye, childish. And foolish. By all that is holy, Callie Rose," he swore, his eyes brimming with both husbandly annoyance and a silent appeal for understanding, "do you not yet realize what has happened? We are married! You are my wife, and as such you owe me complete obedience."

"*What?*" She abruptly ceased her struggles and blinked up at him in astonished disbelief. "Why, you— I don't owe you anything! You tricked me into this marriage, remember?"

"You were a willing enough bride once we were in bed," he reminded her bluntly.

She gasped as though she had been struck. Hot color flew to her cheeks, and her eyes sparked with a deep, near murderous rage. Jerking one arm free, she lifted her hand and brought it across the clean-shaven ruggedness of his cheek in a hard, stinging slap.

"You bastard!" she said seethingly, too angry to think about the consequences of her actions.

Ian's immediate response was to capture her wrist once more, and, surprisingly, lift it to where her hand had left its mark. His manner was one of deadly calm, his eyes gleaming dully. While she stared up at him in breathless expectation, he merely gave her a faint, ironic smile and said,

"Even that will change nothing, sweet vixen. You can flyte at me all you please. You can curse and scream and rain your blows upon me, and *still* I will love you." All traces of amusement vanished when he then advised her, "But never will I let you go. Were you to leave me, I would find you and bring you back."

"No!" She was dismayed to feel her heart flutter wildly again. Shaken by her own longings, she was driven to even further recklessness. "I won't stay here!" she declared, writhing beneath him and trying to pull her wrists free. "I'll do whatever it takes to get away, and you can't—"

"Perhaps it is time you were reminded who is to be the master in this marriage."

"You can go straight to hell, Ian MacGregor!" she cried, her voice rising shrilly.

His gaze darkened anew. With a swiftness that literally took her breath away, he brought one knee upward, pulled her facedown across it, and held her captive with the forceful pressure of his arm about her waist. She gasped, crimsoning when she felt him yank her chemise upward so that her bottom was bared to his searing gaze.

"*Ian!*"

A cry half of startlement, half of indignation broke from her lips as his large hand descended upon her pale, firmly rounded flesh. There was no real desire in him to hurt her, only to teach her that he was a man of his word.

"Stop it, damn you!" she shrieked, squirming and kicking in vain.

"I am no bastard. Nor scoundrel, nor rogue, nor sonofabitch," he proclaimed, a roguish smile playing about his lips as he brought his hand down again.

"*Oooh!* Let me go!" she ground out, her flesh tingling warmly. Considerably more painful was the blow to her pride. Aghast at the humiliating position in which she found herself, she became a swirl of protest across his knee. "I'll make you pay for this! Now let me— *Ian!*"

He spanked her a third time, and yet a fourth, then tumbled her back down to the sun-warmed cushion of grass. She quickly rolled onto her stomach and attempted to scramble to her feet, but he caught her about the hips. Her fiery gaze widened when she felt his mouth upon her bottom, his lips and tongue boldly teasing at the flesh that still flamed from his playful chastisement.

"Damn you!" she whispered tremulously, her eyes

sweeping closed as passion streaked through her like wildfire once more.

"You've a beautiful backside, Lady MacGregor," murmured Ian. His deep-timbred voice was brimming with amusement—and desire.

Moments later, he was urging her to her back and settling the magnificent length of his bronzed, hard-muscled body atop her pliant curves. She forgot all about revenge as his lips captured hers. . . .

It was past noon by the time they headed back to the castle. The sun hung almost directly overhead in a sky that was still clear, yet a gathering of clouds hovered just within sight on the distant horizon.

"Tomorrow, we will pay a visit to your cousin," Ian announced unexpectedly.

"We're going to Inverness?" Callie Rose asked in surprise.

"Aye."

"But, aren't you afraid I'll—?"

"Why should I be?" He cut her off with a sardonic half smile. "After all, you're the bride of a MacGregor. No one would believe you if you stated a desire to leave."

"Someone *will* believe me!" she insisted, her gaze locked in silent combat with his as she rode beside him. "Cousin Martha certainly will. When she hears what you've done, she'll insist that we notify the local authorities at once!"

"And I will offer a full confession."

"You will?" Her eyes widened with incredulity.

"No true Highlander would fault me for putting an end to the blood feud. If, however, I am to be judged

guilty for falling in love with my captive, then so be it."
His own eyes were full of devilment.

"Surely even here there are laws against kidnapping
and forced marriages," she answered quickly, though
without her usual vehemence.

"Aye, but as my kinsmen will attest, you stood before
me at the handfasting and declared yourself to be my
wife," he reminded her.

"Only to gain my freedom!" She heaved a sigh and
shifted uncomfortably in the saddle. "And afterward,
you . . . well, you know what you did. You also know
that it was wrong!" How could something so pleasurable be wrong? that tenacious little voice deep inside
her brain questioned. Doing her best to ignore it, she
charged, "You didn't even have the decency to allow
me a moment alone!"

"No court in the world would convict me for my impatience to begin the honeymoon," he quipped wryly.

She lapsed into pensive silence for a moment, her
whole body suffused with a delicious warmth at the
memories his words evoked. Another sigh escaped her
lips as her thoughts drifted back over the startling, tu-
multuous events of the previous night.

"Who was that other woman?" she asked when an
unbidden image rose in her mind.

"What other woman?"

"The one at the ceremony last night."

"Elspeth MacGregor." His features tensed at the mention of her name, and the look in his eyes grew
guarded. It was clear that he was reluctant to say any
more about her.

"Is she a cousin of yours?" Callie Rose persisted. She

didn't know why, but she was suddenly very curious about the mysterious Elspeth. Frowning, she recalled the belligerent glare the buxom young blonde had turned upon her.

"She is a kinswoman," confirmed Ian, "though the connection is a distant one."

"Why did she leave so abruptly?"

"Perhaps because she was an uninvited guest." Another brief smile touched his lips when he assured her, "She is no discarded paramour, if that is what you suspect."

"I'm sure there are dozens of them!"

"Indeed, I possessed a veritable harem in my youth." Wry humor lurked within his eyes now. He smiled again before remarking, "But even the worst rakehell can be reformed. Indeed, Callie Rose MacGregor, you are woman enough for me."

"For how long?" she shot back, her sapphire gaze bridling at the possibility that he would take another to his heart—and to his bed. She swore inwardly. This time, she recognized her jealousy for what it was.

Why the devil should she be jealous? she wondered. And why did the mere thought of his infidelity fill her with such anguish?

"I'll give you no cause to doubt me," he promised solemnly.

She swallowed a sudden lump in her throat and averted her gaze from the piercing intensity of his. Though it made no sense, she realized that she desperately wanted to believe him.

❧ EIGHT ❧

Callie Rose was grateful for the solitude as she spent the better part of the afternoon in the castle's garden. It was a peaceful, beautiful place—a formal parterre enclosed by a wall with elaborately carved panels and bays. A delightful little structure known as the summer house had been built in a corner of the surrounding stone wall; she knew from a handwritten account of Castle MacGregor's history that it had often served as a retreat for former residents. Perhaps some of those other Lady MacGregors had used it to escape from the constant attention of their husbands, she mused, her eyes sparkling at the thought.

Her own husband (oddly enough, the term seemed natural in her mind) was shut away inside the library with his steward at the moment, going over the account books. It seemed that he had been teasing her when he had led her to believe there were no more than three servants employed to look after the castle. According to what she had overheard on her way outside, there were at least half a dozen others, all of them given a week's paid leave from their duties. He had probably wanted as few witnesses as possible to his treachery, she concluded with a flash of resentment.

She had been left to her own resources for the first time since her arrival at the castle, without benefit of a guard. The freedom both pleased and surprised her. Ian apparently believed her trustworthy. Either that, or he was confident that his warning would be heeded.

She frowned and tucked a wayward ebony curl back into place. Continuing her explorations in the garden, she discovered an ancient bathhouse with a stone tub, a dressing area off to the side, and even a sitting room where ladies had once traded gossip and advice—and had complained about affairs of the heart. A faint smile of irony touched her lips when it occurred to her that certain things had not changed very much since that long-ago time. She could well imagine herself as one of the bathers, besieged by "man trouble" and wracked with confusion.

Wandering among the well-tended shrubberies and tress and a colorful, aromatic burst of blossoms, she drew in a ragged breath. Her thoughts and emotions, ever chaotic since fate had thrown Ian MacGregor across her path, were in stark contrast to the tranquillity of her surroundings. She tossed a restive glance heavenward.

The sun had disappeared behind thick gray clouds, and the air was charged with the fresh scent of rain. It had been much the same the afternoon Ian had carried her off.

Frowning again, she sank down upon one of the stone benches tucked away in a shaded alcove. Her stormy gaze drifted toward the high stone wall. She could try scaling it, of course ... but even if she did manage to escape from the immediate grounds, Ian would find her. He had made it painfully clear that he would never let her go.

I love you. And you love me.

"No!" she whispered, her whole body fairly quaking with the force of her denial. How could she possibly fall in love with a man who had treated her so abominably? Even if they had met under different, far more agreeable circumstances, the fact still remained that he was arrogant and overbearing and bullheaded. Yet he was also witty and charming—and so heart-shakingly tender when it counted. . . .

Alarmed at the turn her thoughts had taken, she leapt up from the bench and scurried back across the garden to the doorway. She would go mad if she didn't stop thinking about him so blasted much. Heaven help her, he controlled her every waking thought—and invaded her dreams. She had to get away. She *had* to!

After a night every bit as passionate as the one before it, and a pleasant enough morning divided between the library and the stables, Callie Rose accompanied Ian to Inverness. She was surprised to discover that the city was only a little more than an hour's ride away, for it had seemed that they had traveled a great distance that storm-tossed afternoon when he had spirited her away from the ancestral estate of the Buchanans.

The countryside was fresh and vibrant in the wake of the brief, torrential rains that had come in the night. Callie Rose felt her pulse leap with excitement when she glimpsed Cromwell's clock tower, the impressive church spires, and the familiar red sandstone castle on the nearing horizon.

"Your cousin has been in very capable hands since you saw her last," said Ian, his mouth curving into a soft smile as he rode beside her.

"How do you know that?"

"Her physician is a kinsman of mine."

"Are you related to *everyone* here?" she queried, with a touch of sarcasm, her eyes meeting his.

"The MacGregors have been in the Highlands for many centuries."

"I suppose they killed off all their enemies long ago," she remarked in the same caustic tone.

"Or married them," he parried dryly.

She colored and looked away. Forcing her thoughts back to the matter at hand, she silently rehearsed what she was going to say to her cousin. She was confident that Martha would help her think of a way out of her present difficulties. And if all else failed, she still had the option of going to the authorities. Even if her marriage *was* valid, she couldn't believe they would approve of a woman—an American, no less—being held against her will.

Minutes later, she and Ian were dismounting in front of the hotel. He took her arm and led her inside, then marched her straightaway down the corridor to the room where Martha Terhune had spent the past three days recuperating from her cold. Callie Rose pulled free, bursting into the room without waiting to knock.

"Cousin Martha, I—" She broke off and stopped dead in her tracks. Her eyes widened in startlement at the scene she had just interrupted.

"Callie Rose!" Martha gasped, every bit as taken back as the younger woman.

She was seated in a chair beside the window with a blanket tucked about her, her hair arranged in a becoming chignon, and her eyes brightly aglow. She looked quite pretty, years younger and not at all on her deathbed. At present, there was a tall, distinguished-looking gentleman in a black serge suit leaning over her. The moment she saw Callie Rose, she blushed rosily and hastened to disengage her hand from the man's warm grasp.

"Oh, my dear, I—I had not expected you so soon!" she stammered.

"You knew I was coming?" Callie Rose demanded in surprise.

"Why, of course!" The petite blonde directed a smile toward Ian, who stood framed in the doorway. "Lord MacGregor was kind enough to send a message informing me of your intended visit."

"You've *met* him?"

"Two days ago," confirmed Martha. She frowned at the strange expression on her charge's face. "Is something wrong? Are you feeling unwell? Perhaps Dr. MacGregor could—?"

"Dr. MacGregor?" echoed Callie Rose. Her gaze shifted to the older, dark-haired man standing beside her cousin. There was, indeed, a noticeable resemblance between him and Ian.

"I am honored to make your acquaintance, Miss Buchanan," the good doctor proclaimed, stepping forward now to offer her a smile and a polite nod. "Mrs. Turhune has spoken of you with the highest regard."

"Has she?" Callie Rose murmured, her head spinning. She became aware of Ian moving into place close behind her. His arm slipped about her waist, and he dropped a light kiss upon her forehead.

"I've some business to attend to, my love," he told her. "I'll return to fetch you within the hour." To an astonished Martha he said, "I'm happy to see that your health has improved, Mrs. Terhune."

"I must be leaving as well," announced the other MacGregor. He turned and gave Martha one last long, intense look. Though his words were of a purely professional nature, his manner was more like that of a devoted suitor. "You should be fully recovered by week's end. Until then, I'd advise you to rest well and continue taking the medication I have prescribed."

"Yes, Doctor," she replied, her color deepening as her eyes fell shyly beneath his steady, blue-green gaze.

Callie Rose waited until both men had left the room, then flew across the room to fall upon her knees before her cousin.

"Oh, Martha, I scarcely know where to begin! Ian MacGregor *abducted* me! He took me to his castle and locked me in the tower and—"

"For heaven's sake, my dear, what are you talking about?" the widow asked, with a breathless laugh.

"I'm talking about what's been happening to me ever since I left Inverness three days ago!"

"You've been visiting Lord MacGregor and his family," Martha stated complacently. A slight frown creased her brow when she recalled the obvious affection Ian had exhibited toward her cousin a few moments ago. "But, it appears that the man has formed an attachment to you—"

"An attachment?" She sprang to her feet and began

pacing distractedly to-and-fro. "Damn it, Cousin Martha, he kidnapped me and then tricked me into marriage!"

"Marriage?" gasped Martha.

"Yes, marriage! Ian MacGregor is nothing but a conniving, silver-tongued scoundrel! He took me prisoner to settle a blood feud between our clans—it all began when my grandfather jilted his grandmother—and he told me that he'd let me go free if I agreed to a betrothal. It wasn't a betrothal exactly," she paused to clarify. "It was a handfasting, which was supposed to be a mere formality. Only, he didn't keep his part of the bargain, and the next thing I knew, I . . . hell's bells, he *forced* me to become his wife!" she concluded in a furious rush.

"But he is a titled gentleman!" protested Martha, visibly thunderstruck by the news she had just received.

"He is no gentleman!" Callie Rose said, seething. Her eyes were brilliantly ablaze as she folded her arms beneath her breasts and whirled to face the older woman once more. "J. D. will have his hide when he finds out what he's done to me!"

"Do you mean he . . . ? Oh, my dearest cousin, did he . . . ?" Martha stammered, her face paling as the awful possibility crossed her mind.

"Yes, by thunder, he did!" Her own face crimsoned hotly, and she felt a sudden shiver course down her spine.

"Then he really is your husband?" the widow murmured in stunned amazement.

"Only under Scottish law," Callie Rose was quick to point out. She heaved an audible sigh and moved to the window, raising a hand to the lace curtains. Her eyes, full of fire, drifted outward to the swiftly flowing river. "You've got to help me, Cousin Martha! I don't know what to do. I don't know what to think anymore, or what to feel—" She broke off and caught her lower lip between her teeth.

Martha's astonishment only increased at that point. She had never seen her young cousin so distraught. She had certainly never heard her admit to such overwhelming uncertainty.

"Why don't you sit down and tell me the whole story, from the very beginning," she urged gently.

Callie Rose did just that, starting with the moment Ian had tossed her over his shoulder and ending with their arrival at the hotel only minutes ago. Martha's heart stirred with compassion for what her cousin had suffered, while her eyes filled with a growing comprehension.

"And so your husband is determined that you remain with him?" she asked, studying the younger woman's face closely.

"Yes," Callie Rose answered. Her eyes fell before she confided, "He said he'll never let me go."

"What about you?"

"Me?" She turned a look of bewilderment upon Martha, who smiled and settled an affectionate, maternal hand up her arm.

"Do you want the marriage to continue?"

"Why, I . . . of course not! How could I?" She jumped to her feet again and resumed her pacing. "How can you even ask me that after everything I've told you?"

"Even the best of unions can have less than auspicious beginnings," Martha replied. "After all, it wasn't so very long ago that arranged marriages were an everyday occurrence. They still are in certain parts of the world. Perhaps there's something to be said for getting to know each other *after* the ceremony."

"I think the medicine you're taking has clouded your brain!" Callie Rose opined, with a sigh of exasperation. She eyed her cousin suspiciously at a sudden thought. "Or has a certain doctor by the name of MacGregor done it?"

"Ewan and I have formed a friendship, nothing more," Martha insisted primly.

"Oh, so the two of you are on a first-name basis already."

"Yes, but— Might I remind you, my dear, that we aren't talking about me at the moment."

"Whatever you do, don't make the mistake of trusting him! He's a MacGregor, and Lord knows what rogues *they* are!" she pronounced irefully.

"You have no right to judge him," Martha admonished, her own voice holding an uncharacteristic edge. She raised her chin defensively. "He is a fine man, an honorable man, and he has been very kind. And anyway, we'll be returning home in a few days' time," she added, appearing anything but happy at the prospect.

"Home," Callie Rose repeated, closing her eyes and turning the word over in her mind. It was strange, but the Diamond L was only a foggy memory, the image of a turreted, fairy-tale castle forced it aside. She gasped, her eyes flying wide again. "We've got to leave today! Right now!"

"I'm afraid that isn't possible," protested Martha. "I am not yet fully recovered, and you cannot leave until you have resolved things with Lord MacGregor."

"Things will never be resolved between us!"

"I'm sure if your father were here, he would encourage you not to run away like a coward," the widow declared, then smiled. "In truth, I think J. D. would be pleased with your choice of a husband."

"He isn't my choice! And *I* say that J. D. Buchanan will have his liver for breakfast!"

"If you're so anxious to leave, why haven't you done so before now?" Martha inquired calmly.

"I—I've tried! But Ian always stops me." She hastily averted her gaze and swallowed hard, disconcerted by the way her cheeks flamed anew. "I'll admit that the man ... well, that I find him attractive." *A vast understatement,* her conscience pointed out. "My mind tells me one thing, and yet my body does another!" she lamented. Though embarrassed to admit to such an unabashedly human weakness, she was desperate for help.

"I think, my dear, that you should examine your feelings and see if, just perhaps, you might have made the right match after all."

"What the devil is that supposed to mean?"

"Only that you should consider making the best of the situation," exhorted Martha. "After all, Lord MacGregor is handsome, wealthy, and an earl."

"Maybe you're impressed by his lofty position in life, but I'm not! And I remember all too clearly the way you threw me at the Duke of Albemarle's head back in London!"

"Oh, but I happen to think your husband a far better catch than the Duke of Albemarle."

"What difference does that make?" She threw up her hands in an eloquent gesture of annoyance. "I can't believe what I'm hearing! Are you actually suggesting that I 'stop crying over spilt milk' and spend the rest of my life married to a man who double-crossed me into his bed?"

"I wouldn't have put it quite so bluntly, but, yes"—Martha held forth in her best straitlaced manner—"that *is* the gist of it, I suppose. However your marriage came about, you are Lord MacGregor's wife now. You are answerable to him. Even if a handfast marriage isn't recognized as legal elsewhere—nor, in my opinion, should it ever be—the fact remains that he is your husband in every sense of the word. And as such, he has the right to command your obedience."

"You're my own flesh and blood, for heaven's sake!" Callie Rose choked out, stung by what she perceived to be her cousin's betrayal. "I would have expected you, of all people, to be sympathetic to my plight!"

"I am very sympathetic," the widow insisted earnestly. "It pains me to know that you are troubled. Yet, I—I'm sorry, my dear, but I can foresee no easy remedy to this tangle," she finished, with a sigh.

"There is only one remedy, and I'm not going to wait any longer to pursue it," vowed Callie Rose. Her eyes lit with fiery determination as she fixed the other woman with a narrow, challenging look. "I'm leaving today. Right this very minute. Are you coming with me or not?"

"Please be reasonable—"

"You're well enough to travel. Don't deny it. Confound it, Cousin Martha, my whole future is at stake, and all you seem to care about is propriety!"

"That isn't fair! I desperately want your happiness, but I also want you to do what's right!"

"Are you coming or not?" she demanded once more. Her heart sank when Martha rose slowly to her feet and shook her head.

"No. No, Callie Rose, I won't be a party to the ruination of your life. And it *will* be ruined if you don't stay here and come to some sort of an agreement with your husband. Oh, my dearest cousin, don't you see? You can't solve anything by running away!"

"Then so be it!"

She spun about and fled from the room. Though she heard Martha calling after her, she ignored the older woman's entreaties and raced back down the corridor. She was oblivious to the curious stares she received as she made her way out of the hotel. Her one thought was to put an end to her inner torment; she forgot all about her baggage and the various difficulties that could beset a young lady traveling alone.

Startled to realize that hot tears were coursing down her cheeks, she dashed angrily at them and unlooped her horse's reins from the post at the foot of the steps. The memory of the previous day's disastrous attempt at escape via horseback suddenly came to mind. With a muttered curse, she flung the reins aside and whirled to direct her steps toward the nearby railway station.

Her gaze shifted anxiously about as she went, searching for any sign of Ian, but she saw nothing of him. His lack of vigilance surprised her. Did he believe he won her over with his threats—or perhaps with his kisses?

God willing, there's a man out there who'll be able to tame you, her father had once said. Ian MacGregor obviously believed himself to be that man. . . .

The ache in her heart grew more intense. She quickened her steps as she spied the familiar outline of the station just ahead. Only dimly aware of the gasps of astonishment she inspired in her mad dash through the city's busy streets, she reached her destination at last and hurried inside to the ticket counter.

"I'd like to go to Edinburgh, please!" she told the agent in a breathless rush. He was a young man, solemn-faced and bespectacled on the other side of the barred window. Taking in the sight of her obvious distress, he shook his head regretfully.

"I'm sorry, miss," he replied, "but the next train to Edinburgh won't leave till tomorrow. Eight o'clock in the morning, to be precise."

"Tomorrow?" she echoed in dismay, her spirits plummeting at the news. She frowned and cast a quick, desperate glance about the station. "But, I can't wait that long!"

"If you're in need of a place to stay . . . ?" he offered helpfully.

"No! No, I—I have to leave Inverness right away!"

"Begging your pardon for asking, miss, but are you in some kind of trouble?" he probed, his voice laced with worriment on her behalf.

"As a matter of fact, I am!" she confirmed. She leaned closer, her bright sapphire gaze holding a silent plea for help. "Someone I wish very much to avoid is looking for me! Time is of the utmost importance! Aren't there any trains leaving today?"

"Aye." He nodded toward the handwritten schedule posted above the small, crowded waiting area. "You could take the three o'clock to Aberdeen. Or else the three-thirty to Fort William."

"I'll go to Aberdeen!" She slipped a hand into the pocket of her riding skirt in order to pay for the ticket, only to realize, belatedly, that she had left all of her money behind in her valise. "Damnation!" she whispered. How could she have been so thoroughly dim-witted?

"Did you say something, miss?" the young agent queried politely.

"I seem to have forgotten to bring my pocketbook," she murmured, her mind racing anew as her eyes swept closed for a moment. What the devil was she going to do now? Ian would be returning to the hotel soon. . . .

"Have you a kinsman here in town? If so, it might be possible for you to apply to him for the funds."

"No, I don't know anyone!" she was quick to deny. She managed a rather wan smile and appealed. "Couldn't you advance me the ticket and then send the bill to my hotel in Edinburgh?"

"Well, I—"

"That won't be necessary."

She gasped loudly at the sound of that resonant, deep-timbred voice. While the color drained from her face, she pivoted about to face Ian. He was smiling down at her, his green eyes brimming with unholy amusement.

"Get away from me!" she cried, extending a hand as if

to ward off the inevitable. She backed away and shook her head in angry, helpless denial while he advanced.

"Do you know this woman, Lord MacGregor?" the ticket agent asked in surprise.

"Aye, Robert, I do," replied Ian. "The woman is my bride." He reached for her, his hand closing about her wrist. "Come now, sweetheart ... it's time we were away."

"No! I won't go with you, Ian MacGregor, I won't!" Unable to pull her wrist free, she tried in growing desperation to summon assistance. "Help! Somebody, please help!"

Her screams brought everyone in the station to their feet. While some of the onlookers appeared ready to come to her aid, most of them evidently believed the commotion to be nothing more than a lover's quarrel. A uniformed policeman hurried forth to investigate, only to smile and touch the brim of his hat deferentially when his eyes filled with recognition.

"I didn't realize it was you, Lord MacGregor. Any problem?"

"I've everything under control, thank you, Murdoch," Ian replied smoothly.

"This man is accosting me!" explained Callie Rose. "Please, make him let me go!"

"Are you not the granddaughter of Angus Buchanan?" the policeman queried, with a slight frown. He'd been able to tell from her manner of speaking that she was an American, and her appearance certainly fit the description he'd been given.

"Yes, but—"

"So you're the lass we've heard so much about," he

murmured, his features relaxing into a smile. He was obviously unmoved by her situation.

"And have you also heard that Ian MacGregor kidnapped me?" she demanded indignantly, still trying to pull free. "Confound it, you've got to do something! I don't care if the whole town thinks he hung the blasted moon, he has no right to hold me against my will!"

"It does appear that Miss Buchanan is reluctant to accompany you," noted Murdoch, his gaze shifting uncomfortably back to Ian.

"It's 'Lady MacGregor' now," Ian informed him, with another brief smile. "We were wed two days ago."

"Oh, aye?" The policeman's brow cleared once more. "Well then, you have my felicitations, the both of you." He nodded, then turned and strolled away.

"Wait!" Callie Rose called after him, her eyes widening in horrified disbelief. "Wait, you can't—"

She broke off with a sharp intake of breath as Ian finally scooped her up in his arms. While she struggled in vain, he carried her out of the station.

"We'll have all of Inverness talking about the 'battling MacGregors,' " he predicted wryly. His eyes twinkled down into hers. "A fine example to set for our children, Rosaleen."

"We aren't going to *have* any children!"

"Are we not?" The merest hint of a smile played about his lips.

"No! Now put me down!"

She squirmed in his grasp, but he bore her relentlessly back toward the hotel. They attracted a great deal of attention—it wasn't every day that a powerful, well-respected clan chief could be seen carrying a beautiful young woman through the streets of the capital of the Highlands.

"How did you find me?" demanded Callie Rose, cursing the way her whole body came alive in his arms. Strangely enough, she felt as though a suffocating weight had been lifted from her shoulders.

"I followed you."

"You never left the hotel at all!" she accused.

"I waited in the lobby," he confessed. "You needed time alone with your cousin."

"If you saw me leave, then why did you let me get all the way to the station before you . . . ?"

"I wanted to see if you would go through with it." He frowned, his eyes glittering dully when he told her, "I thought you were beginning to understand, Callie Rose."

"Understand *what*?" she shot back. "That my whole world has been turned upside-down?" Her voice was edged with a pained bitterness, and she fought back a fresh wave of tears as she found herself confiding in him. "I told Martha what you'd done, and yet she refused to go with me. She insisted that I stay here and— and try to make the best of things. I never would have expected her to turn against me like that."

She released a long, uneven sigh. It seemed that all of the fight had gone out of her now. Resting her head against Ian's shoulder, she allowed her arms to entwine themselves about his neck.

"I'm sorry, lass," he said gently, his heart stirring at her surrender. "But she hasn't turned against you. I think she knows the truth— Aye, and she wants you to be happy."

"She said that I—I'd be ruining my life if I ran away."

"Never that," he replied, disagreeing. He gave her a tender smile when she raised her head to peer up at him in bemusement. "I would not let it come to that. No matter where you went, no matter how long it took, I would find you."

They had reached the hotel again by this time. Callie Rose did not protest when Ian lifted her to the mare's back. She took hold of the reins and watched while he swung up into his own saddle. Her troubled gaze drifted back toward the building where she left a very worried Martha. She considered going inside to speak to her again, but decided against it. For now, there was nothing else to say.

"Ewan has assured me that Mrs. Terhune will be fine," Ian declared. "She is to come visit us as soon as she's feeling up to it."

"She is?" Callie Rose replied in surprise. The thought of her cousin's presence at Castle MacGregor sent a dull flush rising to her face. It was bad enough that Martha knew about her marriage to Ian, but it would be a hundred times more embarrassing for her to witness even a small example of their intimacy firsthand. . . .

"Let's go home, my love," said Ian.

Home. Musing that the word sounded so very appealing on his lips, she heaved another sigh and went obediently along with him.

❧ NINE ❧

They settled into an uneasy truce upon their return from Inverness.

Feeling as though she had been caught in a whirlwind, Callie Rose decided to soak in a hot bath before supper. Ian had taken himself off to the stables, leaving her with a quick kiss and the promise to send Peter to the hotel for the rest of her things tomorrow. She was vastly relieved that he had not insisted on remaining. If ever there was a moment she needed to be alone with her thoughts, it was now.

Recalling everything her cousin had said that afternoon, she sank lower in the tub and closed her eyes. It was true that there was no easy solution to her predicament. Her every attempt at escape had been thwarted, no one appeared willing to believe Ian at fault, the one person she had counted on to take her side in the matter had proven far less than helpful, and, most perplexing of all, she felt no real disappointment at having been intercepted at the train station.

Maybe, just maybe, Cousin Martha had given her some worthwhile advice after all.

He is your husband in every sense of the word. There was no denying the truth of those words. Nor was it possible to escape the fact that, handfast law or no handfast law, Ian considered their marriage everlasting. If she had learned anything at all about him these past few days, it was that he was a man accustomed to getting whatever he had set his mind on.

And he had set his mind on her.

Releasing a sigh, she opened her eyes again, sat up, and reached for the lavender-scented cake of soap. She could scrub her skin raw, and it still wouldn't erase the memory of Ian MacGregor's touch. No, by thunder, he had branded her for life. She knew with a certainty that no other man could ever make her feel what she had felt in his arms. No other man could set her body on fire, or cause her heart to flutter wildly, or toss her very soul heavenward. *No other man.*

Both startled and alarmed by the intense, bewildering emotions coursing through her, she quickly rinsed and drew her glistening curves up from the tub. Her hand had just settled upon the towel when the door behind her suddenly opened. She gasped, her eyes flying wide as she felt a cool rush of air upon her naked skin.

"My timing is ever impeccable," she heard Ian say with a drawl.

Uttering a small, breathless cry of dismay, she sat back down so abruptly that water splashed over the sides of the huge, claw-footed tub. She folded her arms across her breasts in a belated attempt at modesty while turning her head to cast him an indignant glare.

"How dare you! Get out of here!"

"You've nothing I haven't seen before, sweet vixen," he pointed out, his low, resonant voice holding not a single trace of remorse.

His gaze darkened as it traveled lovingly over the graceful curve of her back. She had pinned her hair atop her head, though several rebellious tendrils had escaped to curl becomingly about her face and neck. While she fixed him with another resentful look, he closed the door and lifted his hands to the buttons of his shirt.

"Wha-what do you think you're doing?" she stammered, her eyes growing round as saucers.

"The tub is well able to hold the two of us."

"It most certainly is not!" She blushed fierily and tried to ignore the sudden leaping of her pulse as she looked away. "You're welcome to the bath! If you'll just wait long enough for me to get out—"

"Ah, but that would defeat half my purpose."

"Half?" she echoed in a small voice. She started to ask him to explain but decided she'd be better off not knowing. "I thought I was to have some privacy!" She ventured another glance back at him, only to see that he was clad in nothing but his kilt now. Swallowing hard, she pressed herself as close to the side of the tub as she possibly could. "For the last time, Ian MacGregor, will you please have the decency to go away and leave me alone?"

His response was to toss his kilt aside and climb into the bathtub. Callie Rose shrieked in protest as even more water cascaded onto the floor. Still valiantly attempting to cover the most strategic parts of her nakedness, she started to rise, but Ian's hands caught her about the waist and pulled her back against him while he sat down. She shivered when her bottom came into intimate contact with his lean, hard-muscled thighs— and the undeniably masculine flesh between them.

"Ian!" She breathed harshly, alternately shocked and delighted by his mischief.

"You've let the water go cold," he scolded in mock reproof. "Aye, but I know of a way to warm us both." His strong arms encircled her, his hands smoothing upward to her breasts.

"Ian, stop it!" It was a pitiful excuse for an objection, and she knew it. She gasped again when his fingers claimed the full, rose-tipped globes she sought to conceal. Her arms slipped back into the water, her eyes closing as he bestowed slow and gentle caresses.

"Your breasts, Lady MacGregor, are entirely too delectable," he pronounced, his tone brimming with more desire than amusement. "I could well devour them."

A soft moan rose in her throat while passion set her whole body aflame. She could not help but be aware of her husband's arousal; his manhood throbbed against the roundness of her buttocks.

"Ian, please!" she whispered, not at all certain if she was offering up a demurral or a plea for more of the same. He pressed an ardent kiss to the silken column of her neck.

"I'll never let you go, Callie Rose," he vowed once more, his voice low and splendidly vibrant. "Never!"

He turned her about then, his mouth crashing down upon the parted softness of hers as he swept her against him. She trembled with pleasure and gave herself up to the sweet ecstasy again. *No other man . . .*

They were late for supper that night.

Afterward, when the castle was dark and the moon had risen to bathe the countryside in a soft, silvery light, they lay together in the carved four-poster. The candles had burned low, and the fire was nothing more than a glowing pile of embers. Downstairs, the willfully inaccurate clock chimed eleven times.

Listening to the sounds of the night, Callie Rose was surprised at how light her heart felt. She sighed and snuggled closer to Ian's hard warmth. He smiled, his green eyes gleaming tenderly as he tightened his arms about her.

"Someday, my love, we'll look back on these several days past and laugh at our *spracails*."

"Will we?" she said challengingly, though without her usual flash of spirit.

"Aye. We'll have grand stories to tell our children."

A slight frown creased her brow. It was the second time that day he had mentioned children. She didn't want to think about that possibility. Not now, not when each day was still full of such turmoil and uncertainty. For heaven's sake, she reflected with another sigh, she didn't even know if she would still be in Scotland a week from now, much less a year. Or two years or ten years or twenty . . .

"You've never told me if you have any brothers or sisters," she noted in an attempt to steer the subject onto safer ground.

"I've a younger brother—Gavin. He has been traveling for more than a year."

"Traveling?"

"Having no interest in the family business, he decided to find his own way in the world," Ian explained. There was a discernible edge to his voice, and his eyes glinted dully as he frowned in remembrance. "I fear my brother and I have little in common."

"I have four brothers, all of them older," she told him, her fingers tracing a light, repetitive pattern across the bronzed expanse of his chest. "They're a bit hot-tempered, and perhaps a little too bullheaded at times, but they're good men. Loyal to a fault, and fiercely protective of me. If not for them, I'd probably still be at that awful school back East. They were the ones who convinced J. D. to let me come home."

"You're very fond of them," he observed, his handsome features relaxing. " 'Tis easy to see that. And do you hold your father in affection as well?"

"Yes, of course. J. D. Buchanan is a force to be reckoned with, but his heart is usually in the right place." The one exception being his insistence upon packing her off to Europe for the summer, she added silently. No question about it, his heart had been in the wrong place then ... and look what had happened as a result. Now that she thought about it, her father was to blame (at least in a roundabout way) for her present difficulties. She couldn't wait to let him know it, either.

"You've said he will be displeased by our marriage," Ian recalled, with a faint smile.

"It isn't our 'marriage' that will set him off!" She raised up on one elbow and peered narrowly down into his face. Her eyes kindled with sudden fire while her thick raven tresses swirled about her. "Damn it, Ian MacGregor, you had no right to run roughshod over me! Even if you did think you'd fallen in love with me!"

"Do you still doubt it?" he demanded, startling her when his hands suddenly closed like bands of iron about her upper arms. His gaze burned into hers. "By all that is holy, woman, what will it take to convince you?"

"If you really loved me, you'd let me go!"

"That I cannot do."

"You mean you *won't*!" She struggled in his grasp, then gave a soft, breathless cry as he abruptly rolled so that she was beneath him.

"I neither can nor will!" he ground out. Seizing her wrists, he imprisoned them above her head while she glared up at him in angry defiance. He battled the urge to kiss her, knowing full well that if he did so they'd get no more talking done that night. "When will you admit that we belong together? I will have all of you, Callie Rose MacGregor—your body, your heart, even your soul. You are mine!"

"People don't own each other!" she stormed, writhing furiously beneath him.

"Do they not?" He entangled a hand within her hair and forced her to look at him. "We are bound to each other, now and forever," he decreed softly, his emerald gaze locking with the fiery sapphire depths of hers. "You cannot change it, lass. You can only accept the truth—and thereby free the love that is every bit as strong as my own."

"I'll never love any man!" Even to her own ears, the denial sounded like a hollow one.

"You'll love *this* man," he insisted, his tone dangerously low and level now. "Aye, and you'll share his bed and bear his children and grow old at his side."

She opened her mouth to offer a scathing, ultimately defiant retort, but instead found herself speechless. Her heart leapt within her breast at his words, her body filling with a sweet warmth that made her quiver. Dear God, what was happening to her?

Ian released her wrists and lifted his body from hers. He rolled to his back, frowning up toward the canopy, and left her battling a sudden, overwhelming tendency to burst into tears.

Her eyes sought him out in the candlelit darkness of the room. A long, highly charged silence rose between them. And then the storm of weeping could be held back no more. While she choked back sobs, Ian swore underneath his breath and gathered her close.

She cried as she had never cried before, her tears glistening on his naked chest. He cradled her lovingly against him. His heart ached for the torment she was suffering; he cursed himself as an impatient fool. She'd had so much to contend with these past few days. . . . By damn, he had no right to expect her to surrender so easily. Indeed, one of the things he found most appealing about her was her fierce, indomitable pride. Exasperating though it might be at times, her stubbornness attested all the more to the fact that she was his perfect match in every way.

"Let the tears come, Callie Rose," he murmured soothingly, a tender smile tugging at his lips. "You've more than earned a right to them."

"I—I *hate* emotional females!" she said, her sobs finally diminishing.

"I'd say the two terms are inseparable." He gave a quiet chuckle and gently smoothed the tangled mass of curls from her face. "Were you not female, you would lack the emotions that set you apart. Of course, there are other things about you that are wholly, unmistakably feminine. I can think of at least three." His deep voice brimmed with roguish humor.

"Stop laughing at me, you bastard!" she ordered, though it was uttered with a surprising lack of rancor. She took a deep, shuddering breath before drying her eyes with the sheet he had tugged over her. "I don't know what the devil got into me, crying like that. I never used to be so blasted weepy."

"You've no cause to be ashamed," he insisted. A surge of protectiveness had welled up within him at the first sign of her tears, and he scowled darkly when it occurred to him that someone—her father, if he had to venture a guess—had made her feel uncomfortable with her womanhood. Her next words only served to confirm his suspicions.

"Growing up, we were never allowed to cry. Tears were a sign of weakness." She released a sigh, her eyes clouding again. "Sometimes, I think J. D. would have been much happier if he'd been blessed with five sons."

"Come now, my love, you know that to be untrue."

"I suppose I do," she admitted, with a nod. "But still, I wonder if it might not have been better for everyone concerned if I were a man. It certainly would have been easier for *me*."

"Easier, perhaps." He pulled her up so that he could search her face, his gaze lighting with such incredible warmth that she caught her breath on a gasp. "Yet can you honestly say that you would change things now?" he asked.

"No," she whispered, surprised at how readily she could deny it. "Whenever I— Confound it, Ian MacGregor, whenever I'm in your arms, I forget about everything else!"

"As well you should." His mouth curved into a slow, thoroughly captivating smile.

Though melting inside, she frowned and tried to make sense of the enchantment, still not realizing that some things in this world defy reason.

"Yes, but that could happen even if all there was between us was . . ."

"Physical attraction?" he supplied, then shook his head slightly while his green eyes glowed. "It isn't only your sweet body that responds to me."

"Maybe not," she allowed in a tremulous little voice, "but I don't know what it is I'm supposed to feel. You *are* the only man I've ever . . . been with."

"I did not doubt it." He suppressed his smile this time and glided a compelling hand down to her naked hip. "Another old saying we have: 'There belongs more to a bed than four bare legs.' Aye, we've more between us than this alone."

"Damnation," she muttered, with another sigh. "You are without a doubt the most smooth-talking man I've ever known. I'm not at all sure my father and brothers would know what to make of you." *Especially if they saw you in your kilt,* she added silently, her eyes sparkling with wry amusement at the thought.

"Well then, we must put them to the test."

"Put them to the test?" She stared up at him in puzzlement. "What do you mean?"

"I mean, my lady wife, that come September, we'll be paying a visit to your family. I am anxious to meet them. And to see the ranch you hold so dear."

"But, you can't possibly come to Texas!"

"Can I not?"

"No! I . . . well, I intend to leave long before then!" She quickly sat up, pulling the sheet over her breasts.

"I'm afraid September is the earliest we can hope to make the journey," he insisted calmly.

"We?" She paled at the thought.

"Peter can look after things well enough while we're gone. And after a visit of a month, perhaps two—I've no wish to share you any longer than that—we'll return to Edinburgh for the winter. Winters here in the Highlands can be quite harsh. I doubt if you've experienced the like in Texas. We could always go to London, of course, though I must confess to a marked preference for *'Auld Reekie,'* " he concluded, his voice underscored with affection for the city that had been Scotland's capital for more than five hundred years.

Callie Rose listened to the sound of his voice, listened to his plans for their future together, and found herself smiling. But the smile was replaced by yet another frown when it struck her that he had no right to assume she would still be here in the winter. Hadn't she made it perfectly clear that she was still intent upon leaving—alone? And yet, what was so terrible about the prospect of spending the cold winter months in the warm, loving circle of his arms?

Heaven help her, she couldn't go on this way, torn between the urge to flee and the increasingly powerful temptation to stay. Her mind told her one thing, while her heart told her another. And it was only getting worse.

"It would not surprise me if your cousin decided to

remain until September as well," remarked Ian, his mouth twitching. "Unless my instincts prove wrong, Ewan might finally have found a woman willing to put up with his crusty, skinflint ways."

"You MacGregors are cocksure about everything, aren't you?" she charged, her sapphire gaze bridling. She gasped when he masterfully drew her back down to him.

"Cocksure—or perhaps merely aware of our own limitations," he murmured. Before she could do anything more than fix him with a wifely glare, he laughed softly once more and kissed her. The last coherent thought in her mind was that he didn't *have* any limitations. . . .

The truce continued for the next three days.

Never one for a life of leisure, Callie Rose decided that she'd had quite enough of idleness. She knew she had to do something or else go mad with boredom.

Ian was closeted in the library with his steward a good deal. He was reluctant to spend any time apart from his bride, but it was the busiest time of the year for the shipping industry, and equally critical for the tenant farmers who worked the MacGregor lands. Callie Rose was sorely tempted to inform her husband that she, a "lowly female," possessed a remarkable head for business and had kept the account books for the Diamond L since the age of fourteen. She said nothing, however, owing to the simple fact that she was still uncertain about her role here. Did she consider herself to be a prisoner—or was she truly Lady MacGregor, mistress of the castle?

Molly and Jenny were only too happy to solicit her preferences when it came to the running of the household. In fact, they gave every indication of wanting to defer to her in all matters. Though not particularly domestic, she was more than capable of offering an opinion, and even discovered (much to her own surprise) that she actually liked conferring with them about meals and cleaning and the numerous other everyday details to be seen to. She no longer viewed the two women as "friendly" adversaries, either. They were doing their best to make her feel welcome; it was obvious they were delighted with Ian's marriage, even if the long-awaited miracle had come about through highly unusual means.

Her life evolved into a precarious calm. While the mornings were spent indoors, the afternoons were reserved for solitary walks in the garden, visits to the stables, and long rides with Ian. He showed her the countryside as she had never seen it before, entertaining her with tales of "broonies" and "silkies" and other supernatural beings who, depending upon the turn of their spirit, either lured people to their deaths or taught them valuable lessons about charity. The culture and folklore of the Highlands came alive for her, and she found herself increasingly enchanted by the special, mystical region where Angus Buchanan had once made the fateful mistake of breaking a young girl's heart.

Of course, her dilemma only worsened as a result. The more she got to know her husband, the more susceptible she became to his charm. He was a truly fascinating rogue, she reflected with a soft smile of irony as she sat alone in the drawing room on the second evening following their journey to Iverness. He could be strong and gentle at the same time, sweetly compassionate one moment and infuriatingly implacable the next, and always, *always* irresistible.

Her thoughts had often returned to her conversation with Cousin Martha. They did so now. And almost before she realized it, she began to contemplate what it would be like if she did stay, if she accepted Ian's love as real and finally toppled the barriers she had erected about her own heart. Could she love him in return? Did she already?

"Love Ian?" she whispered, her breath catching in her throat at the possibility.

"Are you offering up a prayer on my behalf—or consigning me to the devil again?" Ian said behind her.

She jumped in startlement, guilty color staining her cheeks as she got up from the sofa and whirled to face him. He had bathed and dressed for supper, and now stood framed in the doorway with a mocking smile playing about his lips. Her eyes filled with a soft, beguiling glow when they met his.

"Neither!" she retorted saucily, lifting her chin.

"Yet I am certain you spoke my name." His gaze darkened as it raked lovingly—possessively—over her. She was wearing a gown of robin's-egg-blue gauze, its tiny puffed sleeves and low, rounded neckline accentuating her ripe bosom and the creamy perfection of her shoulders. Her hair, arranged in the fashionable waterfall chignon, shone like black silk in the lamplight.

"Are you really so conceited that you think I can speak no *other* man's name?" she taunted on sudden impulse.

He was across the room in three long strides, snaking an arm about her waist and hauling her roughly against him. She gave a breathless, halfhearted protest and raised her hands to his chest.

"Ian MacGregor, what—?"

"Tease me at your own risk, my lady," he warned, with a mock scowl of displeasure. "I could easily take it in mind to toss up your skirts here and now and remind you that I am your true lord and master."

"You wouldn't dare!" she gasped, her luminous gaze widening as it shot apprehensively toward the doorway.

"Would I not?"

With purposeful unhaste, he released her, sauntered back across the room, pulled the double, oak-paneled doors closed, and turned to survey her with a tenderly wolfish smile.

"Never dare a MacGregor, sweet vixen," he murmured, advancing on her once more.

"Ian, no!" Backing away, she shook her head and tried to ignore the familiar warmth stealing over her. "You can't possibly—it's nearly time for supper!"

"Supper can wait."

"But, what if someone should come in?"

"Then they will get an eyeful."

A faint cry escaped her lips when he swept her up against him once more and bore her down to one of the chairs with him. While she squirmed weakly in his grasp, he made good on his threat. He settled her on his lap so that she was facing him, her legs straddling his. He pulled her skirts free and tossed them all the way upward, muffling her shocked protests with a cloud of filmy blue gauze.

"Ian, I— No, please, you— *Ian!*"

She inhaled sharply, trembling from head to toe as he moved his hand between her thighs. His fingers easily found their way inside the opening of her drawers. A moan rose in her throat. She battled the enveloping folds of fabric, and finally succeeded in pulling them away from her face just in time to see him lowering his head toward the exposed curve of her breasts. His lips roamed greedily across the creamy, delectable flesh, while his fingers stroked and teased at the moist pink softness that longed for his touch. She closed her eyes and shivered with passion, her hands closing upon his shoulders.

The position was yet another new one, wickedly appealing, and she blushed at the thought of how she must look. Ian's arm clamped about her waist, holding her steady for his pleasure and her own. He parted her legs wider with the gentle pressure of his, and she gasped when she heard the sound of fabric tearing. But she was beyond caring about the damage to her undergarment . . . she was beyond caring about anything other than the desire coursing hot and strong through her body. Her response was utterly, blessedly *female*. These past few days with Ian had taught her so many things, but perhaps most significant of all, she had learned to revel in her womanliness instead of being ashamed or even afraid of it.

They were both on the verge of begging for mercy when he finally took her. He had only to flip up his kilt, lift her slightly with his hands about her hips, and bring her down upon his waiting hardness. She breathed his name as his manhood plunged within her welcoming passage. His mouth captured hers in a deep, thoroughly intoxicating kiss, his fingers digging into the firm roundness of her bottom while she delighted in his thrusts and felt the heavenly rapture calling her once again.

The fulfillment was so complete and powerful that she gave a soft scream and collapsed weakly against Ian. He sought his own pleasure in the next instant, then held her for several long moments afterward, his eyes gleaming with both love and triumphant satisfaction as he smoothed a hand along the graceful curve of her back.

Her clothing required a considerable readjustment when she finally removed herself from his lap. She noted with a flash of irritation that he had only to tug his kilt back down into place.

"I'm afraid I must leave you in the morning," he announced unexpectedly, a faint smile touching his lips while he watched her attempt to shake some of the creases from her gown.

"Leave?" She looked up and frowned in bemusement. "What are you talking about?"

"An important matter awaits me in Edinburgh." It was his turn to frown as he explained, "I received a message from one of my business associates only a short time ago. It seems the man has suffered some sort of accident and requires my help."

"How—how long will you be gone?" Surprised to realize how unhappy she was at the prospect of his absence, she hastily averted her gaze and fidgeted with the lace trim on her bodice.

"A day or two, no more."

"What makes you think I'll still be here when you get back?" she murmured, trying to mask her own unaccountable reluctance to be parted from him. Why in heaven's name did her heart ache so?

"You'll be here," he asserted confidently. His eyes twinkled down at her as he stepped forward and raised a hand to cup her chin. "I will, however, charge Peter with your safekeeping. Aye, and Jenny and Molly will do their part as well. They would not wish to lose their new mistress. They've waited long enough to see me wed."

"If you don't trust me, then why don't you take me with you?" she blurted out. Coloring, she held her breath and watched closely for his reaction.

"What, and put myself through hell searching for you all over Edinburgh?" He gave a low, mellow chuckle and leaned down to brush her cheek with his warm lips. "No, Callie Rose MacGregor, I'll not risk 'misplacing' you among so many other lost souls."

She did not resist when he slipped an arm about her shoulders and led her toward the doorway.

"Will you miss me, lass?" he challenged mockingly.

"As much as I'd miss the plague!" came her impertinent rejoinder.

"Your tongue is in need of further schooling."

He emphasized the point with a hearty swat on her backside. She gasped and pulled away, rounding on him with her beautiful eyes indignantly ablaze.

"Damn you, Ian MacGregor, you—"

"Since I'm to be away for a while, I think we should make the most of the time left to us. I'll instruct Molly to send our supper up to our room."

"You'll do no such thing!"

"Would you care to offer me yet another dare?"

"Would *you* care to spend the night in one of the guest bedrooms?" she parried, hands on her hips.

"Is that a threat, you little shrew?" His tone was deceptively low and level.

"It's a promise!" She raised her head to a proud, defiant angle and folded her arms beneath her breasts.

" 'Tis no more than I deserve for taking an American to wife," he murmured wryly.

She was caught off-guard when he suddenly tossed her over his shoulder and carried her toward the staircase.

"Confound it, you arrogant scoundrel, you can't keep doing this!" she exclaimed, wriggling in protest. "Ian, please. We just—"

"Do you yield, Lady MacGregor?" he demanded.

"Yield?"

"Aye. Will you admit that you've no desire to keep me from your bed?"

"Ian!"

"Supper is waiting," he reminded her.

"All right!" She capitulated with an ill grace.

He set her on her feet again. She yanked her skirts down into place and raked several wayward strands of hair from the flushed smoothness of her face.

"Perhaps I should take you to Edinburgh with me after all," he mused aloud, drawing her against him. His tanned, chiseled features had grown serious now, and his eyes burned down into hers.

Callie Rose felt her heart leap anew, felt her body swaying even closer to his. There was something about the way he was looking at her that made her want to implore him not to leave her behind. But the words would not come.

He said nothing more about it as he gave her a quick kiss, then finally escorted her to the dining room. And when they went upstairs to the privacy of their bedchamber after the meal, neither of them spoke of what the morning would bring. They were content to share the magic of the night. . . .

❧ TEN ❧

Ian left just after dawn.

Callie Rose stood at the window in the library and watched as he rode away through the castle gate. Her eyes clouded with the memory of his good-bye.

He had awakened her with a kiss and a whispered assurance that he would hasten his return. And then he had told her that he loved her. Still too confused by her own feelings, she had offered nothing more than a brief, wordless nod in response. But once he had slipped out of the room, she had impulsively scrambled from the bed, tossed a wrapper about her shoulders, and crept downstairs just in time to see the great front door closing after him.

He was gone now.

Beseiged by a sudden, sharp feeling of emptiness, she heaved a sigh and turned away. She was alone at the moment. Jenny and Molly were busy in the kitchen, and Peter was on his way back inside for a cup of his future mother-in-law's coffee. He would, of course, remain vigilant in his duties to Ian, but neither he nor the two women expected their new mistress to indulge in any further escape schemes. It was obvious to them that she had reached an acceptance (however uneasy) of her marriage, and they were confident they would not be called upon to act as reluctant jailers any longer.

Tying the belt of her wrapper, Callie Rose allowed her troubled gaze to drift back toward the window. She could make a run for it. . . . She could throw open the window and be on her way out to the stables before anyone even realized she had come downstairs. But she couldn't summon the will to do it.

A bird in a gilded cage, she mused with a faint smile of irony. Contradiction though it was, she was a willing captive. And by thunder, she couldn't break the bonds.

Another sigh escaped her lips as she wandered out of the library and back up the staircase to the bedchamber. She bathed and dressed, then headed into the dining room for breakfast. Ian's handsome face swam before her eyes at every turn, and she soon discovered that her appetite had fled. She managed to finish off a cup of tea and an oatcake, however, before telling a casually watchful Peter that she wanted to break with her usual routine and spend the morning alone in the garden.

He was accompanying her across the great hall when a lone rider approached the castle. A knock sounded moments later, and Peter opened the door to reveal a young woman cradling a baby in her arms.

Callie Rose recognized her immediately. It was the same pretty, well-endowed blonde who had attended the handfasting ceremony. The same uninvited guest Ian had been reluctant to talk about.

"I've come to speak with Miss Buchanan," announced Elspeth MacGregor. Her opal gaze hardened when it moved behind him to Callie Rose.

" 'Tis *Lady MacGregor* now," Peter corrected, with

all manner of politeness. He swung the door wide and stood at attention as Elspeth swept haughtily inside.

"What is it you want, Miss MacGregor?" Callie Rose asked, wondering what could have prompted the woman to come calling so early in the day. She smiled when Elspeth drew closer and the baby—a little boy about six months old with a remarkable head of auburn hair and deep green eyes—made a happy, gurgling sound. He was dressed in a white cotton gown, with a blanket of the MacGregor plaid wrapped about him for warmth. "Is this your child?"

"Aye. But you'd best be asking about the father instead of the mother!"

"The father?" Callie Rose echoed in bewilderment.

"Lord MacGregor is away at the moment." Peter hastened to intervene at this point. He frowned and told Elspeth, "I think he would not be pleased—"

"What do I care about pleasing him?" Elspeth shot back angrily. "I'll not leave until I've had a *private* conversation with Miss Buchanan!"

"It's all right, Peter," said Callie Rose. Though a warning bell sounded in her brain, she calmly suggested to Elspeth, "We can talk in the drawing room."

Peter started to voice yet another objection, but realized there was little he could do. He could only hope his new mistress would not take anything Elspeth MacGregor said to heart; he knew the woman was all too capable of stirring up trouble. Nodding at Callie Rose, he turned and strode away, back to the kitchen to inform Jenny and Molly of the situation.

Callie Rose led the way into the drawing room. She

took a seat in one of the chairs while Elspeth settled herself on the sofa.

"Your son appears to be quite healthy," remarked Callie Rose, another smile rising to her lips as she watched Elspeth tug the blanket away.

"He is a true MacGregor," the other woman declared proudly. She set the baby on the floor at her feet and gave him a cracker to teethe on. When she looked back to Callie Rose, her eyes grew cold. "You remember me, do you not?"

"Yes. You were here the night—"

"The night you were handfasted to the man who should by all rights be *my* husband!"

Callie Rose blinked across at her in astonishment.

"What are you talking about?"

"Did you not wonder why I left so suddenly?" Elspeth demanded in a tone that was both hostile and challenging.

"Ian said it was because you hadn't been invited."

"That, at least, was the truth!" the blonde proclaimed, with a bitter little laugh. "He did not want me here, but I would not be kept away! As soon as I heard that he meant to take another to wife, I knew I had to come. But then I could not bear to see him with you, to see the way he kissed you and—" She broke off abruptly, and her features became suffused with dull, angry color. "Ian MacGregor promised to marry me!"

"You and Ian were betrothed?"

"More than that!"

"I don't believe you," Callie Rose told her, with a composure that masked the sudden turmoil within her.

"What reason have I to lie?" demanded Elspeth.

"I don't know. But I don't believe Ian ever promised to marry you." *There have been no others,* he had once told her. Still, a tiny seed of doubt had been planted. And Elspeth MacGregor was determined to see it through to a full harvest.

"Are you really such a fool?" Elspeth charged scornfully. "Did you think he had lived the life of a monk these many years past? You've shared his bed, have you not? If so—and I do not doubt it—you know that he is far too hot-blooded to be without a woman. Aye, he is like all the other men of our clan, only *he* is the best of the lot!"

Callie Rose felt sick inside. Her cheeks burned at the woman's words, and her head spun dizzily. She was tempted to leave, to flee the room and listen to no more, but some invisible force compelled her to remain.

"I was not the first, of course," Elspeth continued, her eyes glittering harshly now. "I've little doubt Ian has broken many a girl's heart."

Hadn't she herself once accused him of the same thing? thought Callie Rose. The knot in her stomach tightened as Elspeth went on.

"We've known each other since we were bairns. Our fathers had planned the match for years. Everyone expected us to wed long ago."

"Then why didn't you?"

"Because he betrayed me! He stole my innocence, he deceived me with sweet words, and then he tossed me aside as though I were little better than one of those painted strumpets down in Edinburgh!"

"No!" Callie Rose gasped out, shaking her head in a stunned denial. "Ian wouldn't—"

"Would he not?" hissed Elspeth. Her gaze was full of such hatred that Callie Rose inhaled upon a soft gasp. "You do not yet know him as I do! He can be cruel and heartless when it suits him!" Her mouth curved into another humorless smile. "He and his brother are two of a kind. They are the most devoted of lovers for a time, but as soon as they tire of a poor lass, they turn cold!"

"So that's why you're here? To tell me that you're one of my husband's former mistresses?" Callie Rose demanded, her own eyes flashing.

"I am here to see a wrong righted!"

"And what 'wrong' is that?"

"Ian promised to marry me!" Elspeth declared once more. "If not for you, I would be his wife now!"

"What makes you so sure of that?"

"I am the mother of his child!"

"What?" Callie Rose gasped, thunderstruck.

"Aye, you've only to look at our son to see what was between us!"

"No, I—I . . ." Her voice trailed away as a terrible pain suddenly gripped her heart.

"You cannot ignore the evidence before your own eyes!" insisted Elspeth. She quickly scooped the baby up in her arms again and placed him on her lap. Her eyes gleamed with malignant triumph. "My Jamie is the very image of his father!"

Callie Rose felt her throat constrict as she looked to the child. His hair was the same color as Ian's, his eyes the same deep, emerald green. And most damning of all, his features bore an incredibly striking resemblance to Ian's.

Dear God, it was true.

"The very day before Ian brought you to Castle MacGregor, he had finally agreed to give Jamie his name!" Elspeth told her.

"Why didn't he—why didn't he marry you when he found out you were carrying his child?" Callie Rose stammered, her voice quavering with emotion.

"We quarreled," the other woman replied, with a shrug of her shoulders. "Ian was pleased with the news at first, but then he began to doubt me. I've a fearsome temper. I sent him away, and I did not see him again until after Jamie was born." Her smile this time was one of satisfaction. "With us, it has always been either hot or cold! Seven years now I've waited for him to keep his promise. He was away for months at a time, and yet I welcomed him with open arms each time he returned. It did not matter that he had been so cruel, that he had enjoyed the 'company' of others."

"How could you do that when—?"

"Ian's kisses can be very persuasive. Would you not agree?" She heaved a dramatic sigh. "And after so long, 'tis hard to say no."

"So you've been his lover for seven years," Callie Rose murmured. Her blue eyes were clouded with anguish as she listened to the blood pounding in her ears.

"Aye. I've never loved another in all that time. No, nor has Ian—not truly! He admitted as much to me only last week." She lowered the baby back to the floor and flung Callie Rose another proud, inescapably victorious look. " 'Tis no real dishonor for a lass to bear the child of her betrothed. Our kinsmen knew our marriage would take place eventually. Ian claimed responsibility for his son from the very first."

"Did he?"

"He did indeed. Jamie is the firstborn. Bastard or no, he will take his rightful place as the next chief of Clan MacGregor!"

"Were you Ian's handfast bride as well?" Callie Rose choked out. Perhaps her marriage to Ian wasn't legal after all. Why did the possibility fill her with misery instead of relief?

"No," Elspeth confessed reluctantly. "But our love has been no secret!"

"I see." She pulled herself up from the chair and swallowed hard before demanding through a haze of pain, "How can I know if anything you've told me is true?" It was hopeless and she knew it, yet her heart wanted desperately to believe otherwise.

"Ask Peter if you don't believe me! Or Jenny, or Molly! Aye, they'll bear witness to the truth!" the blonde exclaimed, lifting Jamie in her arms again as she stood and glared belligerently at Callie Rose. "Go on, *Miss Buchanan*, ask them!" She closed the distance between them now, her features twisted with mingled rage and disdain. "You are not his wife! You do not belong here! You have stolen what is mine!"

"Why didn't you speak up when you were here the other night? Why did you let us go through with the ceremony?"

"I saw that Ian wanted you. He is not a man to be swayed by tears or tantrums. I fear his wrath like no other's. I had no choice but to let him take his pleasure where he would. But I knew he would come back to *me*! He always does!"

"Then why are you here today? What did you hope to gain by telling me—?"

"It is I who should be mistress of Castle MacGregor! Once you are gone, Ian and I can be wed! He will be angry when he learns of my visit— Aye, but I can wait no longer!" Her tone was laced with venom when she said with a sneer, "Go back to America, Callie Rose Buchanan! You never should have come to this place! Go back before Ian breaks your heart as he once did mine!"

Callie Rose felt hot, bitter tears starting to her eyes. She allowed her gaze to move back to the child who looked so much like Ian, and realized in that moment that Elspeth's warning had come too late.

With a strangled cry, she spun about and raced blindly from the room. Elspeth MacGregor smiled in her wake.

Once upstairs, Callie Rose threw herself facedown across the bed she had shared with Ian. She wept long and hard, muffling her sobs with the pillow as she poured out her sorrow. Her heart ached terribly; she had never experienced such intense, gut-wrenching pain.

The truth had come to her at last.

She was in love with Ian MacGregor. She had loved him from the very beginning, from the first moment he had swept her up in his arms and carried her away to his castle. He had known it ... by thunder, he had known it all along.

She sat up and swiped angrily at her tears. Everything made sense now. Finally she understood why she had been unable to resist him, why his very touch set her afire. She wasn't shameless and weak willed after all. She was a woman in love. So desperately, completely in love with Ian that she had given up trying to escape. She had vowed never to feel this way about any man, but it had happened just the same. No matter how much she had fought against it, Ian had stormed her heart every bit as thoroughly as he had stormed her body.

That was why Elspeth's words hurt so much. Heaven help her, she loved him!

But the realization brought no joy—only torment. He had betrayed her. He had promised his love to another. And worst of all, he had allowed his son to be born a bastard. *His son*. Dear God, he had made love to Elspeth . . . he had taken the woman to his bed for seven long years. How many others had there been? She wasn't a complete fool; she knew he hadn't been celibate before their marriage, but she hadn't expected *this*.

She closed her eyes again, battling a fresh wave of tears as Ian's image rose in her mind. The memory of his words, of his passionate kisses and caresses, sent another pain slicing through her heart like a knife. He had said that he loved her. He had told her that he had never loved anyone before. Yet how could she believe him? How could his love for her be true when he had so cruelly deceived and mistreated Elspeth MacGregor?

It couldn't. He didn't love her. And she'd end up just like Elspeth. . . .

The thought made her eyes kindle with a potent mixture of vengeful fury and anguish. As had been the case all too often in the past, her emotions vanquished any hope of reason. She was a true Buchanan, hot-tempered and impetuous, ready to act first and think later. Under normal circumstances, she might well have confronted Ian MacGregor with the discovery of his treachery. She might have been more inclined to doubt Elspeth's claims. But the circumstances were far from normal. God help her, she had never been so vulnerable before. Her love was still too new—too fragile—to weather any storms just yet.

It was so very difficult to think clearly when her heart was breaking. Dragging herself from the bed, she moved across to the fireplace and stared, unseeing, down at the ashes. They were all that remained of the roaring blaze that had only a short time ago joined with Ian's arms to protect her from the early morning chill.

She had to do something, and she had to do it now. She couldn't possibly stay at the castle any longer. Not when Ian belonged to another. She loved him, but she didn't want to. If this was love, then by heaven, she didn't want any part of it!

She must go home.

Home to Texas, home to the Diamond L. It was the best place to sort things out. What other choice did she have? She had fallen in love with a man who was truly a scoundrel and a rogue, a man who was apparently every bit as arrogant and selfish and unprincipled as she had once accused him of being. And yet, she recalled with a ragged sigh, he had been so tender, so loving and charming. In spite of the fact that he had abducted her, she had come to believe him a man of honor. Indeed, he had seemed to be the man of her dreams. How could she have been so stupid?

It briefly crossed her mind to confront Jenny and

Molly (or even Peter) as Elspeth had suggested, but she abandoned the notion. She could not count on them to tell her the truth, for they were fiercely loyal to Ian. And she didn't want them to suspect that anything was wrong. She'd stand a better chance of getting away if she maintained an outward show of equanimity and said nothing.

Her emotions agonizingly raw, she hastened to retrieve her valise from beneath the bed. She set it atop the mattress and threw it open, then pulled her gowns and undergarments from the wardrobe and flung them inside. She was already wearing her riding habit; she had planned to visit the stables and perhaps go for a ride with Peter later in the day.

She closed the valise, buckled its narrow leather straps, and carried it to the doorway. Her gaze was drawn inexorably back toward the massive, canopied four-poster when she paused with her hand on the doorknob.

Oh, Ian, why couldn't you have told me the truth? she lamented as his face swam before her eyes again. Maybe if she had known about Elspeth and Jamie ... but no, she still wouldn't have had any right to love him. And he still wouldn't have had any right to force her into marriage when he was already bound to another.

"You bastard," she whispered brokenly. Filled with a white-hot anger for his betrayal, she cursed herself for ever having been fool enough to trust a man. Ian MacGregor had stolen her heart, he had taught her the meaning of passion, and now he had given her every reason to hate him. She would never forgive him for what he'd done. *Never!*

She drew in a deep, steadying breath, opened the door, and swept determinedly from the room. Keeping a watchful eye out for the servants, she hurried downstairs and across the great hall to the drawing room. Thankfully Elspeth was gone.

She eased open the window and dropped her valise outside, then closed the window again. Dashing impatiently at the tears that lingered on the flushed smoothness of her cheeks, she forced a smile to her lips and went in search of Peter. She found him in the kitchen, stealing a kiss from Jenny. The two of them jumped apart in guilty startlement when they saw her standing in the doorway.

"Are you all right, my lady?" the young housemaid queried. Glimpsing the telltale redness about Callie Rose's eyes, she frowned in genuine concern. "I hope Miss MacGregor did not—"

"I'm fine," lied Callie Rose. "She came to congratulate me on my marriage, that's all. And to show me little Jamie."

"Elspeth MacGregor has always been one for creating mischief," Peter opined, his voice holding a discernible edge. It was on the tip of his tongue to ask what Elspeth had said, but he decided it wouldn't be proper to question his new mistress. If the woman *had* stirred up trouble, he'd do well to trust Lord MacGregor to put it to rights. Besides, he and everyone else at the castle had been sworn to secrecy long ago. . . .

"I'd like to go out to the stables now, if you don't mind," Callie Rose told him in a remarkably level tone.

"Of course." He and Jenny exchanged a last warm, affectionate look before he followed Callie Rose out of the room.

They strolled outside and crossed the well-manicured grounds. Callie Rose stole a glance back over her shoulder as she accompanied him, satisfied to note that her valise was concealed within the shrubbery beneath the drawing room window. Her heart was thundering painfully in her chest, and she continued to waver between fury and sorrow while Elspeth's hateful, earth-shattering words echoed in the turbulence of her mind.

"Would it be possible for us to go for a ride today?" she asked Peter when they stepped inside the hay-scented coolness of the stables.

"Aye, my lady. Your husband said I was to grant your every request. Provided, of course, that you did not ask to go anywhere alone," he informed her, with a crooked smile. "I'll saddle our mounts right away."

"There's no hurry."

She held her breath, watching as he entered the tack room to the right of the doorway. He carried a saddle out into the main part of the building, set it atop one of the wooden rails, and headed back for the second saddle. She waited until he had disappeared into the room again. Then she made her move.

With a swiftness that took him completely by surprise, she darted forward and closed the door behind him. She turned the key in the lock, tossed it aside, and spun about to fly down the cobbled run to the stall where *Ban-sith* was nibbling peacefully at the bucket of oats Peter had given her earlier.

"What are you doing? Please, my lady, let me out!"

Peter shouted from within the tack room's darkness, pounding insistently on the door. "You musn't try to leave! Your husband will thrapple us both! Please, open the door!"

Callie Rose ignored his entreaties, catching up a bridle and reins from the peg above the mare's stall. She opened the gate and led the horse out. In no time at all, she had the beautiful, mahogany-colored animal saddled.

"Lady MacGregor?" Peter called out again. He rattled the knob and tried his best to force the door open, but to no avail. "Are you still there? Can you hear me? Please, you cannot—"

"You can tell my *husband* that I'll be damned if I'll let him play me for a fool any longer!" she shot back in a loud, wrathful tone. Clutching the reins in one hand, she quickly led the mare outside and across the grounds to where she had left her valise. She tied the small banded suitcase to the back of the saddle, then mounted up and placed her feet in the stirrups.

Her gaze sparkled with renewed tears as she took one last look at the fairy-tale castle rising like a beacon above the rugged, green-mantled beauty of the Highland countryside. It seemed a lifetime ago that Ian had brought her here, yet it had in actuality been nothing more than a week. *Seven days* . . . Ian MacGregor had destroyed her whole world in only seven days.

Muttering a pained, bitter curse, she reined the horse about and rode hell-bent for leather through the castle gate.

🐉 ELEVEN 🐉

"Damn it, girl, you've been home two weeks now, and all you've done is mope about like a gnat flying backward," J. D. Buchanan complained gruffly.

"You shouldn't have sent her away in the first place," Sam Buchanan was brave enough to reiterate. He was the oldest (and the one most like J. D.), so he was unfazed by the narrow, vitriolic glare his father sent him.

"You keep the hell out of this!"

"Sam's right," said Clay, the youngest of the four brothers. "Callie Rose ain't been the same ever since she came back. Seems to me she'd have been a whole lot better off staying put."

"Don't say 'ain't,' boy," Jake said with a lazy drawl. Fourth in line in the Buchanan male hierarchy, he was the nearest to Callie Rose in looks if not age. His blue eyes were alight with devilment as he grinned broadly and cast her a knowing wink. "Our baby sister's gone and gotten herself some culture. I figure the least we can do is practice real live manners from here on out."

Callie Rose was able to manage only a weak smile in response. She tossed her napkin down beside her half-empty plate and allowed her preoccupied gaze to travel over the five handsome men surrounding her at the long, linen-covered oak table in the dining room. Her heart, still aching as it had done since she had fled Scotland more than a month ago, momentarily stirred with both pride and love as she surveyed her unique family.

There was Jake, full of life, slender and wiry with hair as black as her own ... Billy, quiet and introspective, built like a bull, his blond hair and brown eyes earning him a lifetime of teasing about having been "found under a haystack"... Clay, still boyish in many ways, with sandy-colored hair, gray eyes, and an alarming tendency toward violence ... Sam, rakishly attractive yet not at all vain, his blue-green eyes and dark brown hair, in addition to his toughness of character, making him the most readily identifiable as his father's son.

And last, but definitely not least, was J. D. Buchanan himself. Her eyes fell beneath the searching, almost angry intensity of his.

"What is it?" he demanded, with a scowl. "What happened to you over there? By thunder, did one of those fancy, sweet-smelling sonsabitches get too—?"

"No!" she denied vehemently, the lie provoking a rush of guilty color to her cheeks. She hastened to compose herself once more. "Nothing happened. I'm just a little tired, that's all."

"Like hell!" her father snapped, disbelieving.

"Can't you see she doesn't want to talk about it?" Billy finally spoke up. Seated next to her, he reached over and covered her hand with the sympathetic, rope-calloused warmth of his. "Confound it, Pa, you can't force someone to confide in you."

"J. D. can," muttered Clay, raising another forkful of mashed potatoes to his mouth.

"Damned right I can!" their beloved, hard-as-nails patriarch asserted. He abruptly pushed away his own plate and leaned back in his chair, folding his arms across his chest. In spite of what he'd said, his steely gaze softened as it fastened on Callie Rose's face again. "Would to God I could understand what's got you looking so peaked," he remarked in a far more compassionate manner.

"I told you, I'm just tired," she insisted, with an audible sigh. "I haven't been sleeping very well lately, and the trip home was not a pleasant one."

That was certainly the truth. She had spent most of the time alone in the ship's cabin, alternately crying and cursing, trying without success to forget she had ever set eyes on Ian MacGregor. And on the rare occasions when she had ventured into the brisk sea air above deck, she had stood at the railing as though transfixed, her grief-stricken sapphire gaze drawn out to the rolling, whitecapped vastness of the sea, her mind plagued by memories both sweet and bitter . . . memories of a week spent as the bride of a man who had showed her that love was good for nothing but pain.

Martha had provided what little comfort she could, of course. Although the widow had finally agreed to accompany her young cousin home—she'd had no choice when confronted with the shocking news of Ian's treachery—she had granted her escort reluctantly. Indeed, before they had boarded the early afternoon train from Inverness to Edinburgh (where Callie Rose had prayed that fate wouldn't be so cruel as to let her cross

paths with Ian), she had insisted that Callie Rose at
least send word of her plans back to Castle MacGregor.
But her pleas for common sense and reason had fallen
on deaf ears. She had given up trying long before they
had reached Bristol and booked passage on the first ship
bound for America.

In the end, the two of them had agreed never again to
speak of what had taken place in Scotland—either to
each other, or to anyone else. *Especially J. D.*

"Maybe I'd better have a word with Martha," J. D.
pondered aloud, his thoughts running startlingly parallel
to his daughter's.

"No, you can't do that!" Callie Rose blurted out. She
swallowed hard and made a valiant attempt to keep her
tone casual while explaining, "She's been under the
weather, too. The poor thing always becomes violently
ill during ocean voyages."

"All right. I'll give her another day or two," he replied, pulling himself up from his chair now. "But then
the three of us are going to sit down and have a pa-
laver."

"That won't be necessary." She blanched at his threat
of a three-way discussion. Cousin Martha had never
been able to keep anything from J. D. Hell's bells, she
mused with an inward groan, the woman would probably spill her guts as soon as she walked in the door.

"There's still plenty of work to be done before sun-
down," pronounced J. D., bestowing a collective frown
on his four strapping sons.

Amid much scraping of chairs and dropping of forks
onto plates, they got up from the table and returned to

their duties outside. Callie Rose remained behind, lifting one hand to her throat as she closed her eyes.

"You are not finished, senorita?"

She looked up to see the new cook/housekeeper standing across the table from her. The woman's plump, honey-colored face was kindly, and there was such concern in her gaze that Callie Rose felt tempted to spill her own guts then and there. But she did not.

"I wasn't very hungry tonight, Elena," she murmured by way of apology.

"*Sí*, you have not been hungry for many days now," Elena noted, shaking her head. "Soon, you will be as thin as your brother Clay."

"Well, I—I have things to do," stammered Callie Rose, rising to her feet at last and hurrying from the room. She headed outside to join the others.

Grateful for the breeze, she paused on the front porch and twisted her thick braid of hair up under her hat. The sun, broiling and merciless on this late August evening, hung low on the horizon. It had been a dry summer. The grass was parched and yellow, the bluebonnets and other wildflowers having long since disappeared from the gently rolling countryside near the Clear Fork of the Trinity River. The leaves on the giant twin oak trees standing guard in front of the house were drooping sadly as a result of Mother Nature's neglect. And from dawn to dusk each day, the heat took on a life of its own, rising from the land in great, undulating waves.

A far cry from the cool, green beauty of the Highlands, Callie Rose reflected with another sigh.

"Don't!" she muttered, then swore with a self-directed wrath at her continuing failure to purge her mind of such thoughts.

The situation had only worsened since she'd arrived home. At every turn these past two weeks, Ian's face had driven away all other images. He would not be forgotten.

She had tried her damnedest. She had worked harder than ever before, spending countless, downright exhausting hours alongside her brothers out on the range or at the ranch proper. She had even taken to doing a good many of the chores inside the house (except the cooking, which she had wisely left in Elena's capable hands). But nothing had helped.

The nights were the worst.

She would lie abed in the darkness and stare up at the low, plastered ceiling, feeling terribly lonely in spite of the fact that the house was full of people who would rather die than see her hurt. The normally soothing sounds of the house creaking, the gentle night wind rustling through the trees, and the crickets chirping beneath her window would go unnoticed in the face of her disconsolate reverie. And even if she did manage to fall asleep before midnight, her dreams would be haunted by visions of a green-eyed, fiercely appealing Highlander who suddenly appeared out of the mist to carry her away on his magnificent black steed.

The yearning deep inside her was not only real, it was constant and painful. Her heart cried out to Ian. No matter how often she reminded herself of his cruel betrayal, she was powerless to stop the flood tide of longing that washed over her as soon as she closed the door of her room each night. She wanted to feel his arms about her, to listen to his voice and gaze upon his face and feel alive once more. *Dear God, how she wanted him.*

But it was impossible. She could never go back.

"Jezebel's about ready to drop her foal!" Jake called out to her from the doorway of the stock barn.

Mentally consigning Ian MacGregor to the devil for at least the hundredth time that day alone, she squared her shoulders and set off to join her brother.

A short time later, Martha Terhune unexpectedly came calling. Callie Rose's throat constricted with alarm when she emerged from the barn and caught sight of the familiar buggy rolling to a halt in front of the whitewashed, two-storied house.

"Speaking of the devil," she muttered underneath her breath, wondering why in the world her cousin had chosen that particular evening to show up out of the blue. She hurried across the yard to issue a warning.

"Callie Rose!" the widow exclaimed, with pleasure, as she alighted from the buggy and smoothed her skirts down into place. "I was hoping—"

"You promised!" Callie Rose reminded her in an annoyed, cautious undertone. Her eyes flashed when she took the older woman's muslin-covered arm in a firm grip and led her a safer distance from the house. "Confound it, you promised to stay away for a while! J. D.'s been asking all sorts of questions!"

"Calm yourself, my dear." Martha responded with a reassuring smile, patting her hand. "There's no need for you to worry. I simply happened to be passing by on my way home from Mrs. Ballinger's, and although it *is* getting rather late, I thought I'd stop to pay your father my respects. I haven't yet thanked him properly for sending me to Europe with you."

"Write him a letter!"

"Don't be silly. Now let's go inside. It's much too hot to stand out here arguing." She gently disengaged her arm and looked around, satisfied to see that they were alone for the moment. "I wanted to seek your advice about . . . well, about a highly personal matter."

"You can have all the advice you want, just as long as you don't let the cat out of the bag," Callie Rose told her, with another quelling frown.

While Sam and Billy waved a greeting from the corral, Martha linked her arm companionably through her cousin's and urged her across to the front steps of the house. J. D., Jake, and Clay were still somewhere outside, so the two women had the parlor all to themselves.

Martha settled herself on the sofa, but Callie Rose was feeling much too restless to sit. She folded her arms beneath her breasts and wandered across to the huge limestone fireplace, then pivoted to face Martha again.

"Have you enjoyed your homecoming?" the widow asked, though she could well discern the answer for herself. She had never seen Callie Rose looking so pale and unhappy. There were dark shadows underscoring the poor girl's eyes (which lacked their usual brightness), and she appeared to have lost weight.

"Of course," Callie Rose replied flippantly. "Why wouldn't I?" Lying was getting to be a necessary habit; she hated it.

"Well, I thought . . . that is, after what had happened, I was afraid you might still be suffering the ill effects—"

"*I* thought we had agreed not to talk about it anymore."

"We had," Martha admitted, with a faint smile. "But you don't seem at all like yourself."

"Don't I?" She forced a smile to her own lips and hastened to change the subject. "You said you wanted my advice about something."

"Yes. I know it would be terribly forward of me, but I am considering the prospect of a correspondence with Dr. MacGregor. I would have to be the one to initiate it, you see, and I—"

"You can't!" Callie Rose exclaimed, hot color flying to her cheeks. "For heaven's sake, you can't write to him!"

"He was very kind to me," Martha reminded her. "I'm sure he must be wondering why I left without saying good-bye. And though he never brought up the subject of payment for his services, I feel honor-bound to settle the matter."

"No!" Callie Rose unfolded her arms and began pacing distractedly back and forth. "Don't you see, it will only serve to stir things up all over again! It's best to let the matter lie as it is, to—"

"Would stirring things up really be such a tragedy?" Martha challenged her gently.

"How can you even ask that?" Callie Rose demanded, her gaze bridling with vengeful fury. "After all Ian did to me . . . ? Damn it, I said I didn't ever want to talk about it again!"

"Very well. We won't talk about your husband."

"He isn't my husband!"

"He is in the eyes of God," Martha asserted primly.

"Well, God will just have to *close* his eyes!" she retorted, yanking the hat from her head.

"Callie Rose!" Shocked at such out-and-out blasphemy, the widow rose to her feet and fixed her young cousin with a stern, reproachful look. "Your marriage to Lord MacGregor was one in fact if not in name—I believe the legality of it is still in question—but you cannot pretend as though it never happened. Sooner or later, my dear, you'll have to seek some professional advice on the matter. And a bit of spiritual advice certainly won't hurt, either!"

"I don't need anyone's advice," Callie Rose insisted stubbornly. "Ian MacGregor can do whatever he needs to do back in Scotland. Now that I'm home, I intend to put it all behind me." *Ah, but intentions have a way of losing themselves,* Ian had once told her. Great balls of fire, she thought with an inward groan, why did she have to keep remembering?

"But what if you should want to marry again someday?" asked Martha. "How do you know if you will be free to do so?"

"I don't care about that."

"Of course you do," her cousin said, disputing her. "I know your 'experiences' have left you troubled, but you'll meet someone else—"

"I'll never marry!" she vowed, with considerable feeling.

"The hell you won't," J. D.'s voice suddenly rumbled forth from the doorway. He had arrived upon the scene too late to eavesdrop much, but what he *had* heard provoked him to anger.

Callie Rose frowned in dismay as she whirled to face her father. Martha, however, offered him an affectionate smile.

"How nice to see you again, J. D. I've been wanting to thank you for allowing me to accompany Callie Rose to Europe. If not for your generosity, I'm quite sure I would have been required to spend the entire summer helping Dorcas Ballinger sew quilts for the church raffle."

"You did me a favor," he proclaimed, never one for accepting gratitude easily. Tugging the hat from his head, he sauntered toward the sideboard while shooting Callie Rose a speaking glare. "Up on your high horse about marriage again, are you?" he accused, pouring himself a drink.

"I am," she willingly confirmed. "And I'm going to stay there, too!"

"You know I was hoping you'd find her a husband," he said, shifting his steely gaze back to Martha. "I was hoping she'd come home with her new in-laws in tow. Looks to me like I wasted good money again." He downed the shot of whiskey in a single gulp.

"It wasn't a waste," Martha assured him. She did not miss the way Callie Rose stiffened with apprehension. "There's nothing like traveling abroad to remind us how unimportant we are in the vast scheme of things."

"Is that why she's been so moody ever since she got back?" he demanded, his voice edged with displeasure.

"Moody? Well, I—I suppose we may have overdone it a bit," Martha stammered—unconvincingly, to Callie Rose's ears. "We saw a great deal in the few weeks we were gone. And I don't know if your daughter has told you, but she created quite a sensation in London."

It was said innocently enough, for she had not heard about the scandal that had erupted in their wake. Callie Rose, however, found herself plagued by yet another memory, that of Ian telling her he was aware of her reputation as a heartless flirt. Her mouth curved into a faint smile of bitter irony.

"She hasn't told me a thing," J. D. ground out. "Not a damned thing."

"Because all you wanted to know was whether or not I was still an old maid!" Callie Rose parried defensively.

"Maybe I ought to send you back to that school," he threatened.

"Come now, J. D., she's no longer a child." Martha sought to reason with him. "Indeed, she's a grown woman, capable of making her own decisions, and certainly intelligent enough to realize that one should never allow pride to overrule one's heart—"

"Remember, Cousin Martha, you said you wanted to get home before dark." Callie Rose intervened at this point. She took the startled widow's arm and propelled her firmly toward the doorway. "Thanks for stopping by. I'll ride into town in a couple of days to see how you're getting along."

"Come for supper tomorrow, Martha," J. D. said. It was a decree, not a request. "It's time you and me had us a nice long talk."

"She can't!" Callie Rose answered for her.

"Of course I can!" Martha corrected her with a soft, breathless laugh. She pulled her arm free and turned back to J. D. "Thank you very much for the invitation. I'll be here at six o'clock sharp."

Callie Rose offered up a silent oath, then followed Martha outside. She watched as her cousin climbed up into the buggy and settled her skirts about her.

"By the way, my dear, I've decided to write to Dr. MacGregor after all," Martha announced, taking up the reins.

"And it isn't merely because you want to settle the bill, is it?" Callie Rose heaved a sigh and remarked, "I could tell there was something between the two of you that day Ian and I came to the hotel."

"I'm not at all sure of that. But, to be honest, I *am* hopeful," conceded Martha, blushing. Her expression grew wistful in the next instant. "I've been so lonely since Franklin died. There are times when I long for the sound of a man's voice in the house." A sad, knowing little smile touched her lips when she exhorted, "Don't let what happened in Scotland turn you against love, Callie Rose. You're still young. You have your whole life ahead of you. Being alone is fine for some women, I suppose, but not for me. And not for you."

"You can't know that," Callie Rose murmured defiantly, her heart twisting nonetheless.

"I knew it when I saw you with Lord MacGregor."

She smiled once more, snapped the reins together above the horse's head, and drove away without another word. Callie Rose stared after her, feeling more confused and restless than ever.

She was up early the following morning. Jake had announced plans to fetch the new saddle he'd ordered

from one of the many saddlemaker's shops in nearby
Fort Worth, and she had been glad of the opportunity to
accompany him.

The two of them rode beside each other on the
uncushioned wooden seat of the buckboard, making idle
conversation about the hellish weather, cattle and
horses, and the phenomenal changes the newly arrived
railroad had made in the area. When they drove into the
bustling activity of the city center less than an hour
later, Jake guided the wagon to a halt in front of T. R.
Calhoun's Saddlery and secured the reins.

"Want to come inside with me?" he asked his sister,
jumping agilely down. A cloud of dust greeted his boots
when they met the boardwalk. "It might take awhile."

"No, thanks." She gathered up the skirts of her faded,
tight red calico dress and allowed Jake to swing her
down beside him, then tightened the strings of the old
broad-brimmed felt hat she had borrowed from Clay.
She cared little about her appearance now that she was
home again; if not for J. D.'s timely intervention, she'd
have shocked the good citizens of Fort Worth by wearing a pair of men's denim trousers. "I think I'll go for
a walk. I haven't had a chance to look around much
lately."

"Suit yourself." He grinned and tipped his own hat
farther back on his head. "Just don't go getting any
ideas about visiting your *compadres* down in Hell's
Half Acre," he warned teasingly.

"As if I'd go near that godforsaken place," she retorted, with an expressive grimace. Unbeknownst to her
father, she had ventured into the infamous red light dis-

trict with Clay one evening last summer. Her brother
had ridden his horse inside the Longhorn Saloon (taking
advantage of its "bar service in the saddle"), leaving her
outside to gaze about in mingled disgust and fascination
at the crowds of gamblers, outlaws, cowboys, soiled
doves, and desperadoes swarming about the dance halls,
saloons, and brothels. It was a wonder she hadn't come
to any harm, especially since shootings and fistfights
and other highly inventive forms of assault were daily
occurrences.

The memory of that ill-conceived excursion prompted
yet another thought of Ian. She could well imagine what
he would have to say about her placing herself in such
danger. God have mercy, she mused as a sudden lump
rose in her throat, it had been over a month now. When
would the pain stop?

"I'll meet you back here at the buckboard in half an
hour," Jake told her. She nodded a wordless agreement
and watched as he disappeared inside the false-fronted
building.

Heaving a sigh, she turned and set off at a leisurely
pace. The streets were crowded with wagons and horses
even at that early hour of the day, the boardwalks already teeming with a varied mass of humanity. Prosper-
ity had returned to the city at long last, bringing with it
new hotels, churches and schools, stores, livery stables
and lumberyards, lawyers and photographers and char-
latans, and a thriving trade for the railroad. The main
focus was on cattle—the old trails were once again
alive with the bellowing of longhorns and the moneyed
optimism of the ranchers. The railroad had successfully

revived Fort Worth's dream of becoming the "Queen of the Prairies."

Callie Rose wandered past the colorful storefronts, absently scrutinizing the merchandise displayed in the windows. She gave a preoccupied smile to all those who spoke to her, and she could summon only a mild interest even when she strolled inside the elegant, gilded splendor of the new Mansion Hotel. When she emerged outside again, she squinted against the sun's unrelenting brightness and headed back toward the saddlemaker's. She had traveled only a few steps when she stopped dead in her tracks.

"Dr. MacGregor?" She gasped, her eyes widening in disbelief. A man walking along the boardwalk on the opposite side of the street looked amazingly like Ian's kinsman. Of course, she had caught only a glimpse of him, and it was difficult to be certain at that distance, but still . . .

With her heart racing, she hurried to make her way across the wide, dusty street. The object of her pursuit was clad in a black serge suit, and he wore a black bowler on his head. She tried her best to keep him in her sight as she dodged the steady stream of wagons, buggies, and horsemen. By the time she finally reached the other side, the man had disappeared into the crowd.

"Damnation," she swore underneath her breath, then told herself with a frown that her mind was playing tricks on her. Ewan MacGregor was thousands of miles away in Inverness. She had only conjured him up because of Martha's visit yesterday.

Feeling incredibly foolish, she crossed the street again and continued on her way to meet Jake. He was waiting for her in the buckboard, his new saddle in the back.

"See anything interesting?" he asked lazily while she climbed up to take her place beside him.

"Plenty," she retorted. Her eyes strayed back toward the spot where she had last seen Dr. MacGregor's lookalike.

"Well, let's get to it," said Jake. With an expert flick of the reins, he urged the horse away from the boardwalk and soon headed the wagon due west.

Callie Rose said very little on the homeward journey. Once back at the ranch, she changed into a pair of Clay's trousers and one of her own white lawn blouses. J. D. would probably rake her over the coals if he caught her "parading around in man's britches"—he claimed it wasn't decent—but she was willing to take the risk.

She hurried outside and across the yard to the stock barn. The long, tin-roofed bunkhouse next to it was empty, waiting for the need to take on extra hands in the fall. There was another barn for storing hay nearby, and two split-rail corrals. The place looked deserted at the moment. Sam and Clay had ridden off with their father immediately after breakfast to check on the herd, Jake was already trying out his new saddle, and Billy was in the barn, inspecting the day-old colt.

"Where are you going?" he asked when Callie Rose stepped inside and fetched her saddle from the tack room.

"I thought Guinevere could use some exercise," she replied, carrying the saddle to the stall where a beautiful, dapple-gray mare stood whinnying softly at her approach.

"I always did think that was a strange name for a horse," Billy commented wryly.

"It didn't seem so strange when I was twelve," she said, her eyes sparkling at the memory. She had read a story about King Arthur, and in the process had found herself carried away to a time of chivalrous knights and damsels in distress. It had all made quite an impression on a young girl. Maybe that was why she had liked Scotland so much. And why she had begun to feel at home within the walls of Castle MacGregor . . .

"You want me to come with you?" her brother offered. He was concerned by the sudden shadow he'd seen crossing her face.

"I'd be glad of the company," she admitted, relieved that he was the one who had remained behind. Billy was the least likely to pry, and the most likely to listen if she felt the need to confide. She pulled the cinch tight and looked up to see that he was already fetching his own saddle. "Billy?"

"Yes?"

"Why haven't you or any of the others married yet?" she asked on sudden impulse, then watched as his mouth curved into a slow, crooked smile. His brown eyes were alight with humor when he moved past her to the next stall and lifted his saddle to the back of an Appaloosa stallion.

"I guess none of us have been roped by the right girl yet."

"What about the women you've . . . the ones you've been acquainted with? I mean, what will happen to them once you do find the right one?" She adjusted the stirrups and settled the flaps, all the while feigning only a casual interest in the subject.

"I don't know." It wasn't a heartless answer, just an honest one.

"If you, or Jake or Clay or Sam, found out you were going to be a father, would you marry the woman who was carrying your child?"

"This isn't your way of telling me you're—?" Billy demanded, his eyes widening in sudden, brotherly dread.

"No!" She colored and gave a vigorous shake of her head. "No, confound it! I'm just asking a simple question!"

"Well now, I can't speak for the others, but my answer's yes. What kind of man would I be if I let my own child be born a bastard?" He said nothing more on the subject as he led the Appaloosa out of the stall.

Callie Rose felt sick inside again. Her blue eyes clouding with despair, she hesitated only a moment before following with Guinevere.

She and Billy rode down to the river, following its tree-lined banks for a while before pausing to allow their horses to drink long and thirstily. The heat was as oppressive as ever, but staying within the shade helped a great deal. After they had spent a few quiet moments at the water's edge, they headed out across the open range.

When they rode back toward home a little more than an hour later, their horses were covered with sweat and they were both looking forward to the prospect of a visit to the water pump in the front yard.

"Pa will skin us alive for taking off in the middle of the day," remarked Billy, though without any real trepidation.

"We've been skinned for worse. And less." Callie Rose sighed. She looked ahead as they neared the ranch, her eyes narrowing as they fell upon the men gathered beside the larger of the two corrals. "It looks like they're all back."

"Not only that, but we've got company." He nodded significantly toward the group. Sure enough, Callie Rose realized as she made a quick count, there were five men instead of the expected four.

"I wonder who ... ?" she murmured, her voice trailing away while she frowned pensively to herself.

"Let's go find out," said Billy. He urged his mount to a canter.

Callie Rose touched her heels to the mare's flanks, keeping pace with her brother as they rode ever closer. It wasn't until she had reined Guinevere to a halt beside the corral, swung down from the saddle, and started leading the horse forward that she finally learned the identity of the man who had only minutes ago arrived at the Diamond L.

He stood tall and proud before the Buchanans. Callie Rose drew to an abrupt halt when realization hit her full force. Her eyes grew enormous while all the color drained from her face.

"Dear God!" She held her breath. It wasn't possible ...

But the impossible had happened. He was here. He was actually here.

The merest hint of a smile touched his lips when his gaze captured hers.

She shook her head in stunned disbelief. Her traitorous heart leapt wildly within her breast.

And the other five pairs of Buchanan eyes fastened on her.

❧ TWELVE ❧

Ian had come for her.

Feeling perilously light-headed, she blinked hard and struggled to regain control of her highly erratic breathing. Warmth and happiness and love flooded her body. For a moment, she forgot that he had betrayed her, forgot everything and everyone else. She wanted to run straight into his arms, but her legs were threatening to buckle beneath her. She stood as if rooted to the spot, her wide, luminous sapphire gaze traveling up and down the whole magnificent length of him.

He was the same Ian MacGregor she remembered— and yet he wasn't. This was the first time she had ever seen him wearing anything other than his usual Highland attire. Indeed, he seemed almost a stranger in his blue cotton shirt, denim trousers, cowboy boots, and tan Stetson. Yet he was as devilishly—breathtakingly— handsome as ever. And he was looking at her as though he couldn't wait to get his hands on her.

She trembled, her very soul taking flight while she yearned to cross the scant five feet separating them. But the sudden, horribly vivid memory of Elspeth's words brought her crashing back to earth. The pleasure of seeing him again quickly gave way to a renewed burst of righteous, vengeful fury. Damn his eyes, he had played her for a fool! He had broken her heart—and for that alone she could never forgive him.

"Callie Rose, Mr. MacGregor here says he's a friend of yours," J. D. put forth, with a grim expression. He and the four other Buchanan males were still watching her face closely. "And he claims he's come all the way from Scotland to see you."

Her pulse raced with dread as she looked to her father. The nightmare had become reality; the moment of truth had finally arrived. Her first inclination was to deny any acquaintance with Ian at all. But she knew J. D. and her brothers would still suspect otherwise, and it would be extremely difficult to hold fast to a denial with the arrogant rogue standing right there before their eyes. He obviously hadn't told them anything yet. God willing, maybe there was a way she could keep the worst of it from them.

"Yes, I— Cousin Martha and I met him when we were in Inverness," she replied, her voice only a trifle unsteady. She shifted her gaze back to Ian's—and caught a glimpse of what she could have sworn was pain in their fathomless green depths. "I did not expect to see you again, Mr. MacGregor," she murmured. Acutely conscious of her family's scrutiny, she battled the impulse to swing back up into the saddle and ride away.

"Did you not?" Ian parried in a low, vibrant tone that sent a shiver dancing down her spine. He leisurely reached up and tugged the hat from his head now. The sun lit gold in the thick, richly hued darkness of his hair, while his eyes darkened to jade and burned across into hers. "I told you a MacGregor always holds what is his."

She groaned inwardly, dismayed to feel hot, telltale color staining her cheeks. His words had effectively killed all hope of concealing the awful truth.

"What the hell's that suppose to mean?" Clay demanded angrily, then rounded on his sister. "What's he talking about, Callie Rose?"

"I—" She tried to answer, but could not.

"Somebody had better do some explaining," Sam asserted, his own voice holding a discernible edge.

"Maybe it ought to be this foreigner," drawled Jake. Hooking his thumbs in the front waistband of his trousers, he eyed Ian narrowly.

"Callie Rose?" Billy's forehead creased into a deep frown of perplexity as he looked to her for enlightenment.

"The truth, girl," J. D. ordered. His eyes glittered dully when they moved back to her face.

"I . . . the truth is, I . . ." She stammered indecisively, still wavering between confession and at least a partial denial. Her own gaze kindled with fiery resentment as she glared at the man who had hurt her more than anyone had ever hurt her before. *Why did I have to go and fall in love with him?*

"Who the hell are you?" Clay demanded. He stepped menacingly toward Ian. "What right do you—?"

"I am your brother-in-law, Mr. Buchanan," Ian declared, with another ghost of a smile. His green eyes brimmed with ironic humor. "Aye, Callie Rose is my wife."

His announcement was met by a long moment of

stunned silence. All eyes turned to Callie Rose once more. She swallowed hard, cursed the tremor that shook her, and shot Ian a murderous look.

"I'm *not* your wife!" she retorted hotly.

"By damn, I want the truth!" J. D. ground out.

"It is the truth!" she cried.

Her breasts rose and fell rapidly beneath the delicate white cotton of her blouse, and she was at present unaware of the way the mere sight of her in the tight, formfitting trousers sent desire, furious and white-hot, coursing through Ian's body.

It had been several long weeks since he had last held her in his arms . . . more than a whole blasted month of searching for her by day and burning for her each night. By all that was holy, he swore silently, he would make her pay for the hell she had put him through. But first, there was her family to be dealt with. And from the look of them, he'd do well to call upon what he had learned in his boxing days at Cambridge.

"He isn't really my husband!" Callie Rose exclaimed, her voice rising on a shrill note of panic. "Our marriage isn't legal!"

" 'Tis legal," Ian decreed, with maddening calm.

"Only in Scotland!" she retorted.

"No, sweet vixen, in America as well." His smile this time was real and warm and perfectly devastating. "It has been duly recorded in both our countries."

"Did you or did you not get yourself hitched?" J. D. demanded impatiently, his gaze slicing back to his daughter.

"Yes, but—"

"Why in tarnation didn't you tell me about all this before now?"

"Because I had no intention of ever seeing him again!" She drew in a deep, shuddering breath and felt hot tears stinging against her eyelids. "You might as well know the whole story! *Ian MacGregor kidnapped me!* He imprisoned me in his castle and then he—he forced me to marry him!"

"The hell you say!" Jake and Billy burst out in near perfect unison. Clay and Sam, the nearest to Ian, already had their hands balled into fists when their father snapped a warning.

"Hold on, damn it!" There was barely controlled fury in his own eyes when he turned to Ian again. "Well, MacGregor? What have you got to say for yourself?"

"Only that I've come to fetch my wife home."

"You yellow-bellied sonofabitch!" growled Clay, his temper flaring to a dangerous level. His brothers looked every bit as ready to attack, all of them tensed and waiting for a sign from J. D.

"I'll never go back!" Callie Rose vowed passionately. "You lied to me, you bastard! You betrayed me, you betrayed Elspeth and your own son! I hate you, Ian MacGregor! I loathe and despise you, and—"

"Believe what you will of me, Callie Rose MacGregor, you are *still* my wife," he reminded her in a tone laced with steel.

"I want a divorce!"

"There will be no divorce."

"Then I'll get an annulment!"

" 'Tis a little late for that, is it not, lass?" He challenged her softly.

She gasped as though she had been struck. Her face crimsoned, her eyes flying wide.

And then all hell broke loose.

"That's torn it, you bastard!" Clay pronounced through tightly clenched teeth.

He was the first to make a go at Ian, but Jake and Sam were hot on his heels. The three Buchanans cared little about outnumbering their mutual opponent. Whenever one would fall beneath Ian's skillful defense, another would be there to take his place. Billy, meanwhile, remained at his sister's side, his perceptive gaze seeing a lot more than the others'.

Callie Rose watched the scene in horror. A sharp, breathless cry broke from her lips when she saw Jake land a punishing blow to the clean-shaven ruggedness of Ian's chin.

"Stop them!" she impulsively entreated her father. She rushed forward to grab his arm, the tears spilling over from her lashes now. "You've got to make them stop! They'll kill him!"

"Thought you hated him."

"I do, but that doesn't mean— For heaven's sake, you can't let this go on any longer!"

"It looks to me like he's doing well enough for himself," observed J. D., his eyes full of begrudging admiration as he watched his new son-in-law deflect yet another blow. Clay, fed up with the way things were going, suddenly tackled Ian to the ground.

"Damn it, Clay Buchanan, fight fair!" Callie Rose cried indignantly. She would have thrown herself in the middle of the skirmish, but her father's hand shot out to grasp her wrist.

"All right." He acquiesced with the merest hint of a smile tugging at his lips. "Maybe it *would* be better if we let him live." Releasing Callie Rose, he strode unhurriedly to where he had left his horse's reins tied to the uppermost rail of the corral, drew his rifle from its scabbard behind the saddle, and fired a single blast into the air. "Enough!" he directed in a booming voice nearly as loud as the preceding gunshot.

Jake and Sam obeyed immediately, but Clay needed an extra dose of persuasion. While his two brothers and Ian climbed to their feet, he seized advantage of the opportunity to launch yet another assault. Ian, however, dodged the younger man's fist entirely and sent him sprawling facedown upon the cracked, sunbaked earth.

"By thunder, I said enough!" J. D. reiterated. He scowled as Clay picked himself up off the ground, and, swearing roundly, moved away.

Dashing at her tears, Callie Rose looked back to Ian. His handsome face was only slightly bruised and battered, but it was enough to make her heart ache. And judging from the dangerous light in his eyes, he intended to make other parts of her ache as well.

"Come on, MacGregor," said J. D., starting for the house now. "I want to hear your side of the story."

"*His* side doesn't matter!" Callie Rose protested, with great feeling.

"You'll have your turn soon enough," her father told her.

"Aye. You will indeed," promised Ian. He bent and retrieved his hat from the ground, slapped it against the powerful hardness of his thigh, and gave her one last long, thoroughly unsettling look before following her father into the house.

She felt her throat constrict in renewed alarm. Still reeling from all that had happened in the past few minutes, she was scarcely aware of the fact that Billy stood behind her. He hadn't spoken at all during the fight, but he did so now.

"Do you love him?"

"No!" she denied a bit too vehemently.

She turned to see that Jake, Clay, and Sam were leading all seven of the horses over to the water trough near the barn. She had expected them to rant and rave at her, to scold her for keeping the truth from them, but instead they seemed intent upon avoiding her. For the moment, anyway.

"Oh, Billy, I—I don't know what to do!" she acknowledged with a heavy, ragged sigh. "I was hoping Ian would never find me!"

"I'm not surprised he did."

"How the devil am I going to get rid of him?"

"Are you really so sure you want to?" he asked, searching her face again. He knew her better than any of the others.

"Of course I'm sure!" she proclaimed. But she was unable to look him squarely in the eye. "After what he did—" She broke off, reluctant to disclose the true extent of Ian's crimes, even to Billy. "You heard what he said. He means to take me back with him!"

"Well, then, guess I'll have to shoot him for you."

"Confound it, Billy, I'm serious!" She whipped the hat from her head, and directed a worried, wrathful glare toward the house. "I wonder what lies he's telling J. D.," she muttered.

"I don't think Pa's going to be able to settle this for you," opined Billy, his mouth curving into a faint smile. He removed his own hat, ran a hand through his damp blond hair, and headed off to join his brothers. "Sooner or later, baby sister, we've all got to learn to stand on our own two feet."

Callie Rose frowned after him. Her emotions were in a veritable uproar, and her mind was filled with too many conflicting thoughts to be trusted.

'Tis legal. Those two words returned to haunt her. If they were true, then the situation was even more complicated than she had counted on. And under the law, Ian MacGregor would have every right to take her back to Scotland with him. By force, if necessary.

The thought provoked another shiver. She told herself it was from outrage and nothing else. Absolutely— positively—*nothing* else.

She waited for what seemed like hours. Finally, her father appeared at the front door to summon her inside. Feeling more nervous than she'd ever admit, she marched up the steps and across the porch into the house.

Ian was standing at the window when she entered the parlor. She had little doubt that he had been watching her. Her eyes flashed their brilliant, deep blue fire when they encountered the penetrating steadiness of his.

"Sit down," J. D. instructed her, giving a curt nod toward the sofa.

"I'd rather stand." She lifted her head to a proud, defiant angle and angrily folded her arms beneath her breasts.

"She was ever disobedient with me as well," Ian remarked, his deep-timbred voice brimming with wry amusement.

"*You* never had the right to order me about!" she shot back.

"Yes, he did," her father contended disloyally. "Fact is, he still does."

"What?" she gasped, her eyes widening in horrified disbelief. "Surely you're not—?"

"Hold your horses," J. D. cut her off. "We're going to have this out before we set anything in stone." He moved to take up a stance before the fireplace and frowned sternly at Ian, then Callie Rose again. "Now both of you, sit down."

Callie Rose obeyed this time, though with an ill grace. Plopping down upon the sofa, she watched as Ian sauntered forward to take a seat in the chair opposite. He bent his tall frame downward and set his hat on the table beside the chair. She caught her breath when he turned his piercing, gold-flecked emerald gaze upon her once more.

"You should not have run away, my love," he said quietly.

"I'm not your love!"

"First things first, damn it!" snapped J. D. He looked to his daughter. "Ian tells me—"

"*Ian?*" she echoed resentfully. "Hell's bells, the two of you got to be friends awfully fast, didn't you?"

"I swear, girl, I'll tan your hide if you don't let me get on with this!" her father threatened in a low growl.

"That particular honor falls to me now," Ian pointed

out dryly. His eyes held a dangerous light as they raked over his beautiful, recalcitrant bride.

"If you dare to try it, you black-hearted bastard, I'll—" she started to counter.

"Pipe down!" J. D. bellowed, his weather-beaten features reddening furiously. His words had the desired effect of silence, at least momentarily. "By damn, Callie Rose, MacGregor has owned up to what he did! He told me about the blasted feud, and about how he carried you off!"

"Did he indeed?" She challenged J. D. with bitter sarcasm, her eyes blazing anew. "Did he also tell you how he lied to me and deceived me? Confound it, J. D., I didn't want to marry him, but he forced me into it! We struck a bargain, and he double-crossed me!"

"Did anybody hold a gun to your head?" her father demanded harshly.

"No, but—"

"Then what you did, you did of your own free will."

"It wasn't like that! Ian MacGregor told me that if I'd go through with the handfasting, he'd let me leave!"

"The way I understand it, this 'handfasting' was a real, honest-to-God wedding. Is that the right of it—or not!"

"Not exactly," she answered, with a heavy sigh. She refused to look at Ian now, and a dull, guilty blush crept up to her face when she explained to her father, "It's supposed to be sort of a—a betrothal."

"You stood before witnesses and said you were his wife, didn't you?"

"Yes."

"Sounds like a wedding to me."

"There wasn't a parson there!" she hastened to point out.

"Still, you gave your word," he observed inflexibly.

"Yes, but I never intended to keep it!"

She regretted the confession as soon as it rolled off her tongue. With an inward groan of dismay, she watched her father's expression grow cold and distant.

"You gave your word."

"Aye, she gave her word." Ian intervened now. Loving her as he did, he could not help rising to her defense. His handsome features took on a grim look when he told his father-in-law, "But the fault is mine, not hers. If you're of a mind to place blame, Mr. Buchanan, you'd best cast your eyes in my direction."

"Hell, yes, I'll cast them in your direction!" J. D. agreed testily. "You deserve to be horsewhipped for what you did to my girl, and by thunder, I'm just the man to do it! But right here and now, we've got to face facts. What's done is done. The two of you are married, and I'll be hanged if I can figure out how to untangle this mess." He sent Callie Rose another paternal, disapprobative scowl. "You should have told me about this when you first got home."

"I know, and I'm sorry! But I was hoping— Oh, never mind what I was hoping!" she cried in exasperation, then flung a suspicious glare toward Ian. "You can't trust a word he says! Just because he claims our marriage is legal—"

"You can examine the records if you like," Ian suggested, with infuriating equanimity.

"I'll do that!" she retorted.

"Why did you leave him?" J. D. suddenly demanded. He knew the answer already, but he wanted to hear it from her. And he wanted his son-in-law to hear it as well. The sooner they got it all out in the open, the sooner they could make up.

"Because he . . ." Callie Rose began.

Her voice trailed away when she once again found herself filled with an inexplicable reluctance to expose him as the scoundrel he really was. Looking away, she was acutely conscious of his eyes upon her. Another sharp pain gripped her heart. On the one hand, she longed to be able to understand what had happened, while on the other, she wanted to make him pay for his sins. And there were plenty of those.

"Isn't it obvious?" she answered her father at last, masking her confusion with an indignant tone. "After everything he's done, he is the last man in the world I'd ever want for a husband!"

"I'm the last man in the world who will ever *be* your husband," Ian decreed.

"Is it true what he said about an annulment?" J. D. then startled her by asking. He regarded her steadily as she crimsoned anew and nodded an unwilling affirmation. "Then it might also be true that I'm finally going to become a grandfather." The prospect made his gaze warm with the first real pleasure he'd known in a long time.

"No!" Callie Rose denied, her own eyes growing enormous within the flushed, delicate oval of her face.

" 'Tis possible," said Ian. "And highly probable."

"But, we—we were only together a few days!" she stammered weakly.

"A single night would have been enough," he noted, his mouth twitching.

"Well?" her father prompted her. "Can you say for sure that you're not—?"

"I can't believe you're asking me this!" Both furious and profoundly embarrassed, she stole another quick glance at Ian. He didn't appear at all uncomfortable with the subject at hand. No, indeed, his green eyes were virtually dancing with amusement. "All right, damn it, yes! I can say for sure!" she lied. She hadn't wanted to think about it these past several weeks. . . . Good heavens, what if *that* was the reason she hadn't yet gotten her monthly flow? The thought tumbled her into even further chaos.

"Well, then, I don't know exactly how yet, but we're going to have to work this out. One way or another," J. D. pronounced in conclusion. "Until we do, MacGregor will stay on here at the Diamond L."

"You can't be serious!" Callie Rose protested. She sprang up from the sofa and faced her father with an angry, incredulous expression. "Please, you—"

"There's never been a divorce in the Buchanan family," he remarked somberly. "And being raised on the Good Book, I've always held to the belief that marriage vows are sacred. But God knows, your marriage didn't come about like it should have." He paused and shook his head. "I can't say I'm proud of you for breaking your word, Callie Rose. MacGregor was wrong to do what he did, but you still shouldn't have made that bargain. And you shouldn't have run off like a coward."

"I had no choice!"

"You had a choice," he disputed, still wishing she

had confided in him sooner. "But I'll make you a fair deal: If after a week's time you still want your freedom, I'll do whatever it takes to see that you get it."

"There will be no divorce," Ian reiterated. His eyes gleamed dully as he drew himself up to his full— ultimately superior—height. "Callie Rose is my wife. I'll never let her go."

"You have yourself a deal!" she told her father, shooting Ian a triumphant look. "You've wasted a lot of time and money coming to Texas, *Lord* MacGregor! You'll soon be on your way back to Scotland, and I'll be able to forget I ever had the misfortune of knowing you!"

"You could never forget, Rosaleen," Ian said softly. He smiled, his gaze brimming with a familiar combination of desire and humor. "And is it not said here that one should never count one's chickens before they are hatched?"

"It's time I left you two alone for a while," J. D. declared, fighting back a smile of his own.

"No!" Callie Rose exclaimed. Her pulse leapt in alarm. "I don't want to be alone with him!"

"He's your husband, girl. For now, anyway. I don't think it's too much to ask for you to sit down and hear him out. Could be you'll learn a thing or two."

"I've already learned more than I ever wanted to know!" she hissed.

"I seem to recall that you were an apt and willing pupil," quipped Ian, his gaze holding a silent challenge. Another faint, mocking smile touched his lips at the sight of her fiery blush.

"You're a Buchanan, damn it," J. D. reminded his

daughter as he headed for the doorway. "And no Buchanan ever backs down from a fight."

"If he lays a hand on me, I'll kill him!" she vowed.

Though it was on the tip of his tongue to say that she'd be more likely to kill him if he didn't, Ian moved back to the window with deceptive nonchalance. He waited until J. D. had gone, then turned to face the woman who had led him an even merrier chase than he had anticipated. Torn between the urge to turn her across his knee and the much more agreeable impulse to sweep her into his arms, he forced himself to refrain from either course of action.

He was determined to win her back. By all that was holy, he would woo her with a vengeance! He would make her accept him in spite of what she believed, in spite of her willingness to think him a man of so little honor.

"You might as well leave now," she told him in a low, simmering tone. Her fingers tightened upon the back of the chair he had just vacated, her eyes ablaze with mingled pain and fury. "I don't know why you came, but it won't do any good. I'll never go back with you!"

"I came because I love you."

"The hell you do."

"Why did you leave without so much as a word?" He folded his arms across his chest, his manner at once authoritative and benevolent.

"Ask Elspeth MacGregor!"

"I did," His gaze smoldered at the memory.

"Oh? And what did she say? Did she tell you that she brought Jamie to the castle the morning you left for Edinburgh? Damn your eyes, Ian MacGregor," she stormed hotly, "you were with her for seven years. You let your own son be born a bastard!"

"Jamie is not my son," he stated in a low and level tone.

"I'm not at all surprised to hear you deny it! She said you accused her of—of falseness. Though how you could expect her to remain true to you while suffering such cruel treatment is beyond me!"

"I have never loved Elspeth. No, nor treated her with anything other than respect." At least until he had learned of her treachery, he added silently. Elspeth had borne the full brunt of his wrath; never again would she seek to cause trouble for him. The threat of an arranged marriage had proven quite effective.

"I don't want to hear . . ." The words trailed away as she flung away from the chair. Her brow furrowed with uncertainty, her mind churning with renewed doubts about Elspeth's claims. She swept across to the sideboard and grabbed the decanter of whiskey. It wasn't until after she had poured some of the amber-colored liquid into a glass that she remembered her intense dislike of the stuff. With a muttered oath, she slammed the decanter back down and rounded on Ian again. "I'll never forgive you for what you've done! *Never!*"

"Is your anger for Elspeth's suffering—or your own?" He challenged her in a maddeningly complacent tone.

"Both!" Her face flamed as she said accusingly, "You took her to your bed. By thunder, you did to her what you did to me!"

"No, sweet vixen, I did not. But even if I had, you

would have driven all memory of it from my mind." He started toward her now, the urge to touch her too powerful to deny any longer. "You should not have left without giving me a chance to explain. Aye, and Peter was none too pleased at spending an entire morning locked away in the stables," he remarked, a faint smile of irony playing about his lips.

"It served him right for being so loyal to *you!*" Another tremor of alarm shook her as he drew closer. But, recalling her father's admonition about the courage of the Buchanans, she proudly stood her ground. "I'm not afraid of you!" she insisted, her outward show of bravado in direct contrast to the trepidation within. "We're not in Scotland now. You can't intimidate me here. All I have to do is scream, and my brothers will come running!"

"Are you not capable of fighting your own battles, Callie Rose MacGregor?"

"Don't call me that! And you know damned good and well that I can—"

"Tell me, lass," he interrupted, with a frown, "why it is that you are trying to be a man."

He came to halt mere inches away, towering above her. His gaze darkened as it traveled boldly—intimately—over her enticing curves. The borrowed trousers she wore stretched tight across her hips and molded every inch of her long, shapely legs. The delicate white fabric of her blouse clung to her breasts, offering a provocative hint of the rose-tipped peaks beneath her chemise.

" 'Tis an impossible task you've set yourself," observed Ian, his eyes searing down into hers. "And did I not teach you that it is far more pleasurable to be what God intended? You are a woman, and one fashioned perfectly for me."

"Why, you conceited bastard!" she ground out.

"I can see you need to be reminded of a good many things."

He reached for her at last. She gasped and tried to move away, but it was too late. Her whole body trembled when his strong arms gathered her close, and even though she raised her hands to push at his chest, he held her captive with very little effort. Before she could do anything more than utter a breathless cry of protest, he brought his lips crashing down upon the parted softness of hers.

She melted against him, all the love and longing in her heart prompting her surrender. He kissed her deeply, hungrily, his mouth devouring hers. One of his hands swept down to her hips, and his fingers curled with a fierce possessiveness about the firmly rounded curve of her bottom, displayed to maddening, delectable perfection by the pants she wore.

The desire that had been simmering within him for the past four weeks blazed tempestuously to life; he wanted nothing more than to take her right then and there. It was much the same for her. She had ached for him these many days and nights, trying to convince herself that she hated him, while at the same time recalling every kiss, every caress and stroke and endearment he had bestowed upon her. The memory of his lovemaking had made her toss and turn restlessly in the loneliness of her bed. . . .

She was on fire again now. A low moan of passion

rose in her throat. Raising her arms to entwine about his neck, she pressed her body into even more intimate contact with the virile, hard-muscled warmth of his. Her mouth welcomed the hot invasion of his tongue, and she returned his kisses with an answering fervor that was every bit as intense as his own.

And then she remembered Elspeth.

"No!" she cried hoarsely, tearing her lips from his. "No, damn you! Let me go!"

She struggled violently within his grasp. His arms tightened about her, until she thrust a knee upward in a vengeful, albeit not entirely successful attempt to inflict pain upon his manhood (It struck her as a fitting retaliation for his betrayal.) He bit out a curse and seized her arms in a punishing grip, holding her captive while his eyes, filled with a near savage gleam, bored down into the furious resentment of hers.

"By heaven, woman, I should thrash you well and proper for what you've put me through!" he told her, his handsome face thunderous.

"It's no more than you deserved!" Glaring defiantly up at him, she ignored the traitorous fluttering of her heart and vowed, "That was the last kiss you'll ever force on me, Ian MacGregor!"

"Force has never been necessary."

"Oooh, how I hate you!" she said, seething.

"Hate me if you will," he replied, his eyes gleaming dully as his tanned, rugged features became inscrutable. "But know that you are mine. Now and forever." He released her with such unexpected swiftness that she stumbled backward against the sideboard. She clutched at the edge of it for support, her breasts heaving while she fought down sudden tears.

"Why didn't you tell me about Elspeth?" she demanded impulsively. Her lips still tingled from his kiss, and she rubbed at her arms where his hands had scorched her skin even through the protection of her sleeves. *"Why?"* she repeated, her voice threatening to break.

"Elspeth's story was not mine to tell." He was sorely tempted to elaborate, but something within him prevented it. No, he mused to himself as his gaze darkened anew, when she came to him it would have to be in spite of everything. In spite of Elspeth's lies and her own damnable pride. He would be sure of her love. And by all that was holy, never again would she doubt him.

"Aren't you at least going to try to explain what happened between the two of you?"

"Would you believe me if I did?"

"No," she answered truthfully. "Probably not."

"Could you not have trusted me, Callie Rose?" he asked, his own voice slightly raw with emotion.

"How could I trust you when I—I didn't even know you?" she responded, with a heavy, ragged sigh. Her eyes clouded with confusion once more. Maybe, just maybe, she shouldn't have been so ready to believe the worst of him. "Everything happened so quickly. . . . One minute you were holding me prisoner to settle a feud I didn't even know existed, and the next we were married. We're *still* little more than strangers!"

"We know each other better than many who have been together a lifetime." The merest hint of a smile touched his lips before he frowned again. "But no matter what you believed, you had no right to steal away like a thief in the night."

"You're a fine one to be throwing stones!" she shot back. "And after everything you'd done to me, I had every right to leave! Elspeth's visit made me realize that—that I had been a blind, weak-willed fool!" If only that were truly all she had realized.

"You were never weak willed," murmured Ian, his green eyes aglow.

"It doesn't matter now! The only thing left to be done is to end a marriage that was a terrible mistake from the outset. Though I'm not even sure it was a marriage at all!"

"You are my wife." He battled the impulse to remind her of it in a way even she could not deny. *Patience*, he cautioned himself. "You hold my heart in your hands, you bear my name—"

"I don't want your name!" She raised her chin in a gesture of proud defiance once more, her eyes flashing with their usual spirit. "You heard what my father said. One week. One week, and then I'll get a divorce!"

She expected him to argue, to repeat his vow of eternal bondage, but he did not. Instead, he sauntered across the room, took up his hat, and turned back to her with an expression that struck fear in her own heart.

"Anything can happen in a week's time," he warned quietly. "Aye, anything at all."

Raising the hat to his head, he tugged the front brim low and gave his wide-eyed, reluctant bride one last hard look. Then he left her alone.

Callie Rose stared breathlessly after him, her pulse racing and an alarming heat filling her body. She felt branded by his gaze as well as his kiss. . . . The memory of it made her groan aloud.

Casting an agitated glance heavenward, she headed back to the sofa and sank weakly down upon it. Her eyes swept closed for a brief moment, and she released a long, pent-up sigh.

Why, oh, why did he have to come? she lamented silently. Given a little more time, she might have been able to forget. . . .

Now and forever. Damn him. Damn him straight to hell. It was painfully obvious that he was determined to bedevil her again. But she wasn't the same naive, unsuspecting virgin he had dealt with before. No indeed, she was sadder and wiser, and definitely not a "spinster" any longer. He had seen to that. Yes, by thunder, she mused bitterly, he had brought about the transformation on all three counts with a thoroughness that could not be undone.

And still her heart cried out for him.

Another groan of dismay escaped her lips. Drawing herself up from the sofa, she quickly crossed to the window. Her gaze clouded anew when it fell upon Ian, who was striding toward the barn to fetch his things. He moved with the same easy, masculine grace she had noticed that first day when he had taken her to Castle MacGregor. That first day when he had swept her into his arms and kissed her—and taught her the meaning of passion.

"One week," she whispered. God help her, it was going to be the longest week of her life.

❧ THIRTEEN ❧

That first day proved to be even more of an ordeal than Callie Rose had expected—so much so that she wondered how she could possibly endure six more just like it.

She managed to avoid Ian (and her father) for a while by slipping out to the barn a short time after their "discussion" in the parlor. Quickly saddling her horse, she rode off alone to the familiar peacefulness of the river again. She stayed there until well past time for the noon meal; her appetite was certainly showing no immediate signs of improvement.

Upon her return to the ranch, she was surprised to discover that her unwanted guest was gone.

"Said he had some business in town," Billy revealed. He, Sam, Clay, and Jake were on the front porch, taking a well-earned break from their chores. J. D. was nowhere in sight at the moment.

"Business?" Callie echoed, with a frown of bemusement. Having already unsaddled and rubbed down her horse, she tugged off her hat and climbed the steps to join her brothers in the shade. She was hot and tired, and so emotionally on edge that she knew it would take very little to set her off again. "Did he say when he'd be back?"

"Nope." This came from Sam. He had always been a man of few words, but he did bestir himself enough to demand, "Is MacGregor really your husband?"

"Yes. I mean, no. Hell's bells, *I don't know*!" she uttered, with a heavy sigh, throwing herself down into the old wooden porch swing beside Billy.

"Sam has a problem with his love life, too," Jake said with a drawl. He stood leaning negligently against one of the columns, his eyes full of a teasing light when they shot to his older brother. "He can't keep his women straight."

"You're a fine one to talk," Clay piped up. He settled back in his chair and stretched his long legs before him. A slow, crooked grin spread across his face. "You've got yourself an even dozen gals looking to put their brand on you. And I'll bet you ten dollars cash money you're the first one to get roped."

"You're on," Jake replied, with a nod. "It'll be the easiest ten dollars I ever made."

"Confound it, can't you talk about something else?" Callie Rose snapped, her temper flaring at the sound of their congenial banter. She found nothing the least bit amusing about marriage—or the studied avoidance of it.

"All right," agreed Sam, frowning sternly down at her from where he stood near the door. "Why don't you start off by telling us what you're going to do about that funny-talking greenhorn you may or may not be married to?"

"He isn't funny-talking," she shot back. "He's a

Scotsman. And there isn't anything I *can* do. Not yet, anyway. J. D. said he can stay a week."

"You want us to light a fire under him?" Clay offered. Though he was speaking figuratively, he wouldn't have thought twice about making the threat a reality. He was always ready to right a wrong, especially when the wrong had been done to his sister.

"No," she said, shaking her head. "You know as well as I do that J. D. would never allow it."

"What happens at the end of the week?" Billy asked, his gaze full of compassion as he turned his head to look at her.

"I'll be able to get a divorce."

"A divorce?" Sam repeated in obvious disapproval. "No Buchanan's ever gotten divorced."

"Well then, I'll have to be the first!" she retorted defensively. "And how in tarnation is that any worse than what the four of you are doing? Everyone says the Buchanan brothers are the scourge of the county! At least Ian MacGregor married me before he took me to his bed!"

"Damn it, Callie Rose, it ain't right for a decent woman to talk about such things!" Clay scolded.

"Maybe I'm not so 'decent' after all!" She stood and confronted them with her blue eyes splendidly—righteously—ablaze. Indeed, she looked somewhat like an avenging angel—albeit a windblown one. "I'm no different than any other woman! We want to be treated with kindness and respect, to know that we're loved, to know that—that what a man shares with us, he shares with no one else. And all of you would do well to remember that the next time you promise a girl the moon and then leave her with nothing more than a broken heart!"

"Did that husband of yours do that?" Jake challenged her sharply.

"That's none of your business!"

"It's our business, right enough," Sam contended, his eyes narrowing. "He made it our business when he showed up here at the Diamond L."

"I say we ought to ride him out of Texas on a rail!" Clay suggested, with his usual bloodthirsty zeal.

"Don't be an idiot, boy," advised Billy.

"You call me 'boy' one more time, William Jeremiah Buchanan, and I'll beat the hell out of you!"

"Nobody's going to do any beating around here!" Callie Rose maintained, her voice rising perilously. "All we have to do is wait him out! And then he'll go on back to Scotland where he belongs, and everything will get back to the way it used to be around here!"

"You think it'll be that easy, do you?" Billy queried, with a faint smile in her direction.

"You know, MacGregor didn't look to me like the kind of man who'd let it go at that," murmured Jake.

"Just what the blazes *did* he do to make you run off after the two of you got hitched?" The question was put forth by the ever curious Clay.

"He—he still cared for another," Callie Rose stammered disconsolately, sinking back down onto the swing.

"You mean he was out tomcatting around while you—?" Clay demanded, already riled at the mere thought of it.

"No!" she hastily denied. Alarmed by the feral gleam

in her brother's eyes, she grew pale and shook her head again. "It wasn't that way at all!"

"Pa's coming," Billy announced, squinting toward the lone horseman approaching the ranch. "He's been over to check on the Widow Layne's stock again."

"Maybe our baby sister isn't the only one with marriage on her mind," Jake commented wryly.

"J. D. and the Widow Layne?" Callie Rose gasped in stunned disbelief.

"Why not?" said Sam, a glimmer of amusement in his eyes now. "He may be slowing down a bit, but he's still a Buchanan."

"Hell, don't ever tell him he's slowing down," Billy cautioned.

"I'll bet he doesn't marry her," Clay predicted cynically.

"How much are you willing to lose this time?" Jake was quick to challenge.

"Why do you have to treat everything with so little respect?" Callie Rose complained, her gaze filling with fire again. "The possibility of J. D. getting married isn't a laughing matter!"

Far from it, she added silently. It was difficult to imagine her father with a wife after he had spent so many years without female companionship—although, judging from the snippets of conversation she'd overheard, he hadn't exactly been pining away. *Ian wouldn't pine away, either,* an inner voice expounded gleefully. The thought sent a hot, powerful surge of jealousy through her. She told herself she had no right to it. But it was there just the same.

"And anyway," she added, turning a collectively reproachful look upon her brothers, "how can you sit around here and make jokes when our 'guest' is going to come riding up any minute now and—?"

"Leave him to us," counseled Jake, flashing her a smile of pure devilment. "We'll have him hightailing it back to Scotland so fast he won't know what hit him."

"First thing in the morning, I'll saddle ol' Beezlebub," Clay submitted as he drew himself up from the chair.

"No!" Callie Rose protested in wide-eyed alarm. "I swear, Clay Buchanan, if you dare—"

"Make up your mind." Sam cut her off impatiently, lifting his hat back to his head. "Either you want him gone or you don't."

"I want him gone, not *dead*!"

"We're not looking to kill him," Jake reassured her. "Just rattle him good."

"Billy, please!" She appealed to the most sensible of the four. "Don't let them do anything crazy!"

"I'm afraid you're asking the wrong man," he replied somberly. He stood and pulled her up beside him. "Pa's the only one who can rein them in."

"You made your bed, damn it, now you've got to lie in it," Sam asserted, still angry with her for having kept the truth from them all.

"She doesn't want to lie in it," Jake was obliging enough to point out. "That's why we've got to get rid of MacGregor."

Callie Rose colored furiously and opened her mouth to deliver a suitable retort, but her father was closing in fast. Jake, Sam, Billy, and Clay left her standing alone on the porch as they strode forward to greet the man who had always ruled his hard-won Texas kingdom, and his family, with an iron hand.

Anxious to avoid another interrogation, Callie Rose offered up a silent curse and whirled about to escape inside the house. She felt a sudden and desperate need for a bath. Hurrying upstairs, she fetched a change of clothing from her room and then returned to the bathroom situated on the ground floor near the kitchen. There was no need to heat water; the ground had soaked up so much of the sun's mercilessly broiling rays that the water she pumped into the polished metal tub was far from cold.

When she emerged again, she was feeling considerably refreshed and ready to face her father again. Her thoughts returned to Ian (they had never really strayed), and she wondered if he was back from town yet. Securing her long, damp tresses into another braid, she smoothed down the skirts of her gown—the same faded calico she had worn earlier—and set off in search of Elena.

The afternoon drifted toward evening, and still there was no sign of Ian.

J. D. and his sons called an end to the day's work and washed up for supper. Callie Rose wandered into the parlor after Elena had good-naturedly chased her out of the kitchen. A faint smile touched her lips as she crossed to the window and caught sight of her father and brothers gathered around the pump in the front yard. But the smile quickly faded when her gaze traveled farther, searching the vast, cloudless horizon for the outline of a lone rider.

Where the devil was he? she wondered, her silken

brow creasing into a troubled frown. Maybe he wasn't coming back at all . . . maybe he had believed her when she'd said that she hated him. If so, then all her problems would be solved. She would be spared six more days of anguish, and she could arrange for a divorce that much sooner. Surely it would be easier to obtain a formal separation if her husband simply up and disappeared . . . ?

A sudden, painful lump rose in her throat. Turning away from the window, she released a sigh and headed back toward the dining room. She was in the process of setting the table when she heard the front door open. Assuming that it was merely J. D. and her brothers coming inside for supper, she continued with her task. But she soon became aware of someone watching her. She looked up—and suffered a sharp intake of breath when her eyes encountered the steady, gleaming warmth of Ian's.

"My apologies, sweet vixen," he offered in a vibrant tone, his tall frame filling the doorway. "I hope you were not troubled by my absence."

"Where have—?" she started to question, only to break off and draw herself haughtily erect. "Not in the least!" she proclaimed, virtually slamming the last plate down upon the white linen tablecloth.

"Liar." His disarming smile belied the condemnation.

She cursed the way her knees weakened. Pretending complete indifference to his presence, she sailed back into the kitchen to help Elena transfer the bowls and platters of food to the table. She could have sworn she heard her husband's low chuckle behind her.

J. D. and her brothers materialized in her absence.

She frowned darkly when she emerged from the kitchen and discovered that her father had arranged for her to sit beside Ian. It occurred to her to voice an objection, a very heated one, but she knew it would do no good. And the last thing she wanted was to be drawn into a humiliating scene with Ian MacGregor as a witness.

He gallantly stood and held her chair for her. Although she glared up at him with something far less than gratitude, she nevertheless took a seat. She inhaled upon a soft gasp a moment later when Ian, resuming his place in the chair close to hers, allowed his hand to linger boldly upon the curve of her hip. A fiery blush stained her cheeks, and she cast a swift, anxious glance about the table to make certain his familiarity had gone unnoticed. The look she flung him promised retribution.

"I wouldn't mind hearing more about that feud," J. D. told Ian as he began filling his plate. His four sons were doing the same, and they were startled when he suddenly decreed, "But first, we'll say grace."

"Grace?" Clay blurted out, only to fall silent when confronted with one of his father's bone-chilling glowers.

"Seeing as how MacGregor's the guest," said J. D. "we'll let him do the honors." He looked back to Ian and challenged dryly, "You people do know how to pray, don't you?"

"Aye," Ian replied, with the merest hint of a smile. "We are not quite the heathens some would believe."

Callie Rose bowed her head and listened to him ask God's blessing upon the meal. The sound of his voice made her heart stir and her body grow embarrassingly warm, but she couldn't very well curse him while he was engaged in such a virtuous pursuit. Refusing to meet his gaze afterward, she took the bowl of mashed potatoes from his hands and passed them on to Jake.

"Now. About that feud . . ." J. D. prompted.

Ian was only too happy to comply. While his rebellious bride merely picked at her food, he ate heartily and regaled his father-in-law with tales of the bloody history of both the Buchanan and MacGregor clans. Even Callie Rose's brothers appeared far more interested than they should have been.

She simmered beside him, noting with angry resentment the way her whole family seemed to hang on his every word. She sat there as long as she could, feeling more and more that her allies were all being turned, however subtly and politely and with very little effort, against her. Finally she could bear it no longer. Rising abruptly from the table, she flung her napkin down and surrendered to the impulse to take flight.

"Damn it, girl, get back here!" J. D. called harshly after her.

"Let her go," Ian instructed in a calm, commanding manner.

The four Buchanan brothers exchanged a quick look of disbelief with one another, then sat in anticipatory silence, waiting for the inevitable to happen. No one ever told J. D. Buchanan what to do and got away with it. *No one.*

But it seemed there was a first time for everything. The tough old rancher shocked (and disappointed) his sons when he merely smiled and shook his head.

"By thunder," he remarked, "you might just be the man to tame her after all."

"Never doubt it, Mr. Buchanan," Ian said, his gold-flecked emerald gaze holding the promise of victory.

Callie Rose, meanwhile, had taken refuge on the front porch. She sat in the swing, her arms folded tightly across her chest as she toyed with the idea of going for another ride. It wasn't long before she heard her father, brothers, and husband entering the parlor for the customary evening drink.

Their voices drifted out to her through the open windows. She could easily discern which one was Ian's, and not only because he spoke with such a pleasant, distinctive brogue. He and J. D. certainly seemed to be getting along well. Too well. And why shouldn't they? she asked herself umbrageously. They were both proud and stubborn and overbearing, and there was the added bonus of Ian's title, though she wasn't even sure her father knew about that yet. Never mind that the man was an out-and-out rake. He was a husband, by thunder, the one thing J. D. had wanted most. Well, perhaps not as much as he wanted grandchildren . . . a whole passel of them, he had said. The thought only added to her quandary.

The setting sun had turned the sky into a blaze of color, but she was in no mood to appreciate it. Leaning back in the swing, she closed her eyes and heaved another audible sigh.

"Tha coltas ruisge oirre."

She started in alarm, her eyes flying wide as she looked up to see Ian smiling softly down at her from the doorway.

"I came out here to be alone," she told him. "And you know damned well I don't understand Gaelic!"

"It looks like rain," he translated, giving a nod toward the clouds looming on the far horizon. "We may well have storms before this night is through." He moved forward, and, without benefit of an invitation, took a seat on the swing beside her. The wooden slats creaked beneath his weight, and Callie Rose frowned in displeasure.

"You don't know anything at all about Texas weather." She started to rise, but she was reluctant to turn coward and run again. Besides, she mused with an irritated glance over her shoulder, J. D. was probably straining to hear every word they said. Sliding as far away from Ian as she could, she tucked a wayward strand of hair back into place and tried her best to ignore the erratic pounding of her heart. "It hardly ever rains this time of year."

"Not at all like the Highlands," he recalled for her.

"I'm surprised you can abide the heat here." *Heat.* She felt scorched by his body, even though they weren't touching at all.

"Have you not yet learned that we Scots are highly adaptable?" He allowed another brief smile to touch his lips.

"I suppose you'll be telling me next that you'd go through the fires of hell itself to get me back," she remarked, her voice full of bitter sarcasm.

"Aye, if it would make any difference."

"It wouldn't."

" 'Tis a beautiful place," he opined, changing the subject as his gaze swept across the vast, gently rolling prairie. "But do you never get lonely?"

"Lonely?" She stole a glance at his face, then hastily looked away again. "No, of course not." *Another lie.*

"What about your friends?"

"I have a few." Very few, she thought with an inward sigh. She'd never had much in common with other girls.

"Male or female?" His tone was light and teasing, but the look he turned upon her was deadly serious.

"You're not the only one with a mysterious past, Ian MacGregor," she said, taunting him. "For all you know, I've got an even dozen men lined up, just waiting for the moment when I'm a free woman again!"

"That is something you'll never be," he vowed unyieldingly.

"This little scheme of yours isn't going to work! And you're only asking for trouble—"

"Ah, but you are well worth the risk." His eyes burned down into hers.

"Did you tell Elspeth *she* was worth the risk, too?" she demanded acidly, her throat constricting.

"My conversations with Elspeth have been anything but pleasant."

"You probably don't do much 'talking,' is that it?" She leapt up from the swing and swept irefully across to the outer edge of the porch.

"You've lost weight, lass," observed Ian, frowning as he drew himself upright behind her. The faded, tight-fitting dress she wore revealed curves that were a bit less voluptuous than he remembered. And he remembered them well.

"What if I have?" retorted Callie Rose. "What possible concern is it of yours?"

"*You* are my concern," he ground out, closing the distance between them in two long, angry strides. His hands closed about her slender, uncorseted waist with near bruising force. He yanked her close. "By heaven, woman, why will you not face the truth? You were beginning to when Elspeth filled your head with her lies. Aye, you were near to it when I went away! Do you not think I have cursed myself a thousand times over for leaving you?"

"Keep away from me!" she warned in a furious undertone, struggling in his grasp while at the same time fighting desperately against the urge to surrender. She sliced a narrow, anxious glare toward the parlor windows. "My brothers will kill you if they see you!"

"And have you no desire to be a widow?" He challenged her mockingly.

"No! I— Damnation, let me go!" She was startled when he complied. Retreating a few shaky steps, she tilted her head back to meet his gaze squarely. "Maybe I *was* starting to—to feel something for you, but whatever it was is gone now! How could I care for a man who treated the mother of his own son so shamefully?" Though she kept her voice low, she was trembling with the combination of hurt and outrage, and a deep, secret yearning that would not go away.

"Jamie is not my son."

"Why do you keep trying to deny it? For heaven's sake, the child looks exactly like you!"

"A family resemblance, nothing more."

"A very *close* family!" She balled her hands into fists and planted them on her hips. "Next, I suppose you'll try telling me that his father is Dr. MacGregor, or maybe even your own brother, who's so conveniently God-knows-where at the moment!"

"You're not ready for the truth." His voice was whip-cord sharp, his gaze glinting coldly now. "Someday, Callie Rose MacGregor, you'll realize that no man travels halfway round the world for a woman he does not love."

"Please, just go away!" she entreated in a hoarse, ragged whisper. She folded her arms across her chest again and spun about, her own gaze clouding with pain. "Go back to Elspeth and leave me in peace!"

"I cannot do that." He came up behind and lifted his hands to her arms, pulling her gently back against him. "I love you," he spoke in a low, husky tone close to her ear. *"An comhnaidh."*

She shivered and caught her lower lip between her teeth. Closing her eyes, she battled a wave of desire so intense, so heart-stoppingly powerful, that she was in very real danger of saying to hell with pride and reason and honor. . . . More than anything, she wanted to turn and lose herself in his arms. She was only dimly aware of the continuing murmur of her family's voices; she could easily forget all about them and let Ian take her right there on the front porch.

But, much to her surprise, he broke the spell.

"I've little doubt that tomorrow will offer all manner of trial and tribulation," he remarked wryly, allowing no hint of the desire coursing through him like wildfire. It took every ounce of self-control he possessed to release her. "Good night, Lady MacGregor."

She said nothing in response. Her face flamed, and she struggled to regain control of her breathing. Plagued by an acute sense of disappointment, she listened as he walked back inside the house.

It wasn't much later when she decided to seek the coveted sanctuary of her room. She hurriedly climbed the stairs, only to stop short on her way toward the end of the landing. Her eyes widened in dismay as they fell upon Ian, who stood framed in the doorway of Sam's room. He casually raised his hands to begin unbuttoning his shirt.

"Your father was kind enough to offer me the room next to yours," he explained.

"Where's Sam?" she demanded, her whole body tensing in renewed alarm.

"I believe he's to share Billy's quarters for the duration of my visit." He freed the last button and slowly peeled off the shirt, a roguish smile playing about his lips. "Surely you're not troubled by the arrangement?" He challenged her softly.

"Why should I be?" she parried, with a remarkable composure. Her fiery blue eyes locked in silent combat with the deep, fathomless green of his. "You aren't such a fool that you'd try anything with my father and brothers in the house, are you?"

"Perhaps you'd do well to lock your door."

"Are you trying to frighten me?" Once again, she took refuge in her anger.

"I think you're more afraid of yourself than of me, my love," he told her, his fingers already moving to unfasten his trousers.

She gave him a venomous look. Then, forcing her eyes away from the bronzed, powerful hardness of his chest and arms, she moved past him to her own room.

But as soon as she had closed the door behind her, she leaned weakly back against it and gave a low groan.

Her uneasiness only worsened once she had undressed and slipped beneath the covers of her bed. She lay there in the gathering darkness, unable to refrain from listening to the sounds Ian made as he prepared to retire for the night. The walls had always been thin, but she had taken little notice of it before. She could hear the bedsprings creaking as he sat down . . . could hear his boots falling onto the floor as he drew them off . . . could hear him standing again to remove his trousers. It wasn't at all difficult to imagine him climbing naked into the bed.

Her body grew warm all over. She cursed her own wickedness and rolled angrily onto her side.

Yet sleep eluded her. She tossed and turned in a futile attempt to find a comfortable position. Her eyes traveled frequently to the door. Recalling Ian's "advice" about locking it, she felt another involuntary shiver dance down her spine. There was no lock. There had never been a need for one until now.

The night was turning out to be far worse than any she'd endured since coming home. She was painfully aware of the fact that Ian lay in the next room. He was so close that she could almost hear him breathing, so close that she could call out to him and put an end to her suffering, if only for a night.

God help her, would he make good on his veiled threat of intrusion? And what would she do if he did?

She rolled over again and punched at the unresisting softness of her pillow. *Six more days,* she thought, then muttered an oath.

❧ FOURTEEN ❧

Callie Rose overslept the next morning.

Chagrined when she awoke to find her room filled with a full blaze of sunlight, she flung back the covers and sprang from the bed. No storms had come in the night—*and no Ian.*

Stripping off her nightgown, she quickly washed her face, dressed in a white blouse and divided skirt of soft buckskin, and drew on her boots. Twisting the long, thick mass of raven curls up under her hat, she hurried downstairs. Her steps led her straightaway into the kitchen, where Elena stood at the sink washing dishes.

"Everyone's had their breakfast?" she asked the older woman, though she was already certain of the answer.

"Sí," confirmed Elena. "Long ago." She dried her hands on her apron and asked hopefully, "You would like something to eat?"

"I'll just take one of these," said Callie Rose, snatching up a leftover pancake from a plate atop the worktable. She moved across to the massive black cookstove and poured herself a cup of coffee. Her preoccupied gaze drifted toward the window as she sipped carefully at the hot, aromatic liquid.

"He is at the corral with your brothers," Elena told her, with a knowing little smile.

"Who is?" she responded, feigning ignorance.

"Señor MacGregor."

"At the corral? I wonder what . . . ?" she murmured, then tensed in sudden suspicion while her eyes grew very round. "Damn that Clay!" she bit out. She tossed the pancake back onto the table and slammed the cup down so hard that some of the coffee spilled onto her hand. Swearing roundly, she went storming out the back door.

"You must eat!" Elena called after her.

But food was the last thing on her mind as she raced toward the larger of the two corrals. Her worst fears were soon realized.

There within the split-rail enclosure stood Ian, preparing to mount the great, smoke-colored stallion Sam had, appropriately enough, dubbed Beezlebub. The horse's wild, "unamiable" temperament was legendary; he was often employed to humiliate newly arrived greenhorns. Few riders had ever managed to stay on his back, and even those who *had* met with success had remained distressingly saddlesore for days afterward.

Callie Rose's sapphire gaze flashed to a furious brightness when it sought and found her brothers. All four of them were safely on the other side of the corral, their own eyes alight with gleeful anticipation as they folded their arms upon the top rail. J. D. appeared to be conveniently absent at the moment.

"Stop!" protested Callie Rose. She ran forward, her face flushed with vengeful anger. "Clay Buchanan, I told you—"

"Stay out of this." Sam cut her off.

"This is between us and him, baby sister," Jake insisted, his mouth curving slyly upward.

"No, it isn't!" she argued hotly. "Confound it, he could get killed!"

She scrambled atop the lower rail and looked to where Ian waited with the reins gripped tightly in one hand. Beezlebub snorted, strained at the bridle, and pawed impatiently at the ground. Callie Rose's heart leapt in very real alarm.

"Ian, you can't do this!" she cried. "That horse is loco, he'll—"

"Have you so little faith in my abilities, Callie Rose?" he queried, with only the ghost of a smile. There was something in his eyes that both frightened and thrilled her.

"Maybe it ain't your 'abilities' she's worried about," Clay said with an easy drawl. His remark earned him a quick, speaking glare from his sister.

"Ian, please!" she entreated in growing desperation. "I know you're a good rider, but Beezlebub isn't what you're used to!"

"You're wasting your breath," Billy told her. He seemed to be looking forward to Ian's humiliation every bit as much as the others, she noted resentfully.

"Get on with it!" yelled Clay.

Callie Rose looked on in helpless, angry frustration as Ian finally swung up into the saddle. She closed her eyes and offered up a silent prayer on his behalf, just as the horse beneath him began to move.

And then a miracle happened.

Her eyes flew open at the sound of Clay's muttered

oath of wonderment. She gasped at the sight before her. Beezlebub bucked and pitched and reared, but Ian managed to stay in the saddle. The animal became further enraged, tossing his head and kicking up a furious cloud of dust while he rampaged about the corral. Still, Ian did not fall. Maintaining an iron grasp on the reins with one hand, he lifted his other high and responded expertly to each movement, almost as if man and beast had become one.

"Well I'll be damned," Jake said. Beside him, Sam stood silent and watchful. But there was a faint glimmer of admiration in his own gaze.

"How the hell you reckon he learned to ride like that?" Clay mused aloud.

"Maybe those sonsabitches over in Scotland aren't such greeners after all," said Billy. He turned his head and flashed his incredulous, wide-eyed sister a broad grin. "Pa will be glad to hear he's worth something."

Speechless, Callie Rose looked back to Ian. Beezlebub was slowing down now, starting to tire, and it took only a few more minutes of "persuasion" for him to cease his struggles entirely. In the end, he appeared as tame and easy-spirited as an old mare.

Ian swung down from the saddle, bent to retrieve his hat from the dirt floor of the corral, and sauntered forward. The stallion followed obediently in his wake.

"You're not yet a widow, sweet vixen," he pointed out to Callie Rose. His green eyes twinkled rakishly into the luminous blue depths of hers.

"Can you hunt?" Sam suddenly demanded.

"And rope?" added Clay.

"Aye. I've done a fair bit of both," Ian replied, with

a faint smile of irony. He was not at all surprised that his wife's brothers were putting him to the test. He knew that they were determined to aid Callie Rose. But he was equally determined to have her.

"Good," said Sam, settling his hat low on his head. "Let's go."

"No!" exclaimed Callie Rose. She hastily climbed down from the rail and rounded on her four incorrigible brothers again. "You've done enough, by thunder!"

"Tell J. D. we'll be back in time for supper," Sam instructed her. "We've got a full day's work ahead of us."

"If you're going, then I'm going, too!"

"No, you're not," Jake was quick to deny. "This is man's business."

"I've never let that stop me before!" she reminded him.

"Perhaps not," Ian told her as he opened the gate of the corral and led Beezlebub out, "but your brothers are right. It would be best if you stayed here."

"I didn't ask for your opinion, Ian MacGregor!" she retorted, her temper flaring at his presumption.

"Nevertheless, you'll have it." He drew to a halt directly before her, his gaze smoldering down into hers. "For once, lass, do as you're told."

"Why, I—I will *not*!" she sputtered indignantly. She looked to her brothers for support, only to find that they were, for the first time, in obvious agreement with Ian. While she stood fuming at their disloyalty, they turned away and headed into the barn to saddle their own horses.

"Why did you try to prevent me from riding?" Ian asked her once the two of them were alone.

"Because no matter what you've done, I didn't want to have your blood on my hands!"

"It would not have been on yours."

"What difference does it make? You might very well be lying dead now and—" She broke off and eyed him accusingly. "Why didn't you tell me you could ride like that?"

"You never asked," he replied, his mouth twitching.

"Where the devil did you learn how?"

"California."

"California?" she echoed in astonishment. "I didn't know you'd ever been West before!"

"There are a good many things you've yet to learn about me," he declared softly, his eyes aglow with loving amusement.

She opened her mouth to tell him that she'd done all the learning she was going to do, but the words stuck in her throat. Giving him one last, narrow look, she whirled about and marched back toward the house. If he was so determined to get himself killed, she thought in mingled anger and apprehension, there was little she could do about it.

The morning wore on, noon came and went, and afternoon crept ever closer to evening. Clouds gathered on the horizon, as they had done the day before, holding forth the promise of much needed rain. Yet those who had spent any length of time in that part of Texas knew better than to hope too much. Summer was always a time of difficulty and disappointment. And surprises.

To Callie Rose, the hours seemed to crawl by. She remained uneasy throughout the long day, tormented by visions of Ian lying injured or even dead out on the range somewhere. Though she did not really believe her brothers would intentionally kill him, she knew they were capable of great mischief. And no matter how hard she tried to turn her mind elsewhere, she found it next to impossible to think of anything else. . . .

It was nearly six o'clock when her ears detected the sound of approaching hoofbeats. She hurried outside, only to see that it was Cousin Martha, not Ian, who was driving up to the house. Her eyes grew very round at the sight of the man seated next to her cousin in the buggy.

"Dr. MacGregor?" she whispered in astonishment. So it *had* been him she'd seen in Fort Worth the previous day! Relieved at the thought, and yet wondering why he had accompanied Ian all the way from Scotland, she moved down the front steps and across the yard.

"Callie Rose, look who's come to visit!" Martha exclaimed, with a happy blush. She guided the horse and buggy to a halt and then waited for her tall, distinguished-looking escort to assist her down.

" 'Tis a pleasure to see you again, Lady MacGregor," Ewan pronounced, smiling as he tucked Martha's arm possessively into the crook of his and led her forward.

"This is quite a surprise, Dr. MacGregor," Callie Rose told him. Her bright gaze shifted from one to the other, and she did not miss the way the doctor's eyes had trouble leaving Martha's face.

"I'm so very sorry I couldn't make it for supper last night as we'd planned," the widow hastened to apologize. Her color deepened again. "But Ewan arrived yesterday morning, and I . . . well, I must confess that the matter slipped my mind entirely."

"I've been a bit preoccupied myself," Callie Rose murmured wryly. She did not add that she, too, had forgotten all about J. D.'s invitation.

"Is Ian about at the moment?" asked Ewan.

"No. He's out riding with my brothers." She forced a smile to her lips and said, "Please, come inside. Everyone should be back soon. And I'm sure J. D. will insist that you stay for supper."

"Callie Rose, there's something . . ." Martha began tentatively, her voice trailing away as she exchanged a quick, loving glance with the man beside her.

"Yes?"

"I wanted you to be the first to know. You see, Ewan and I are going to be married."

"Married?" she repeated, her eyes widening again.

"Yes," Martha reaffirmed. "Right away, as a matter of fact."

"But isn't this rather sudden?" Callie Rose asked, visibly stunned at the news. "After all, you've only known each other—"

"A month longer than you knew Lord MacGregor when you were wed," Martha pointed out, not unkindly.

"Aye. Time holds little meaning when the heart renders a decision," Ewan remarked.

Spoken like a true MacGregor, Callie Rose thought with a brief, ironic smile.

"And so, my dearest Callie Rose, it seems we will all four be returning to Scotland together!" said Martha, her face beaming at the prospect.

"I'm not going back to Scotland."

"What? But I thought, since your husband came—"

"Nothing has changed," she insisted stubbornly. "Nothing at all."

"I could not help but be aware of your troubles," Ewan declared in a compassionate manner. "Were I not bound by a promise to Ian, I would tell you the truth about Elspeth MacGregor. What I *can* tell you, lass, is that the man you've married is as fine and honorable as they come. And he loves you truly."

"I—I wish I could believe that," she stammered in a weak voice, her heart twisting anew. But she resolutely squared her shoulders in the next instant and started back toward the house. "Come on. Elena makes the best lemonade in the county. We'll have some of that, and you can tell me all about this wedding you've got planned." At least this one would be legal from the outset, she mused, her eyes bridling at the memory of her own.

She was seated in the parlor with Martha and Ewan when her brothers finally came riding up half an hour later. Her eyes lit with excitement at the sound of their return, and she flew to the window to assure herself that Ian was with them.

He was there all right. And her father, too.

Heaving an audible sigh of relief, she turned back to her guests. They were both surveying her with an attention that was too steadfast for comfort. Dull color stained her cheeks.

"It looks like we can have supper now," she announced, striving to keep her tone nonchalant. She calmly led the way into the dining room, then sat waiting in secret impatience for Ian to appear.

He greeted both Ewan and Martha warmly when he preceded the Buchanans into the room—and took his place beside his wife without a word. She was preparing to ask him how the day had gone, but one look at his face told her he had triumphed once more.

"By thunder, Callie Rose, that husband of yours can damn near shoot the wings off a fly," Sam startled her by proclaiming. He and her other brothers were actually smiling as they sat down.

"Yeah, and he can throw a rope better than Billy," added Clay. There was no denying the admiration in his voice.

"Never thought I'd get me a son-in-law who could hold his own with my boys," J. D. remarked, with a low chuckle. He was obviously in an expansive mood, and even went so far as to inform Ewan that any family of Ian's was, by damn, *his* family, too.

"Too bad you won't be staying on," Jake told Ian, with a frown of genuine regret.

"Could be he'll give some thought to trading in his bagpipes for some spurs," Billy suggested, grinning broadly.

Callie Rose was shocked at the transformation that had taken place. And in the space of a single day, she thought dazedly. It was beyond belief. Her own father, her own brothers . . . they were traitors. Every blasted one of them.

She did not enjoy the meal. While the others entered into a lively conversation, she remained silent, picking at her food with the same lack of interest that had plagued her for weeks. And when everyone showed

signs of lingering at the table afterward, she stood and
fled upstairs with the murmured excuse of a headache.

Later, long after she had heard Martha and Ewan
driving away and her family—and Ian—settling down
for the night, she finally dragged herself from the bed
and tossed a blue gingham wrapper about her shoulders.
She wore nothing but a nightgown of thin white cotton
underneath it, her feet were bare, and her long hair cascaded freely down about her.

Anxious to escape the house for a while, she slipped
out of her room and crept down the stairs. Once outside,
she set a course for the hay barn. It had always been a
favorite hiding place; she had gone there whenever
she'd been troubled and wanted to be alone. Her father
and brothers had respected her need for privacy. Most
of the time, anyway, she recalled with a faint, rueful
smile.

The night was deep, the sky choked with a thick,
boiling mass of clouds that hid the light of a thousand
stars. The wind was uncertain—first gentle and then
gusting fiercely, warm one minute, mercifully cool the
next, carrying the scents of sagebrush, cattle, and rain.
A lone coyote howled plaintively close by, while the
distant bellow of a hungry calf rose in the storm-
charged air.

Callie Rose directed a swift glance heavenward, her
pulse quickening at the prospect of rain as she padded
across the dusty, sunbaked ground. She opened one of
the double barn doors, pulled it to again once she was
inside, and hurried to light the lamp hanging from a
rafter near the door. She struck a match and held it to

the wick. The flame flickered to life, casting a soft golden glow upon the bales of sweet-smelling hay.

Ian. She heaved a sigh as his face swam before her eyes. Tugging the wrapper off, she flung it aside and sank down onto the thick, cushioning pile of hay in the corner instead of climbing to her usual perch in the loft. Someone had carelessly left a pitchfork, business end up, on the floor. With a frown, she turned it over and pushed it close to the wall.

Her frown deepened as she bent her knees upward and wrapped her arms about her legs. Her eyes traveling slowly about the barn, she listened to the sounds of the night and allowed her thoughts to wander at will. It was no surprise when they returned time and again to Ian.

What the devil was she going to do about him? He had won her family over. Yes, indeed, she reflected with a healthy dose of annoyance, he had turned that irresistible MacGregor charm upon them and convinced them that he was the most goshalmighty, wonderful thing to come along since the wheel.

If only she didn't love him so much.

She closed her eyes and leaned her head forward, resting it on her knees. Outside, the wind had picked up velocity. It chased great swirls of dust across the yard and whistled through the cracks in the walls, warning of what was yet to follow. Lightning suddenly streaked across the sky. A loud, earthshaking clap of thunder answered it.

Callie Rose inhaled sharply and lifted her head. The air was charged with the strange, familiar expectancy that comes before a storm. She climbed to her feet, her

gaze drifting toward the rafters while she wavered indecisively between staying and returning to the more sub-
stantial protection of the house. A steady rain was no
danger, but there was always the possibility of an out-
right gully-washer, or even a hailstorm. She had once
seen hailstones as big as quail eggs; birds and rabbits
had been pelted to death, and some of the ranch hands,
caught out on the range, had suffered painful welts and
bruises over most of their bodies before they'd been
able to make it to shelter. The memory of it caused her
to shudder.

Another flash of lightning split the sky. Thunder rumbled mere seconds after it, giving proof that the storm
was near to breaking.

Suddenly the barn door crashed open.

Callie Rose started in alarm. Her heart leapt in her
breast. Her eyes flew wide.

"Ian!"

He smiled softly, the lamplight playing across his
face as he stepped inside and closed the door.

"Did you not know I would come, my love?" His
clothing appeared to have been drawn on in a hurry, for
his shirt was unbuttoned and his feet were as bare as
her own.

"I—I thought you were asleep!" she stammered
weakly. She caught her breath on another gasp when his
bold, penetrating gaze raked over her. Belatedly remembering that she was clad only in a nightgown, she hastened to retrieve the wrapper she had tossed aside.

But Ian was of a different mind. He was across the
barn before she had taken more than a single, unsteady
step, his hands reaching for her. She gave a strangled

cry and spun away. Eluding his grasp, she raced for the door, wrenched it open, and escaped into the heavy, windswept darkness outside. Her long nightgown flapped and tangled about her legs, threatening to send her tumbling to the ground. She gasped when she felt the first cold drops of rain stinging against her face as the heavens opened up at last.

Ian caught up with her just after she had stumbled over to the corral. Seizing her wrist, he scooped her up in his powerful arms and carried her swiftly back to the barn. Lightning crackled again and again, thunder sounded hot on its heels, and the rain slammed earthward in a great, vengeful cloudburst.

Callie Rose's nightgown was soaking wet by the time Ian bore her into the welcoming shelter of the barn once more. The thin white fabric clung transparently to her body, revealing every sweet, enchanting curve, offering a provocative hint of the rosy peaks of her breasts and the delicate curls between her thighs. Tiny rivulets of water coursed down her face, and her damp, thick raven tresses were streaming wildly about her shoulders.

She struggled in Ian's arms, but she could not prevent him from conveying her across to the pile of hay in the corner. A sharp, breathless cry broke from her lips when he tossed her unceremoniously down upon its fragrant softness and then stripped off his shirt. His clothing was as drenched as her own, his flame-colored hair darkened to a rich mahogany by the rain. His magnificent, hard-muscled upper torso gleamed all bronzed and wet in the lamplight, and Callie Rose was alarmed to feel a familiar heat spreading throughout her body as she scrambled into a sitting position and stared up at him.

"What the hell do you think you're doing?" she demanded tremulously, her pulse racing.

"What I should have done yesterday," he replied in a low tone brimming with passion. His eyes glowed hotly down into hers, and a tender, captivating smile touched his lips. "I vowed to be patient, sweet vixen." He began unfastening his trousers now. "I was determined to win you back, to prove myself worthy of the love I know to be in your heart. But I am only flesh and blood. And by all that is holy, I could not allow this opportunity to pass."

He removed his trousers, flung them aside, and stood before her, naked and unashamed, in all his masculine glory. She colored warmly from head to toe, her traitorous flesh yearning for his touch. With a low groan of dismay rising in her throat, she finally came to life again.

"No! No, damn you! I won't let you do this!"

She grabbed the pitchfork and sprang to her feet. Ian smiled, his gaze filled with ironic amusement as she stood aiming the prongs menacingly in his direction.

"Would you run me through, Rosaleen?" He challenged her in a voice that was little more than a whisper.

Overhead, the rain drummed noisily on the tin roof, while the wind tore across the prairie and sent the life-giving drops of moisture into every crack and hollow in the parched ground. The atmosphere inside the barn was a perfect match for the storm-tossed fury outside.

Callie Rose battled her own emotions as she looked at Ian. Her fingers tightened about the handle of the pitchfork. She felt hot tears gathering in her eyes, felt a sharp pain slicing through her heart.

"I love you, Callie Rose. Aye, and you love me. What else matters?"

"I—I don't want to love you!" she declared brokenly. "I don't want to love anyone!"

"Then you might as well use that thing," he told her, his gaze darkening, "for I'll never let you go."

She choked back a sob while he began advancing on her. Almost before she realized it, the pitchfork slipped from her grasp. Ian was there to catch her in his arms when her legs gave way beneath her. She murmured one last futile protest as he lowered her back to the hay and placed his body atop hers.

He kissed her hungrily, mercilessly, pressing her down into the hay while his mouth ravished hers. Desire, raw and relentless and too long denied, flared between them.

Callie Rose knew the battle to be lost.

She was soon as naked as he, her soft, supple curves straining feverishly upward beneath his virile hardness. His hands roamed with fierce possessiveness over her, reacquainting themselves with every beguiling hill and valley, his lips and tongue intent upon the same rapturous purpose as they trailed a fiery path downward.

Though her mind cursed her for a fool, Callie Rose could not find the strength to put a stop to the sweet madness. She wanted him, needed him desperately, and God help her, *she would love him this night if no other*!

Her fingers threaded within the damp thickness of his hair as his mouth closed about one of her breasts. She moaned, her eyes sweeping closed while he sucked greedily and teased at the nipple with the moist, sensuous swirl of his tongue. He did the same to her other breast, then slid lower on her body, his hands impatiently parting her thighs.

A cry of pure pleasure escaped her lips, but it was drowned out by another resounding clap of thunder. She clutched at his head, her legs trembling and her hips moving restlessly beneath the hot, delectable mastery of his bold caress. Burning with desire, she was certain she could endure no more.

"Ian, *please!*" she gasped out.

Her plea for mercy turned his own blood to liquid fire in his veins. With a groan of loving triumph, he slid back up on her body. His hands gripped her about the hips, his gaze smoldering down into hers while the storm raged on. And then he plunged into her at last.

She gasped loudly, feeling as though she had been touched by fire. Her eyes swept closed again. Arching her back, she reveled in his thrusts, her hips matching the expert, provocative rhythm of his while her legs came up to wrap about his waist. She grasped at his shoulders for support, oblivious to the feel of the hay beneath her naked back.

Consumed by a blaze of furious, white-hot passion, they were aware of nothing save each other. Elspeth and Jamie were forgotten, as were J. D. and all the other Buchanans. . . . There was only this mystical, magical ecstasy, part heaven and part earth, a soul-stirring splendor they could find with no one else.

The fulfillment was the most explosive they had ever known. Callie Rose screamed softly, feeling as though a part of her had been snatched back from the very brink of death. Ian tensed above her in the next instant, and she gasped again when his seed flooded her with its warmth.

They were both left panting for breath afterward. He rolled to his back in the hay and tugged her close. She lay against him for several long minutes, listening to the strong, steady pulsing of his heart beneath her cheek and the beating of the rain on the roof above. And then a particularly violent gust of wind shook the barn.

It was enough to bring Callie Rose to her senses once more. She pushed herself away from her husband and climbed to her feet, catching up the discarded nightgown.

"What's your hurry, Lady MacGregor? We've the whole night ahead of us yet," Ian said with a soft smile. He drew his tall, undeniably masculine frame into a sitting position and bent one knee upward, resting an arm across it. His eyes glowed with affectionate humor as he watched her shaking out the uncooperative folds of her nightgown.

"This doesn't change anything!" she insisted. "Not a blasted thing!" Fighting back a fresh wave of tears, she tried, without success, to don the wet garment. Pieces of hay clung to her damp, wildly tangled hair, and her skin was beginning to itch. But worst of all, her conscience branded her as little better than a whore. Never mind that she loved him—she had selfishly taken pleasure from a man who belonged to another.

"Can we not call a truce now?" he suggested, rising to his feet before her. "Why not admit that you love me, and let me explain—"

"There's nothing left to explain!" Draping the nightgown modestly in front of her, she moved past him to retrieve her gingham wrapper. She slipped it on, tied the belt about her waist, and muttered a curse as she flung the nightgown back down to the barn floor. Her eyes blazed up into Ian's while she choked back a sob. "For heaven's sake, don't you understand? What's between us was never meant to be!"

"I understand more than you think."

His heart twisted at the sight of her distress, but he could not be sorry for what had happened. He was tempted to forget about the five days still remaining on her father's bargain and carry her back to Scotland. If not for his desire to please her family—and thereby please *her*—he would have done so that very night.

Callie Rose gazed at him with eyes full of pain. Another faint, stricken cry escaped her lips when she spun about and made her way blindly back to the door. Ian did not stop her this time. She took flight at last, bending her head against the summer storm as her bare feet slipped upon the muddy, rain-lashed ground.

Once at the house, she crept inside and back up the stairs to her room. She did not notice that her father's bedroom door was ajar, nor did she see the way he smiled to himself in purely paternal satisfaction.

❧ FIFTEEN ❧

Callie Rose left before dawn.

She had agonized over the decision, staying awake all night long while her heart waged a furious battle with her head again. Finally she had told herself that there was only one thing to be done.

She would run away. Once she was gone, Ian would realize the hopelessness of his pursuit and return to Scotland. And she would be left behind with a broken heart, hating herself for wanting him so much, hating her father for instilling in her such a damnably keen sense of honor.

Heaven help her, she would go to her grave loving Ian MacGregor. There would never be anyone else. *Never.*

Her eyes, full of anguish, had strayed toward the room where he slept as she had sprung into action. After throwing a few things into a carpetbag and fetching the small amount of money she kept hidden in an old boot, she had dressed in her riding clothes and slipped cautiously out of her room. She had kept her watchful, disconsolate gaze fastened on the door to Ian's room when she'd moved toward the staircase. But he had not stirred. Part of her had been relieved; part of her had felt a sense of disappointment so achingly intense that it had left her shaken.

Quickly saddling Guinevere, she rode away without a backward glance. Yet every fiber of her being called out to her to stop. . . .

The morning sun was casting long shadows upon the rainwashed countryside by the time she finally slowed the mare's frenzied pace. The air smelled fresh and clean in the storm's wake, and she inhaled deeply as she settled her hat lower on her head. Her eyes moved with a will of their own back to the north. Trying to ignore the mingled sorrow and despair burning deep inside her, she frowned and forced her gaze southward once more.

She had decided to head for San Antonio. A distant cousin lived there, a much older woman she had visited nearly two years ago. She doubted that even J. D. would be able to guess her whereabouts. And Ian certainly wouldn't follow her this time.

He would be having his breakfast by now, she mused with an inward sigh. It would probably be another hour or more before anyone realized she was gone; they would assume she had overslept again. Ian, of course, would think it was because of what had happened between them last night.

Her throat tightened painfully at the memory.

"Easy, girl," she murmured as the animal beneath her stumbled a bit. Gliding a gentle hand along the horse's sleek mane, she shifted her hips restlessly in the saddle and tossed a quick look up toward the brilliant blue canopy of the sky. If not for the lingering moistness of the ground, and a few broken branches scattered about, it would be difficult to find evidence of the violent thunderstorm that had ended shortly before midnight. The heat had returned with a vengeance.

She did not pause to rest until the sun hung directly overhead. Reining Guinevere to a halt beside a tree-lined creek, she dismounted and led the mare to the water's edge to drink. She withdrew a leftover biscuit from one of the saddlebags, then sank down upon the soft, grassy bank and tugged off her hat.

The unbidden image of a tall, green-eyed Highlander rose in her mind. She loved him. Dear God, how she loved him. But how could she possibly stay with a man she didn't respect?

Jamie is not my son. If only she could believe him. If only Elspeth . . . But no, the woman had no reason to lie. She had added credibility to her story by offering up Ian's faithful servants as witnesses to the truth.

Closing her eyes, Callie Rose drew in a deep, shuddering breath. Why did she keep torturing herself? It could serve no real purpose to dwell upon what was past. And it would only make the future that much more difficult to endure.

Though she still had little appetite, she managed to eat the biscuit. She hoped it would settle her stomach; she had been plagued by an odd queasiness for the past several days. Drawing herself up from the ground, she moved back to the creek and knelt to take a drink. Guinevere gave a soft whinny, pawing impatiently at the earth.

A faint, rueful smile touched Callie Rose's lips as she swung back up into the saddle and spoke a soft command to the mare. Pulling her hat low upon her head once more, she rode away across the boundless Texas prairie.

The day stretched interminably before her, the monotony of the journey broken only by the few stops she made to rest her horse. She avoided the many small towns and settlements that dotted the landscape, for she knew that being seen would make it easier for J. D. and her brothers if they decided to come after her. It never occurred to her to feel any apprehension at traveling alone. Not only was she too preoccupied with thoughts of Ian, but she was also well prepared in case trouble did arise. She had learned long ago never to ride without a gun.

Darkness was already falling by the time she decided to make camp for the night. Heading beneath a grove of tall cottonwood trees that flanked a narrow stream, she slid wearily to the ground and unsaddled Guinevere. Once the animal was grazing peacefully, she withdrew some provisions from the saddlebags and hastened to build a fire.

The air was filled with the appetizing aroma of coffee and bacon a short time later. Callie Rose unfolded her bedroll and sank gratefully down upon it. Her gaze drifted up toward the starlit panorama of the sky, her heart aching as she became lost in yet another painful reverie.

Why the devil had she run away? she lamented miserably, besieged by doubts while the long, lonely night stretched before her. Her father would curse her for a coward, her brothers would reproach her for failing to trust them to resolve the matter, and Ian would probably never forgive her. It was just as well.

Her eyes swept closed. She buried her face in her hands, feeling completely torn apart—

A twig snapped somewhere in the near distance.

Startled, she opened her eyes and scrambled to her feet. Her pulse leapt in alarm as she looked to where she had left her rifle on the other side of the fire. She flew to retrieve it, her whole body tensed in defensive readiness when she whirled back around with the gun in her hands.

"Who's there?" she demanded in a loud, insistent voice. Her gaze narrowed slightly, her blood thundering in her ears as she tried to see who, or what, was concealed within the darkness of the underbrush. "Who's there?" she repeated. She held her breath and heard the leaves rustling to her left. She raised the gun, her finger moving to the trigger.

"By heaven, woman! Put that thing down!"

"Ian?" she gasped, her eyes widening in shocked amazement. "Ian, is that you?"

"Who else would be fool enough to chase you all over Texas?" he parried, his tone both angry and mocking. Leading his horse into the firelight now, he raked the hat from his head. His handsome, chiseled features were dangerously grim, and his gaze smoldered with barely suppressed fury.

Callie Rose grew light-headed with relief as she lowered the rifle. Her heart stirred joyfully at the sight of him, but joy gave way to indignation in the next instant.

"What the blazes did you think you were doing, sneaking up on me like that?" she charged hotly. "Damn it, I—I might have shot you!"

"You may yet wish you had done so." He looped the reins over a branch, then advanced on her with slow, foreboding purposefulness. "Have you any idea what I felt when I heard you riding away this morning?"

"You—you heard me?" she stammered, her eyes growing very round again. Swallowing hard, she raised her head in proud defiance. The gesture belied the thoroughly chaotic state of her emotions. "You shouldn't have come after me! I told you—"

"Cum do theanga!" he ground out. Towering ominously above her, he wrenched the gun from her grasp and clenched his own fingers about it. "You will hear me out!"

"We have nothing to say to each other!"

"Try my patience no more, Callie Rose MacGregor," he warned in a low, simmering tone. "I have spent these many hours past following you, cursing you for your willingness to believe the worst of me— Aye, and cursing myself for ever having been fool enough to hope you would see reason!"

Another sharp gasp broke from her lips when he suddenly tossed the gun aside and seized her by the arms. His strong fingers dug into her flesh, his eyes burning down into hers. She shivered and felt her whole body grow warm.

"Elspeth MacGregor was never mine!" he declared. " 'Tis true that she sought my bed, but *never* did she share it! I wanted none of her, for I knew her to be coldhearted and deceitful. When she failed to ensnare me, she turned to my brother for solace. Gavin was ever less discriminating when it came to women," he recalled, with a faint smile of irony. "He took Elspeth without benefit of marriage, even though her father was a well-respected member of our clan. And when he discovered that she was carrying his child, he further dishonored her by refusing to give Jamie either his name or his support."

"Jamie is—is your nephew?" Callie Rose asked, her voice quavering.

She read the truth in his eyes.

"Aye. He is Gavin's son." His mouth curved briefly upward again. "I told you there was a family resemblance, did I not?"

"Yes, but, I—I never . . ." The words trailed away while she shook her head numbly.

"You never trusted me," Ian finished for her.

"How could I?"

"How could you not?"

Something in his voice finally pierced the wall of anger and hurt and jealousy she had built around herself. *Dear God, it was true.*

She stared up at him as the realization of it hit her full force. After all these terrible, lonely weeks of doubting him, her mind was clearing again. She would have been hard put to say exactly why she was inclined to believe him now. Maybe it was because he had never given up. Or maybe it was simply because she was tired of denying what was in her own heart. Whatever the reason, she was worn down true and proper. She couldn't fight against him anymore.

"Oh, Ian, I wanted to trust you!" she burst out. "I wanted to believe that the woman was lying, but how could I? She had the baby with her, and—and she sounded so very convincing!"

"Elspeth is well known for her theatrics," he remarked dryly.

"But, why? Why did she do it?"

"Because she had vowed to seek revenge. Though I have claimed the boy as my ward, she demanded that she be installed as the mistress of Castle MacGregor. I refused. She swore to make me pay for my rejection of her." He frowned again, his eyes glinting dully. "I suspected trouble when she appeared at the handfasting, but as the days passed, I thought perhaps she had accepted our marriage. When Peter told me of her visit, I knew she was to blame for your departure. It took little 'persuasion' to have the truth from her."

"She wanted you for herself," murmured Callie Rose, her gaze lighting with comprehension. "That part of it wasn't a lie."

What a fool she had been. What a blind and impulsive fool! Her heart soared, while at the same time a damning, powerful wave of guilt washed over her.

"Molly and the others had agreed never to speak of the matter," said Ian, "yet I am certain they would have found a way to ease your fears if you had gone to them."

"Great balls of fire, how could I have been so naive?" she whispered. Her head was spinning, and she felt her legs growing weak.

Ian had not betrayed her! If only she had waited for his return from Edinburgh, she could have heard the truth weeks ago. And she could have spared herself weeks of agonizing loneliness and grief. Her impetuousness had gotten the better of her again, she reflected, her eyes clouding at the thought. Cousin Martha had warned her about jumping to conclusions, but she had stubbornly refused to listen.

Stricken with remorse, she fought back sudden tears and lifted her hands to her husband's broad chest.

"Why didn't you tell me this that first day at the ranch?"

"You said you would not believe me. And in truth, I wanted to know that you loved me in spite of the fact that I was a villain in your eyes," he confessed, his brow creasing into another frown. He shook his head. "It was wrong of me. I know that now."

"Oh, Ian, I—I'm so sorry!" she choked out. Now that she knew the truth, her heart was free. "I should never have left Scotland! I should have stayed and given you the chance to explain! But I was too uncertain of my own feelings, and I didn't know what else to do!"

"Are you still uncertain, lass?" He challenged her softly. His hands slid around to her back, and he pulled her close. His penetrating, deep green gaze captured the luminous blue fire of hers, his voice raw with emotion when he asked once more, "Are you?"

"No." She swayed against him and lifted her own arms to his neck. The tears spilled over from her lashes to course down her cheeks. But they were tears of happiness this time. "I can't fight against it anymore. I *do* love you! Even if you had been guilty as hell, I'm not at all sure I could have held out much longer."

"I'm glad to hear it."

"You knew it all along." She sighed. "I—I didn't want to love you, but it happened just the same. I didn't realize how I truly felt until the day Elspeth came.

That's why I had to leave. I couldn't bear it when I thought you cared for someone else!"

"I love only you," he told her, his own heart taking flight at the sound of the words he had waited so long to hear. He tightened his arms about her, and his mouth curved into a smile so devastating that she melted inside. "You've led me a merry chase, my 'Wild Rose.' Yet I would gladly do it all again."

"*I* wouldn't!" She wiped the tears from her face and released an eloquent, uneven sigh. "Damnation, Ian MacGregor, I don't think I could stand another month like this one!"

"Nor could I," he agreed, with a low chuckle. His eyes traveled lovingly over her beautiful, upturned countenance. "I vowed I would skelp you when I got my hands on you. Where were you off to this time?"

"San Antonio. And wouldn't you much rather kiss me?"

"I would indeed, but not until we get a few things straight. You will never run away again, do you understand?" Though his expression was tenderly affectionate, there wasn't a trace of amusement in his eyes.

"Perfectly."

"And you will doubt me no more?"

"I won't. That is, not unless you give me reason to," she clarified. Her gaze kindled at the thought. "As God is my witness, I'll scratch the eyes out of any woman who dares to come near you!"

"Aye, I am sure you would." His deep-timbred voice was brimming with humor now.

"We still have so much to learn about each other,"

she noted in a more serious vein. "I know my father and my brothers approve of you, but—"

"We've a lifetime to learn. And 'tis you I've married, not your family."

"But you will bring me back to visit, won't you?"

"I will," he promised solemnly.

"I've only got one more question, and then you can kiss me."

"I would have done so without your permission. But what is it you wish to know?"

"Why it took you so blasted long to find me," she murmured, pressing her body seductively against his as her sapphire gaze issued a sweet invitation.

"Beezlebub may be aptly named, but he does not run as though the fires of hell were licking at his heels."

He smiled once more before lowering his head and kissing her at last. She moaned in wholehearted surrender, her lips parting beneath the warm, deliciously conquering pressure of his.

The sound of approaching hoofbeats rose in the night air.

"What the—?" Callie Rose whispered, pulling away from Ian in renewed alarm. She spun about and caught up the rifle again.

"Unless my guess proves incorrect," Ian said lazily, "I do not think you'll have a use for that." He made no move for his own weapon.

"What are you talking about?"

"Only that, from the sound of it, there are five riders bearing down on us. And I can think of five who have more than a passing interest in your welfare."

He was soon proven right. Callie Rose muttered an

oath of incredulity as her father and brothers swung down from their weary, sweat-soaked mounts and strode into the firelight.

"What the hell's going on?" J. D. bit out. His eyes glittered harshly as they shot to Callie Rose. "First I hear you've lit out, and then Sam tells me MacGregor's up and disappeared too! Now I want some answers, girl, and I want them *now*!"

"I—I was heading for San Antonio!" she explained, coloring guiltily. "And Ian came after me!"

"Is that so? Well, I've had a bellyful of this claptrap!" He scowled and ordered his third oldest son, "Jake, get a rope!"

All four Buchanan brothers exchanged quick looks of bemusement, but Jake hastened to do as he'd been told.

"What do you want a rope for?" Callie Rose asked in a small voice, her face paling at the look on his.

"You wanted your freedom, didn't you?"

"My freedom?" Her wide, sparkling gaze shifted to Ian and then back again. "Damn it, J. D., what are you talking about?"

"You'll find out soon enough."

Jake returned with the rope. He handed it to his father, who proceeded to toss an end of it over one of the tree branches above.

"Pa, what are you—?" Billy sought to intervene.

"Stay out of this, boy!" growled J. D. His eyes narrowed into mere slits as they moved to Ian, who stood tall and silent (and with an unholy light of amusement in his own eyes) on the other side of the fire. "You've done enough to my girl, you redheaded bastard! Since she'll have none of you, we'll settle things here and now." He began to fashion one of the rope ends into a noose.

"You mean you're going to hang him?" asked Clay.

"I am."

"What?" Callie Rose gasped in stunned disbelief.

"Hell, J. D., you can't—" Sam protested.

"This isn't—" Jake spoke at the same time.

"You can't lynch a man for taking off after his own wife!" exclaimed Billy, his voice the loudest of all.

"All right then, we'll say we strung him up for horse thieving," pronounced J. D. "Anyone here recall giving him permission to borrow ol' Beezlebub?"

"Stop it!" cried Callie Rose. She moved protectively in front of Ian, her manner like that of a tigress fighting for her mate. Her eyes blazed across into her father's. "You can't hang him, J. D. Buchanan! By thunder, you'll have to kill me first!"

"And why the hell is that?" her father demanded. "You want to get rid of him, don't you?"

"No! But even if I did, this wouldn't be the way— and you damned well know it!"

"That ain't good enough." He finished securing the knot and pulled the noose head high over the branch.

"I love him!" Callie Rose finally proclaimed for all to hear. She did not see the way Ian's mouth curved into a slow smile of warm, loving satisfaction. "I love him, confound it, and I'm going back to Scotland with him!"

"Well, I'll be damned," Sam muttered in surprise. Jake and Clay had much the same reaction. Billy, however, seemed to have expected her declaration. And J. D. was obviously pleased with himself.

"Does that mean you're going to stay put with him

this time?" he demanded of his beloved, headstrong daughter. "No more running back to the Diamond L or lighting out for parts unknown?"

"I'm going to stay put!" she promised, with all her heart.

"Well then," said J. D., his weather-beaten features breaking into a grin as he met Ian's gaze, "that's all I wanted to hear."

Callie Rose blinked at him in astonishment, then pivoted to face her husband. Without a word, he swept her into his arms once more. She blushed and opened her mouth to remind him that they were not alone, but he silenced her in a supremely effective—and pleasurable—way.

"You weren't really going to hang him, were you?" Clay asked his father.

"Damn it, boy, you've got a lot to learn."

The kiss gave every sign of lasting. J. D. cleared his throat noisily and clapped his nearest son on the back.

"Let's break out some grub. Looks like Callie Rose has done a good job of burning the bacon. She never could cook worth a damn."

Ian finally released her. She was becomingly flushed and bright-eyed, and she turned to smile at her father.

"First thing in the morning, we'll get you two hitched in a church," he decreed in his usual gruff manner, though his gaze softened when it met hers. "Just to be on the safe side."

"Nothing about them's ever going to be 'safe,' " predicted Billy.

And he was right.

❧ Epilogue ❧

One year later:

Callie Rose stretched languidly in the great canopied bed. Her eyelids fluttered open when she smoothed a hand across the mattress and felt the warm indentation where Ian's body had lain beside hers all night long. Soft morning light streamed in through the windows, offering evidence of yet another cool, beautiful summer day in the Highlands.

"Ian?" She sat up, unmindful of the fact that in so doing the sheet fell away from her naked breasts. Her sleepy, searching gaze lit upon her husband. *"Caite bheil thu dol?"*

His low, mellow chuckle drifted back to her. He drew himself up from where he had been kneeling before the hearth.

"I'm only starting a fire, my love," he told her softly. "There's a chill in the air, and I would not have Connell awaken yet." He cast a swift glance toward the cradle on the other side of the room. Satisfied when the fire blazed to life, he returned to the bed and slipped beneath the covers once more. He drew Callie Rose close, smiling as she fitted her soft, beguiling curves against his hard-muscled warmth. "You've mastered the Scots tongue quite well, sweet vixen," he murmured, his tone laced with both pride and affectionate humor.

"I had no choice. How else was I to know what the devil you were saying every time you got angry with me?"

"Aye, we've had our share of collieshangies," he recalled, his eyes twinkling at the thought. "But the making up was well worth what came before, would you not agree?"

"Aye." She sighed, smoothing a hand along the broad, lightly matted expanse of his chest. "That I would." She smiled to herself and tried, without success, to keep her eyes open. "Your son will be wanting his breakfast soon."

"He's a true MacGregor."

"Three months old, and already as impatient as his father." There was no real complaint in her voice.

"Ewan told me that he half expects a son of his own."

"Well, there *are* even odds on it," she pointed out, with a soft laugh of her own. "Speaking of Martha, I still can't believe she's going to have a child at her age."

"She's not exactly ancient," he noted wryly, his fingers gliding along the saucy, well-rounded curve of her naked bottom.

"I know, but . . . it was just so unexpected, that's all."

"It should not surprise you to learn that a MacGregor can father a child," he teased.

"For heaven's sake, Martha had just as much to do with it!" she retorted, pushing herself up a bit so that she could give him the stern, wifely look he deserved. "Why do men always take full credit for—?"

" 'Tis a mystery best left unexplored." He smiled and pulled her down for a quick yet thorough kiss. When she settled her body against his once more, she was flushed and agreeably light-headed.

"I'll pay a visit to Martha tomorrow," she announced. "I doubt if I'll have another chance before we leave."

"Your father will no doubt be pleased to see Connell."

"An understatement if ever I heard one." Her blue eyes sparkled happily. "Maybe those brothers of mine will finally do their duty, too." If Billy's last letter was any indication, all four of them were perilously close to getting roped before winter. It was about time, she mused with another soft smile.

"J. D. is no doubt fighting a few battles of his own with the former Widow Layne."

"Well, at least he won't have to face the dreaded prospect of two women living under the same roof. I suppose getting me married off was all it took. I do wish I could have been there for the wedding." A sudden shadow crossed her face, but it was quickly gone.

"You've not been homesick, have you, lass?" asked Ian, frowning slightly.

"No." She raised her head to look at him again. Her gaze held all the love that was in her heart. "Home is wherever you are, you impossible Highland rogue," she told him.

His own gaze darkened with passion, his own heart soaring with the promise of a lifetime of loving.

"I love you, Callie Rose MacGregor. *An comhnaidh.*"

"Always," she whispered, trembling as he pulled her down for a kiss that would warm them as no fire ever could. *"An comhnaidh."*

J. D. Buchanan got his passel of grandchildren. And well before he had one foot in the grave.